WHY HORSES, MRS K?

by

Blanche Whitney Kloman

Best wishes
Blanche Whitney Kloman

cover artist, Walter Proksa
layout, Wayne Spelius
staff assistant, Anne Brashler
editor, Carol Spelius

LAKE SHORE PUBLISHING

373 Ramsay Road

Deerfield, IL 60015

ISBN #0-941363-35-X
copyright 1995

$14.95

to the children

PRAYER OF A HORSE

To thee, my Master, I offer my prayer:

Feed me, water and care for me, and when the day's work is done, provide me with shelter, a clean dry bed and a stall wide enough for me to lie down in comfort. Talk to me. Your voice often means as much to me as the reins.

Pet me sometimes, that I may serve you the more gladly and learn to love you.

Do not jerk the reins, and do not whip me when going up hill.

Never strike, beat, or kick me when I do not understand what you want, but give me a chance to understand you. Watch me, and if I fail to do your bidding, see if something is not wrong with my harness or feet.

Examine my teeth when I do not eat. I may have an ulcerated tooth, and that, you know, is very painful.

Do not tie my head in an unnatural position, or take away my best defense against flies and mosquitoes by cutting off my tail, or limit my range of vision by blinders so that I am frightened by what I cannot see.

And finally, O my master, when my youthful strength is gone, do not turn me out to starve or freeze, or sell me to some cruel owner to be slowly tortured and starved to death; but do thou, my master, take my life in the kindest way, and your God will reward you here and hereafter.

You will not consider me irreverent if I ask this in the name of Him who was born in a stable. Amen.

Author Unknown

To the Reader

This is a true story but I have changed some persons' names and locales. The horses' names have not been changed.

... Blanche Kloman

Remembering the honest horses and ponies of Arcadia Farm.

Sammy • Katie Twist • Comanche • Colonel • Katie-Did • Sugarfoot • Diamond • Chrystal • Safari • Big Boy • Medal • The Grulla-mare • Star • Stonewall and Andy • Honey • Fire • Firestone • G-G- • Mitzie • Drambuie • Ginger • Tillie • Bobby Socks • Wally • Red • Buck • Colonette • Jack Daniels • Bill the wagon horse • Redwing • Bill • Dakotah • Misty • Ariel • Dusty • Rebel • Frosty • Nina • You-All • Toby • Flame • Domino • Melody • Navaho • Geronimo • Rambler • Gibran • By Request • Hi-lo • Snuffy • Stoney • Laddie • Lady Skelly • Buckshot • Shamrock Mount • Ned • Star • Cheyenne • Tameo • Kono • Buster Brown • Cinnamon • Casey Jones • Comet • Velvet • Champion • King • Chief • Victory • Sioux Chief • Zza-Zza • Jesse James • Marquis • Daisy Mae • Fooler • Betcha • Sandman • Hardship Man • Dial-an-go • Firebuck • Khanoo • Sunshine • Sun-down • Comanche • Rockey • Dinky • Mia • Sonny • Beth • Shannon • Cocoa • Rhoda Bar • Ginger • Major • Brandy • Daiquiri • Cheyenne 2 • Sandy • Tuffet • Rickey • Rusty • Blackie • Mr. Tweed • Gerry M. • Fritz • Our Buddy • Prince • Tayda • Saraam • Thunder • Joker • Skip-a-bob • Misty Mom • Highland Fling • Robin's Joker • Keith • Jump Back • Capri • Sam • Stormy • Scooby-Dooby • Kanoodle and Kaniddle • Ralph • Bounty • Dawn • Sarge • Vacation Plan • Dreamboat • Erradette • Doc • Gypsy • Rhythm • Oakley Vandy • Twist • Aries • Big Red • Holly • Baron • Molly • Heather • Gretchen • Hilo-Tonka • Eddie • Charlie Brown • Downbeat • Easter-bar-bon • Spear • Topeka • Cooney • Peaches • Tanya • Cat-fire • Tasha • Poco • Stewball • Sidewinder • Chocolate • Satin • Angel • Raven • King 2 • Scout • Buddy • April • Friday • Apache Warrior • Hanaaf • Victor • Dancer • Mikado • Montana • Lucky • Sahara • Einar • Beau • Paint Box • Ka-bob • Cricket • Starmount • Pocotante • Skippers Sunday Sue • Revel • Ebony • Blaze • Yankee • Belle • Archie • Patchy • Cotton Candy • Red 2 • Tennessee Lady • Ming • May Day • Baby • Paiute • Trojan • Jo-Jo • Breezy • Yellowstone • Cheetah • Babydoll • Spur • Cobby • Wimpy • Johnny Riley • Abigail • Buffy Brown • Bunky • Dash • Nahja • Tom • Mohawk • Sputnick • Hunky Flame • Apache Dancer • Shawnee • Joy • Autumn • Poco Pica • Shane • Little Al • Dann • Snooky • Lady Godiva • Tabu • Sugar • Candy • Sonny • Georgia

Foreword

Many of those who heard Mother's stories always thought she should write a book. She started the manuscript while still at the farm seated at the round oak table in the kitchen of our fieldstone farmhouse. Her first chapter was about old Bill the pedlar-wagon horse.

Whitney thought she should include headings for each chapter. Lynn helped her keep some appointments for the book. I edited several chapters. Walter Proksa sketched the illustrations. All this with the guidance of Carol Spelius and Lake Shore Publishing.

Mother's book is about friendship. Friendship between her and the individuals who were part of her life during the twenty years she owned Arcadia Farm, and friendship between her and the horses.

Gail

Table of Contents

Chapter 1

In Business

It was hot for June, humid, smothering as only a midwest summer can be. In 1959 there was not the blessing of air-conditioning on public transportation. As the train lurched along on uneven tracks, I leaned my forehead against the dirty window glass and closed my eyes.

The finality of the morning court session -- with its perspiring, impatient attorneys, innumerable papers to sign, and the irritable, muttering judge whose scarcely audible words returned me to single status -- had exhausted me.

An hour later, the conductor called out my station. Clutching my cumbersome briefcase, I staggered to my feet and down the aisle. As I reached the steel stair to the platform I caught my heel and pitched headlong into the conductor's arms.

It was not a propitious beginning to my new life, I thought, grimly. From now on, divorced, with financial responsibility for my children and no special training for making a living, I'd probably stumble often in the days ahead.

Once I was behind the steering wheel and driving by the open fields, and groves of cottonwoods and hawthornes, my spirits lifted. The single lane blacktop road led me past old St. Martha's church. To see its slender Gothic spire and bell tower was comforting to me.

The weathered timbers on the narrow bridge shook and rattled as I drove across it. The creek bed, where once herds of Buffalo watered, was bone dry. I looked ahead for familiar landscapes, my neighbors' farms and my own gently rolling land.

The sound of my car wheels on the gravel brought the children running to the garage. Their faces were sober. While not fully comprehending, they knew that from this day forward our lives would be different.

After a restless night, I slept later than usual. Dressing hurriedly, I went downstairs. The house was quiet, no one was in the kitchen. I took a chocolate doughnut from the breadbox and went outside to look for the children. I heard their voices coming from the far end of the driveway. As I drew closer, I saw they were working on a project.

My son, Whitney, stretched his long arms upward and squinted in concentration as he looped the chain on the hand-lettered sign over the iron arm bracket attached to a stout six-by-six post. The square black letters stood out against the white background. "Arcadia Farm, Horses Boarded".

His younger sisters stood underneath the sign to check the alignment. Gail, holding Melanie, her orange tom cat, hopped around directing Whitney, her fine-boned frame bursting with energy. Lynn, whose lightly freckled face was already beginning to sunburn, brushed a strand of strawberry blonde hair from her eyes and asked, "How much longer, Whit? I'm getting tired holding this ladder."

"Just a couple more minutes. I'm putting in the last bolt," Whitney replied.

When the girls announced their approval, Whitney stepped down from the rickety stepladder and grinned at me. "Well, Mom, looks like we're in the horse business."

I looked at the three of them, my staff. One twelve-year old boy, two little girls, eight and ten. On my next birthday I would be forty-four.

I smiled at them, hoping I looked confident. The day before I had received word from the bank that the mortgage on the farm had been approved, but for two thousand less than I had applied for. That two thousand was to be my cushion against emergencies.

The frowning, stern image of Henry Borchardt, President of the Prairie Grassland Bank, staring at me through gold-rimmed glasses, had remained with me. "Why horses, Mrs. Kloman? Can't you use your barn as it is and buy some dairy cows? That farm of yours was a money-making dairy operation in the past."

"I don't know anything about cows," I had protested, hoping he wouldn't ask me what I knew about horses. I plunged ahead before he could ask further questions. "I plan on having horses, Mr. Borchardt. All I need is enough money to remodel the barn, buy some seed for crops and do a little advertising."

"Well, it's our joint risk," Mr. Borchardt replied gruffly. "I'll take it up with the loan committee and call you."

Now, as I looked into the trusting faces of my three children, I wondered for the hundredth time if I was adequately equipped and capable enough to run a horse farm.

I walked back to the house, the children running ahead kicking up gravel on the curved, tree-lined driveway leading to the stone farmhouse.

In the kitchen I fixed myself a cup of coffee and sat down at the round oak table, my account ledger and checkbook before me. Once again, I reviewed the estimate from Bud Riley, a local carpenter. He had drawn up plans for the conversion from cattle to horse barn.

Two weeks before, Bud and I had walked around the farm buildings making plans for their renovation. The main barn that had once housed forty-eight registered Guernsey milking cows for a former owner was sixty feet long and thirty-six wide. There were two stock pens at either end. Off the main barn was a granary, its grain chutes leading down from metal lined oat bins above. Nearby were the corn cribs with woven wire partitions and ventilated exterior walls. There was also a bull pen made of heavy piping with its own exercise yard.

Bud thought I should make the silo into an equipment room and suggested part of the corn crib be converted into six stalls. He advised me to consider a use for the old bull pen, too.

Bud proposed building thirty standing or straight stalls over in the long machine shed. I expected to use these stalls for my school horses or boarders.

As I looked down the empty shed, I pictured a row of sleek horses -- each horse with his own saddle covered by a clean blanket on a nearby rack, and his bit and bridle in which he worked most comfortably, hanging nearby. There would be crisp hay in their mangers, fresh water and a generous grain ration. These horses would have no cinch or back galls from hasty, slipshod saddling or ill-fitting equipment.

Also on the property, there was an eight stall horse barn, empty except for our Palomino gelding, Kono. There was no lack of space on the eighty acre farm. I couldn't imagine I would ever use it all.

Our tour finished, Bud leaned his back against one of the barn doors and said, "Now, should you get the loan, and I build this and that, and you get the horses in and all, who'll do the work? There'll be a hellava lot of work feeding and cleaning after those horses. Who'll do it?"

I thought a moment before I answered him. Looking down the long aisle of the empty barn, already filled with horses in my mind's eye, I replied with all the confidence I could muster, "I will, and the children will help me."

Bud laughed, shaking his head. "Woman, those kids are pretty young. Your boy's twelve, but the girls can't be more'n seven or eight."

"They're eight and ten," I replied. "They're big enough to feed and water horses. They want to help."

Bud shook his head, his eyes full of disbelief. "Some bales weigh ninety pounds or more."

"The girls will manage just fine. I'll cut the bales and separate the flakes. And they won't always be eight and ten years old."

That night the children helped me compose my first advertisement for a chain of newspapers in neighboring suburban villages: Horses Boarded,

Conscientious Care, Reasonable Rates and our phone number.

Looking into the children's faces, so full of trust, I vowed the project would succeed. It simply had to. It was the only way I would be able to support the family without leaving home. The farm was my divorce settlement. I wanted to live there and be available to the children, still too young to be on their own after school.

And now, I had the loan. In short order, Bud Riley started construction on forty box stalls in the big barn. He brought with him an experienced welder to burn off the iron cow stancheons. Until the stalls were completed, I planned to shelter boarding horses in the stock pens at each end of the barn.

The endless shower of sparks from the welder's torch alarmed me. I continually warned Bud to keep an eye out for fire. He hooked up a length of hose and periodically sprayed the barn walls and ceilings. I worried that an unnoticed spark would reduce my venture to ashes. I was greatly relieved when the welding was finished.

Chapter 2

Mellow Vibrations

I met our first prospective customers -- two pretty girls, one ash-blonde, one dark-haired -- coming out of the big barn with Whitney. He had been showing them around. They were dressed in blue jeans and khaki army shirts with a red 5th Army patch on one shoulder and the word Peace embroidered on the back. Neither of the girls wore makeup . . . or shoes!

These girls, Carrie and Holly, were joint owners of a mare named Bounty. "We're looking for a place to board our horse, a place where the vibrations are mellow," Carrie said, smiling at me.

The vernacular of the sixties was alien to me but before I could say anything, Whitney, obviously captivated by the eighteen year old prospects, said, "We're mellow, aren't we Mom?"

"I guess we are." I said, laughing. I explained our boarding accomodations and rates, the difference between box or tie stalls, and that 'on the rough' meant to board in a paddock with other horses, and with a loafing barn for shelter.

"One more point, girls," I told them firmly. "If you decide to board your horse with us, you'll have to wear something on your feet. Bare feet are not allowed in the barn." I went on to describe the hazards of the tetanus baccilli. They listened intently, wide- eyed as if it was the first time they had ever heard of its danger.

Apparently the vibrations of Arcadia were good. After conferring together, they nodded their heads in agreement. They would keep their horse at my minimum rate, "on the rough." Each paid half her board.

Steadfast friends, the girls had gone through primary, elementary and high school together. They worked as waitresses in a tea room in the suburbs. The mare, Bounty, though dense boned and crude, with hairy fetlocks, proved to have a grateful personality.

My own daughters, Gail and Lynn, although so much younger, developed a strong attachment for Carrie and Holly. Over the years, I considered the older girls good influences with their gentleness and simplicity.

While I spoke with Carrie and Holly that first day, a well-dressed man had parked his Chrysler New Yorker near the barn. He walked toward us, a copy of my newspaper ad in his hand. Chase Harper was about fifty, with a pleasant round face and hornrimmed glasses. He removed his chocolate brown Stetson hat and inquired genially, "How soon can I move in? It seems like a real homey place, Barbie should like it here."

"Immediately," I replied. "That is, if you don't mind using one of the stock pens for a few weeks."

Chase Harper took a picture out of his wallet and passed it around for us to see. He spoke of his pretty little chestnut mare as if she were his closest friend. He was proud of her "Three Bars" bloodline and called her, "Barbie Bar." He said he had no objection to keeping her in a stock pen, temporarily. He mentioned he was District Manager for Chrysler Motors. He did not ask about my boarding rates.

After we had admired Barbie's picture, Chase pointed to Whitney and asked, "Can this fine young fellow show me where to put my saddle? I've got it in the trunk." The two of them walked off in the direction of the silo, now converted to a tack room. My spirits soared. I had my first two boarders.

Within three weeks, I had eighteen boarders and the work on the barn was almost completed. As Whitney said, "We are really in the horse business." We continued to receive inquiries from the newspaper ads and the sign on the road. That so encouraged me that I considered other ways to increase the farm's income.

I decided to buy a few school horses so I could offer trail riding and lessons. Scanning the Sunday paper, I noticed a two line advertisement. "Riding horses, reasonable". The seller's address was on Chicago's far south side, near the Indiana line.

Taking Whitney along for moral support, I set out that very afternoon. After battling city traffic we reached a rundown house trailer adjacent to a large fenced corral. Thirty-five horses, mules and ponies milled aimlessly, indifferently snatching mouthfuls of moldy hay from a manger.

A boy, about fifteen years old, slouched against the fence. An unlit cigarette dangled from his lips. His lean-ribbed hound growled a warning and came toward us as we climbed out of the car.

Whitney, braver than I, walked toward the boy. "Call off your dog," Whitney said. "My mom wants to buy some horses. Some good ones."

The boy whistled the hound to his side, looped a frayed clothesline around its neck, tying the end to the front fender of a beat-up horse van. The boy gestured toward the herd. "Take your pick."

This was my first experience as a horse buyer. I had purchased Kono, our family Palomino, on the recommendation of a friend. I hadn't known what to expect, but I hadn't expected *this*.

Slightly confused and doubtful now about how to recognize sound horse flesh, Whitney and I walked around the enclosure, eliminating horses with obvious disabilities or those in poor condition. Finally, we agreed on two mares, a black and white pinto and a chunky chestnut with a homely head and small eyes. Our third choice was a roan gelding with flaxen mane and tail.

The boy told us the price for each, a total of four hundred seventy five dollars. Then he took a brush from a can of white wash next to the trailer and walked over to the horses we had chosen. He wrote a number on each horse's rump and handed me a crumpled piece of paper on which he had written the same numbers and the selling price. We arranged for delivery the following Wednesday. With a last nervous glance at the horses, Whitney and I climbed into the car and drove home. By the time we reached Arcadia, I had convinced myself that horse trading was not difficult at all. We would see how these horses turned out and return in a few weeks for others.

Chapter 3

Lessons To Be Learned

As promised, a battered cattle trailer rumbled up the driveway on Wednesday, a wiry, unshaven man at the wheel. Gail, Lynn and Whitney crowded around as the driver, hacking and spitting, unloaded the horses. I had promised Gail she could consider the chestnut mare hers -- when not used for business -- if she would keep it groomed.

On the spot, Gail named her Nina. Whitney and Lynn named the big gelding, Blaze.

The cattle trailer and the old man and boy had hardly left the driveway when Gail ran for her saddle. We watched as she mounted Nina, nudged her with a heel to "walk off". The horse lowered her head, planted her hooves in the grass and refused to budge. After promises, threats, and swats with the reins, we accepted the truth that Nina would not leave the yard. Eventually, we learned the only way to get her going was to have someone ride another horse in front of her.

As big a disappointment as Nina seemed to be, Blaze was even more so. Ridden by Whitney, he behaved well for about five minutes, then lowered his head between his stout shoulders and began to buck, twisting his spine like a hooked fish, a "sun-fisher" for sure. Once he started, he kept it up until he unloaded his rider. After his rider had been bucked off three times, unhurt, I insisted Whitney give up and lead Blaze back to the barn.

The pinto mare seemed docile; at least she would redeem my investment. We put her in a box stall and returned to the house for supper. The children were subdued, and I dished out the stew in silence. I began to wonder if I knew as much about buying horses as I thought I did.

When I went into the barn the next morning to feed and water, I heard thumping from the pinto mare's stall and rushed over to her. She was whirling in circles, steamy sweat rising from her heaving flanks. As she swung by, I saw the tip of a tiny cream colored hoof protruding from her birth canal.

I dropped the water pail I was carrying and ran back to the house. My hands shook as I dialed Jeff Roper, our veterinarian. He wasn't in, but the answering service promised to locate him. The service called back to report they had not been able to reach him, but would keep trying. I leafed frantically through the phone book's classified section. I found a vet who worked with large animals and was listed at an address about five miles from the farm. His secretary took directions to Arcadia and I went back to the mare and waited.

A half hour later a sleek Jaguar pulled into the driveway. Out stepped a jaunty, immaculately dressed young man wearing highly polished boots, a designer sports jacket and slacks. He introduced himself as Dr. Hudson. I led him to the barn.

By that time the little pinto mare was in the throes of an abortion. The doctor shed his jacket and knelt by the mare. With each violent contraction, he applied gentle pressure on the foal's leg, now fully visible. He did not speak to me, his silence an accusation. Finally, with a last violent contraction, a dead foal slipped into the doctor's arms. By that time, the doctor was smeared with dirt and blood. The mare, exhausted from her ordeal lay quietly, her sides continuing to heave with uterine contractions.

With the anguished children watching, the veterinarian helped me slip the dead foal into a plastic bag and between us we carried her to a spot in the shade near the hay wagon. I didn't know what might happen next. Dr. Hudson offered no information or explanation. I was so intimidated and shocked that I stood silent while he washed his arms in a pail of cold water, snapped shut his medical bag, and without a consoling word or backward glance, strode to his car and sped down the driveway.

Not knowing what else to do for the mare, I added clean bedding to her stall and sent Gail to the house for warm water to add to her water pail.

Then, the children and I watched helplessly as she repeatedly staggered to her feet only to collapse. Each time she seemed more disoriented, sometimes falling and banging her head against the stall boards. As her actions became more violent, I realized she should be moved to an open area where she couldn't injure herself. With Gail grasping the dock of her tail to steady her, Whitney and I supported the mare across the yard. When we reached a grassy spot, she gave a great sigh, fell to her knees and stretched her neck on the sod, groaning. We squatted silently around her. It was clear that she was dying.

We heard the telephone in the barn. It was Dr. Roper's wife calling to say he was on his way.

I stifled my impulse to hug the familiar vet when he stepped out of his station wagon and hurried over to us. In seconds, Dr. Roper was administering an intravenous solution, supplemented with antibiotics, to the stricken mare. Whitney stood on a bale of straw holding the bottle over his head, while Gail and Lynn stroked the mare's twitching legs.

Dr. Roper asked where I had bought her. After I told him about the ad in the paper he said, "That's a risky way to buy horses. I'd say the little mare had been kicked in the belly or thrown hard against the side of a railroad cattle car. They ship them loose from horse auctions, without feed or water. Injury in this way could have caused death to the foal. Toxemia must have entered the mare's blood stream immediately. She has all the symptoms of 'the blind staggers'."

The vet followed the intravenous solution with a blood transfusion, bending over the suffering animal, frequently lifting an eyelid and peering at her bloodshot eyes.

I fought to keep from crying as I watched the children's white, worried faces and debated about sending them to the house.

The mare's breathing became shallow. Finally, with an almost inaudible sigh, she shuddered and lay still. The children began to cry. We stood with our arms about each other, for comfort.

That night in bed I restlessly tossed, reliving the terrifying day. It was like nothing I had ever imagined. Three problem horses: one pig-eyed and stubborn, one incorrigible and dangerous, and one dead. My self-confidence had evaporated.

I knew I wouldn't quit, but I needed to advance quickly beyond the greenhorn stage. I had been reluctant to admit I might need help. I knew now that I needed help badly. First thing in the morning, I'd call Dr. Jeff Roper for advice.

When I asked him where I could buy reliable horses, he replied in detail. "First of all, Mrs. K, there are few folks from whom I would buy horses in this area. You should drive up to Marion Center, Wisconsin, just over the state line, to the Pike brothers' farm. Those boys bring in decent horses for resale from the Dakotas and North Platt, Nebraska. Both the Pike boys are pretty straight and truthful. Should there be any question about the horse's health, I can go by there and check the horse out for you. Remember, it will be impossible to find perfect horses for what you are able to pay. Tell Justin Pike you want gentle horses and leave it to him. The horses will most likely have a little age on them, but also remember you can fatten up most any horse with decent feed and adequate water."

I felt reassured that Dr. Roper would help me select serviceable horses, checking their vision, legs, and respiratory systems. The advice he gave me about the Pike brothers was some of the best I received during the twenty years I owned Arcadia Farm. In the course of those years I bought over forty head of horses from them. Ninety percent turned out to be satisfactory. At this point, however, the years with their painful lessons to be learned stretched before me, and Dr. Roper would prove, with others, to be a perceptive teacher.

Chapter 4

My Early Years

As I watched my healthy children run and tumble in the twilight on summer evenings in the midwest, catching fireflies in an old mason jar, I thought of my own childhood in the east.

I was a frail child, having contracted infantile paralysis before I was eight. My mother took me to the leading specialists of the day, including the Royal Victoria Hospital in Montreal. The doctors stretched, adhesive taped, measured and manipulated my tortured leg muscles. I had massage with melted cocoa butter, and foot exercises with a masseuse who came to our home. Under protest, I swallowed a daily tablespoonful of countless pints of cod liver oil and liver extract.

I lost so much formal schooling that my parents hired a governess to tutor me over the years. During summers at Camp Arcadia on Rainbow Lake, my good parents also hired Jim, a strapping Adirondack guide, as my nurse and companion.

Jim taught me to fish, to swim and handle a canoe. He saw that I came to no harm in the healthful out of doors which would play such a part in my recovery. It was through Jim's influence that I developed a keen awareness and love for the wildlife in that part of northern New York which my mother lovingly called "God's Country".

Each day there were lessons to be learned as Jim and I explored the many wonders of the forests and lakes. In the restoring sunshine, and with Jim in the stern of the canoe, his paddle scarcely making a riffle on the water, we glided within a stone's throw of working beavers or close to a buck or doe. They stood knee high in the rushes feeding on lily pads, out of reach of tormenting black flies.

When the canoe drifted with the current near a cranberry bog, Jim pointed out a blue heron standing on one leg, making believe he was an upright stick and that we couldn't see him. Sometimes we followed a family of loons all afternoon, watching them disappear beneath the water only to pop up again a long way off, nearer the shoreline.

Often we set the rudder of my toy sailboat, watching it take a true, brave course through the choppy waves. Jim always rescued the little bark before it ran aground in the rocky cove.

Six Adirondack summers at Rainbow Lake under the guide's watchful eye restored me to good health, except for a slight limp whenever I got excessively tired.

Dearly as I loved our Camp Arcadia, one of my tenderest memories was of the ten acre gentlemen's farm in Connecticut, with a saltbox farmhouse dating back to the American Revolution. So vivid is my recollection of that property that, if given the task today, I could lay out the entire plot from memory even though I was no more than six when we lived there, and that only a few months of each year.

I could not forget the towering pines where my single board swing hung from a lofty branch and where stretching and straining my polio-weakened calf muscles I swung higher and higher over beds of golden glow, singing at the top of my voice, songs I made up myself. Rainy days were no hindrance to swinging and singing. The pine boughs above my head were so dense not a raindrop fell on me.

Below my swing, on the lawn, mountain pink spread up and over a huge boulder of silvery gray granite embedded in the earth. Terraces on the west side of the house sloped gently to a row of willows which father planted himself. Crimson, white and delicate pink rambler roses burst over fieldstone walls bordering my mother's flower gardens where beds of purple iris, white peonies, clusters of variegated phlox and peach dahlias bloomed profusely.

It was here too, in a small barn, that father kept Rosebud, an old chestnut steeplechaser, his spirited riding mare. She was always afoam and champing at the bit and I was never allowed near or on her. I watched the two of them from a vantage point in the low-hanging branches of a Queen Anne Cherry tree as my father urged Rosebud to jump post and rail fences over the over again, finally disappearing over the rising slope of the meadow. Although they were out of sight, I knew the mare was leaping across the brook which ran through a neighbor's pasture.

Often at supper father would regale us with accounts of Rosebud's courage: how she scaled a high wall or without hesitation scrambled down the rocky embankment near the old quarry. Father always said if Rosebud wasn't in Heaven when he got there he wasn't going to go through the gates himself. In later life I understood what he meant.

It would be many years before I had a horse of my own but the seed planted by my father's words grew and blossomed in my mind. There could be nothing more wonderful or exciting than to own a horse! My heart was set on it.

Passing years saw me married and settled in the midwest, eventually buying rural property. To my city-bred husband, our farm was a canny investment, but to me it was a dream fullfilled. I would live once more in the out-of-doors and have my children close to me. We could have a dog, a cat and maybe a horse.

Years later, when the farm on Allendale road became mine in our divorce settlement, it provided support for the children and me.

I made great plans for my own Arcadia Farm. I too, would have broad well-kept lawns and lush flower gardens, just like my parents did. Where I would get the resources did not occur to me. I dreamed my fantasies. Multiflora rose hedges, lilacs and forsythia already bloomed generously near the road. It was a good start. Formal flower gardens would have to be left to the future.

The best we ever managed was to mow the lawns, let a good bit of them revert to hayfield and plant tubs of red geraniums and white petunias at the front door. However, I did not compromise on the lawns. They always looked well cared for, thanks to Whitney. He maintains he spent most of his teen years walking behind a lawn mower.

Chapter 5

Farmin' and Such

Renting out acreage to a neighboring farmer would probably pay my taxes and little more. I finally decided to farm the land myself, since income was my primary goal. That meant I would need someone experienced to plant, cultivate and harvest the crop.

One late summer morning I was at the Farm Bureau Supply Company buying water pails for the horse stalls. In the course of our conversation about the merits of different weights in galvanized buckets, I asked the owner if he knew anyone who might be interested in working for me. He reflected a few seconds, then disappeared into his office and returned with a small pad of paper in his hand. "Maybe my brother-in-law Josie. He's retired, but he's looking for something to do. Knows all about farming and such. Doesn't drink or smoke. Chaws a little." He laughed as he handed me the writing pad. "Make me a little map where you live."

The next morning Josie came to see me. Just turned sixty-five, he had finished thirty years as an employee of a large tractor plant. He looked more like fifty-five, strong, energetic, active. His steel grey hair was neatly trimmed in a crew cut. His penetrating blue eyes never left my face as he listened to what would be expected of him.

Josie knew all about farming. "Like a book," he informed me. He knew how and when to plant soy beans and field corn. He could handle the tractor with plow, disk and drag. The corn planter was not the mystery to him that it was to me.

First, we looked over the machinery. I had inherited an old International diesel tractor with the farm. Josie proposed tuning it up before fall. The list of new parts he needed was staggering, particularly

with money in short supply.

"Always like to do some plowing in the fall. Land works up better come spring," he explained. "Don't like this here model too much," Josie stated flatly, inspecting the motor of the diesel.

"It will have to do, it's all I have," I replied defensively.

Even though Josie was opinionated, He was the answer to my need. After our talk he left to think about the job. I hoped against hope that his decision would be favorable.

He was back the next day. With him was his rosy cheeked, plump wife. She must have weighed two hundred pounds. Ida Mae had come to look me over. "Joseph says you're as green as grass when it comes to field work, but never you mind, honey. As I always say, you can't be good lookin' and smart at the same time." There was no malice in her remarks but I couldn't agree with her theory. I had always thought you could be both.

Josie decided to "Give it a try" as he put it. Ida Mae was a bonus. She was one of the best cooks in the county. Many doughnuts -- that she called crullers --, apple and peach pie, and fluffy angel food cake found its way into my brood's grateful stomachs. The hungry "little shavers," Josie called them.

Throughout those years when Josie worked for me, (I preferred to put it, worked with me,) I could not have run the farm without him even though his pessimism was sometimes enervating. He became to the "shavers" the patient grandfather figure. As the years passed I relied on him more and more.

"Can you teach Whit to run the diesel?" I asked Josie one morning. "Wouldn't surprise me none," Josie answered, surveying my skinny son. "His arms are a mite puny. Come here sonny, let's see if you can turn the wheel."

On the high tractor seat, Whitney grasped the big, black, steel wheel. The veins on his forearms stood out with effort as he barely managed to turn the front tires slightly to the left and right.

"This old junker will build your muscles," Josie laughed as he patted Whitney on the shoulder.

Old as it was, after the tuneup the big International made quick work of the field chores. At first Josie did all the plowing. Later, Whitney disked and dragged the field to ready it for sowing. In a few years, he had mastered the hydraulic lift and was plowing, too.

Once in awhile Whitney would stop the tractor to rest, looking up at the sky where jets were flying. Whitney wanted to be a commercial pilot. The responsibilities of our business kept him earthbound but his heart was in the skies. Over the farm, his keen eyes followed the aircraft on their flight patterns into O'Hare Field. As he grew older, he talked constantly about taking flying lessons. I promised him some day I would see he got them.

Chapter 6

No Time For Conversation

I awakened every morning around five o'clock to the familiar, strident crow of cock ring-necked pheasants. They roosted at night in the tall Colorado blue spruce near my front door. If I got up right away at the male's first rasping cry and looked out my bedroom window, I saw the birds strutting like peacocks on the front lawn, trailing their shaded, brown-striped tail feathers on the ground, their emerald green and white collars a vivid contrast to the dull grey morning mist.

Sometimes it was hard for me to leave the warmth of my Hudson Bay blanket and down pillows, especially if I had spent most of the night in a cold barn with a sick horse or a new mother.

When I hugged the soft wool pile of the blanket against my cheek and closed my eyes, its warmth brought a memory of Rainbow Lake in the Adirondacks. There, the best sleeping was on the sleeping porch, screened on three sides, high among the fragrant pines. When rain beat on the roof at night nothing equaled the sense of security the blanket provided. There was something romantic about the legend of the blanket for which the Indians traded four beaver pelts.

Usually I took a hasty morning shower, dressed in a flannel shirt, jeans and boots and went downstairs quietly, leaving the children a half hour more to sleep.

Munching on a slice of toast, I made breakfast. Hot cereal, toast and cocoa was our usual fare. There were seldom any complaints about its lack of variety. While the children ate, I made school sack lunches. At the same time, I made mental notes concerning the chores ahead of me.

During the school year, the children had limited time to help with morning chores, so we moved right along with little conversation. Whitney put hay in the long manger for the outside horses, our "roughers", kept in a paddock in the winter with a loafing shed for shelter. I fed in the small barn and then the two of us joined Lynn and Gail feeding in the main barn and corn crib. I helped the girls water while Whitney

finished up caring for the annex horses.

Back in the house, after their showers, Gail fed the cats while Lynn fed our dogs, Stuart and Ashley. Beds were made in haste, soiled clothes thrown down the laundry chute.

Gathering up books and lunches they ran for the school bus at the end of the long driveway. Lester, the driver, was often waiting for them. At that point I sat down at the kitchen table, transferring my mental notes to a written list for the day.

Josie was on the place by the time I went back to the barns at eight-thirty. He and I watered all the stock once again before he started daily chores, field work or maintainance. Next, I tackled the mountain of laundry in the cellar.

Chapter 7

A Perfect Police Horse

"Put 'im back in the barn, I ain't in'trested in thet ole crowbait," scoffed the seedy looking man, spitting a stream of tobacco juice on the ground. We were at the Pike brothers' farm looking for horses. Other customers were there as well. The rough looking man, several days' growth of beard on his leathery cheeks, continued to spit tobacco juice and comment in a loud voice, "That one will be a hard keeper! Look at them rafter hips."

I took a good look at the big bay gelding who was the subject of these disparaging remarks. He looked to me like a horse who could stand a square meal, -- painfully thin in neck, barrel and hind quarters. I remembered what Dr. Roper had said about fattening up the "good" ones. I watched the bay being ridden by one of the Pikes. He did everything asked of him, jogging slowly on a loose rein, backing up without sticking his nose in the air. He seemed to be a "real good broke horse" as Justin Pike put it, quiet, gentle, willing.

There was something else about him. The way he held his head, the alert, intelligent look in his eye. Suddenly, a childhood memory engulfed me: From a little girl's vantage point, I was standing on the sidewalk looking up at another bay horse who seemed very tall indeed. Under his highly polished English saddle, lay a military blue saddle pad with the initials, N.Y.P.D. stitched in gold thread. The letters glittered in the afternoon sunlight.

Each day between three and four o'clock the horse and rider were at the corner near the residential Gramercy Park hotel. So were my nurse and I. My family spent January and February in New York to ease the stress of father's commuting to his law office during those strenuous months.

Our stay at the elegant small hotel was particularly important after the stock market crash, from which Father sustained heavy losses and failing health.

Billy, the doorman at Gramercy Park, must have seen and understood a little girl's passion for the police horse. One day as my nurse and I crossed the lobby he surprised me with a membership card in the "Society for the Prevention of Cruelty to Animals", and a large membership button. I wore it constantly, even on my nightgown.

One memorable day Billy lifted me up in front of the mounted policeman. How different the world looked from between the ears of a horse! I stroked the horse's muscular neck, fingering the leather pouch tied to the saddle. Into it the officer put all the treats well-meaning New Yorkers gave him for the horse. He told my nurse that if he fed all the sugar lumps, carrots and apples pressed on Commander, the horse would surely die.

Now, thirty years later, a long way from Gramercy Park, this childhood heart-stirring memory stunned me. I caught my breath at the impact of the astounding similarity between the two bay horses.

The shabby looking man kept up a running commentary, disparaging everything about the bay from the size of his head to the sparceness of his tail.

At one point he "lowed the horse would "Make good mink food, if the mink weren't too choosy."

That remark made me so angry I called out to Jake Pike, "Jake, include that big gelding for Arcadia Farm."

The disagreeable man gave me a pitying look, spat on the ground and snarled, "Girlie, you don't know a damn thing about buying horses."

The horses were to be delivered to the farm in a few days. When the stock truck arrived, there, wedged between two others, was my "rafter hipped" skinny one. As Jake led him down the truck ramp, suddenly the horse's glands under his jaw broke. Pus literally poured down his neck and chest. It was my first experience with shipping fever, distemper in horses. It would not be my last.

Apologetically, Jake said, "I'll take him back to my place until he's clear if you want." I looked at the horse. He was in sorry shape. In addition to being just skin and bones, he had messed on the ramp in front of his new owner.

"I still want him," I said, "and I'll pay his board until he's clear."

I appreciated Jake taking the horse back to avoid exposing my other horses to shipping fever. Future experience would teach me it is almost impossible to keep the virus from spreading. Watching Jake reload the horse, which had scrambled willingly up the steep ramp, I was upset by the plight of the animal. Already the bond between us was forming.

It was three weeks before I saw the bay again. Once the ramp was lowered, he inched his way down the steep incline. Jake handed me the lead rope and I led the gelding into the barn. It was my first real contact with him.

"Come on big boy," I encouraged the scrawny creature. He followed me eagerly. Big Boy . . . that was it, a perfect name, and so the bay horse became one of my first school horses.

Big Boy's condition meant we must take steps immediately to rehabilitate him. Dr. Prince gave him a thorough physical, wormed him and floated his teeth. When he opened Big Boy's mouth and pulled his huge tongue to one side to get a better look at his molars he called to me, "Look here, Mrs. K, see this."

Horrified, I saw for the first time scar tissue on Big Boy's tongue. It had been almost torn in two at one time. Dr. Prince thought the injury had been caused by too severe a bit in the harsh and heavy hands of a careless rider.

Grazing through the summer on good pasture, Big Boy fleshed out. In time he developed into a solid heavy horse, weighing about eleven hundred seventy five pounds. He became the anchor horse of the business. Six year olds could rein and turn him at a walk or jog. Over the years, officers from the Army base at Fort Sheridan led the Fourth of July parade on Big Boy. He behaved in an alert, regal, unruffled manner in spite of the bands, fire engines and screaming spectators. Big Boy would have made a splendid police horse!

Chapter 8
Louie the Llama

Lester Rowe's grain farm touched my northern boundary. Les, an uncomplicated man with a warm smile, drove the school bus. For several years I bought Kono's hay from him. He delivered the timothy bales in his pickup truck, right to the horsebarn. Whitney and I helped unload it into a vacant stall.

Les was a reference resource for almost anything I needed for the farm. He directed me to the Farm Bureau store for supplies, salt blocks, fly repellant, even an aluminum gate. I asked Les where I could buy supplementary sweet feed for my Palomino gelding.

Chewing on a wisp of timothy, he answered me. "You better go over to Chester Hayes' place. Chester's got about everything you'll need for your horse." He laughed. "Or for rabbits, ducks and chickens too." He added, "It's a real interestin' place, Chester's warehouse. Take the kiddies with you. There's lots for 'em to see."

Chester Hayes owned a small scientific animal farm. He raised white mice, rabbits and a large assortment of exotic birds. Much of his stock found their way into zoos throughout the country.

One day, as I was leaving his warehouse after buying Kono's sweet feed, he asked me to follow him into his office. He sat down behind his cluttered desk, rubbed his forehead as if he had a headache. Then, he peered at me through his thick glasses and said, "Got a big favor to ask you, Mrs. K. Hope you can help me out!" I was looking through a plate glass partition, distracted from what Chester was saying by the sight of three pair of coral flamingos preening and bathing in the indoor pool. He repeated his statement and I realized he was waiting for a reply. "What is it you need, Ches?" I asked, not taking my eyes off the fascinating birds.

Chester leaned back in his chair and said, "It's about my llamas. I've got ten females and two males. This one male I call Louie, is so tough and mean he won't let us in the pen with the females to clean or feed. Bought the villian at an auction. He's a fine specimen, but he's not working out. Hate to get rid of him. Wondered if you'd take him over to your place for a spell. I believe he'd be okay alone, and you might gentle him down."

I stared at Chester, dumbly. Could he be serious? Up to that point I had only seen llamas in a zoo! "Well, I don't know about that," I said, playing for time.

Suddenly, Chester sprung to his feet. "Come with me," he said. "Take a look."

Skirting several tall dressers, each with drawers overflowing with squirming white mice, I followed Chester into the yard. He led me down a gravel path past pens of foxes, skunks, and raccoons. Behind a ten foot cyclone fence grazed the llama herd. Several of the animals were lying down, chewing their cuds. Near these females, standing guard, was a male llama. "That's Louis, the old rascal," Chester whispered under his breath.

"What does he do that is so bad?" I inquired innocently. By that time we were right up to the fencing. "I'll show you, but you stand back," Chester said.

He walked up to the gate and called "Here Louie, here Louie." The llama turned his head, tipped back his camel-like head, filled his mouth with saliva and spit a stream of brown juice toward  Chester who knowledgeably stepped back out of range. The stench from the spit was foul. At the same time the llama let out a kick at the wire fencing with both hind feet. The steel posts reverberated. Obviously, Louie was a real terror.

"He'll have to go. That's all there is to it. I won't put up with this." Chester shook his head sadly from side to side. I had to laugh, for in the pen, Louie was imitating Chester, shaking his head, twitching his nose and growling.

Then Chester said, "Louie was raised in a children's zoo. I guess they teased the hell out of him."

Suddenly, I felt sympathy for the llama. I felt myself weakening. "I'll take him to the farm on a trial basis, Chester," I heard myself saying. "But you'll have to get him there. Bring some grain along. I have plenty of hay."

Chester said he would tranquilize Louie, put a halter on him and deliver him to me the next day.

At supper that evening, I told the children about our new boarder. They were excited. Gail said she had been studying about llamas in class. "You can ride them, you know, Mom. They're beasts of burden, just like camels and donkeys." Whitney and Lynn were exchanging knowing glances.

The next day, Chester brought the llama in a stock trailer. The llama was dopey from the tranquilizer.

With Chester leading him, Josie pushing on one side and Whitney on the other, they shoved the beast down the barn aisle into the bull pen. We slammed the heavy pipe gate behind him. The llama promptly lay down with his legs curled beneath him and began to chew his cud rhythmically. His long, silky eyelashes covered his eyes with every chaw. I thought, this isn't so bad, but what will happen when the tranquilizer wears off?

An hour later, there was loud kicking at the bull-pen walls and piping. Louie had looked into the horsebarn and didn't like what he saw. I watched with growing consternation as the llama lashed out with both hind feet over and over again. From the outside, Whitney vaulted the twelve foot bull yard fence and slid the door to the bull pen open. This gave Louie access to the outdoors and sunshine. The cantankerous beast calmed down and began to eat hay.

Caring for the llama fitted into our regular feeding routine. It was no problem at all to include him with a flake of hay when I fed the horses. It took but a minute to fill his water pail and slide a shallow cake pan of grain under his gate. I impressed upon the children not to prolong their chores with the llama, allowing him to settle into his new surroundings for a time. Above all, I cautioned everyone not to provoke or tease him. I wanted to put an end to his disgusting spitting!

We moved the barn radio into his quarters so Louie could ruminate contentedly to the popular music of the day. Whether or not Louie enjoyed his own company or was a loner, he did like being alone. He spent most of the time out in his bull yard basking in the sunshine. When we cleaned his area we put grain in the outside pen and slid the door between us so he couldn't surprise us.

One morning, as I was changing light bulbs in the ceiling of the main barn, Josie interrupted me. "Come with me, Mrs. K. Come see what that there 'lima is up to," he said with a glint in his eye. I put the stepladder away and followed Josie to the bull pen apprehensive about what mischief Louis might have gotten himself into.

My heart almost stopped beating at what I saw. There was Whitney leading Louie in circles in the bull yard. Astride the llama's plush back, her legs entwined around the animal's neck sat Lynn, my youngest.

Seeing the concern on my face, Whitney stopped dead. "Mom, it's okay. Louie likes it. He hasn't spit once!"

Lynn pleaded, "Mom, watch me. Louie's a good boy. Really Mom!"

I couldn't argue with them. The llama appeared almost placid and manageable. The children had his confidence. What could I say?

Admonishing them to take extra care, and to restrict the llama- riding to no more than five minutes, I retreated to the barn and called Chester on the phone.

"Can't believe it," Louie's owner declared. "You mean to tell me that old rascal let those kids ride him? That's really good news." Later in the afternoon, the whole riding performance was repeated for Chester with Whitney riding the llama and Josie leading him. After this display Whitney dismounted.

Chester was impressed. "What can I do for these kids?" Chester asked me. "They're better trainers than many I've seen."

Whitney looked toward the ground, not his usual talkative self. Lynn had a wistful look on her face.

"Tell me, you two," Chester urged. "What kind of a reward can I give you for taking such good care of Louie and training him to boot?"

Lynn's face brightened. "You could give Louie to Whitney and me!"

I was embarrassed at such a direct answer to Chester's question. I put my arm around their shoulders saying, "Oh no, children, Louie has to go back to Chester's. He's too valuable an animal."

Lynn's eyes filled with tears.

Chester, his brow wrinkled in a frown, seemed to be wrestling with a decision, torn between the value of the llama and the children's feelings. "Tell you what," he said, "I'll give you one of the first babies that Louie fathers. How would that be?"

Lynn stopped crying as she ran toward Chester and hugged him around the waist.

"We'd like a girl," declared Whitney. "We want a girl llama. Okay, Lynnie?" Lynn nodded. "A girl would be fine," she said, smiling at Louie.

That evening as I washed supper dishes I reflected on my decision to take the llama in the first place. I had not anticipated that one could learn to love a llama, especially one as naughty as Louie. He had won our hearts: even mine.

One week later, Chester decided it was time to take Louie home. He was anxious to find out if Louie's manners had improved. A few weeks later, Chester called to report that, once home, Louie reverted to his old cantankerous self.

Unfortunately, Chester had Louie gelded so I never had to cross the bridge of raising one of Louie's offspring. It was a disappointment to Lynn and Whitney who chorused, upon hearing of Louie's surgery, "Gee whiz, Mom! And just when we were looking forward to raising our own llama."

Chapter 9

Darkness Before Dawn

Our stone farm house, built on a gentle knoll, had two wings divided by a long hall. On the left were two bedrooms, a bath, and the stairs to the second floor. At the end of the hall was the family room with its honey pine paneling and stone fireplace.

The other wing, off a short vestibule, included the living and dining rooms with cove ceilings and marble window sills.

We seldom sat in the living room and used the dining room only on special occasions or holidays. We ate all our meals at the round, oak table in the kitchen.

There were times, however, when I retreated to the living room, alone. It was from the living room windows that I could see the full-crowned Norway maples and stately blue spruce, and beyond, the broad lawn leading to the mares' and foals' pasture. The living room also held my mother's antiques. After any emotional or traumatic experience, being near mother's graceful furnishings had a stabilizing, comforting effect on me. The elegant Federal mahogany pie crust tea table held a delicate handpainted china tea service with yellow roses. Many of the accessories in the room had been my mother's wedding presents when she was married in 1907.

Father had said more than once that the sofa table, its drawers faced with satinwood, was Duncan Phyfe. He pointed out the cabinet maker's trademarks in design, the clustered wheat ears and reeded legs. Father's favorite piece, a Chippendale spinet desk, constructed from Honduras mahogany with tiny drawers and pidgeon holes supported by heavily carved legs, stood against one wall, flanked by two of mother's wing chairs. One was upholstered in dusty rose velvet with tiny fleur de lis woven in the fabric. The other was covered with pale green striped damask. Rarely did anyone from our family sit on them. Our jeans were too rough for those delicate, worn fabrics.

This room was a good place to collect my thoughts. Being near the familiar, graceful furnishings had a comforting affect on me. Seated in one of Mother's chairs by the dim light of an ivory Majolica lamp, I'd sort out my problems. I could almost hear her voice admonishing, "Don't forget, it's always darkest before the dawn." or "Faint heart never won fair lady." Mother had such pronouncements for any occasion.

How often she told me, "The only limitations you have in life are those you impose on yourself". I tried to believe this as I struggled with the day-to-day problems of Arcadia Farm.

Chapter 10

The Boys

In addition to the horses, we always had a large inventory of small animals at the farm. Our isolated location made us vulnerable to people abandoning dogs and cats at the entrance to the farm. We became home for innumerable strays, as well.

In August, 1960, several trail riders reported they had seen three or four abandoned pups in a ditch along the roadside. Lynn and Gail searched for the dogs without success. The pups, we suspected, had scampered into the tall cornfields across the road. However, one Sunday morning Chase Harper, on the trail with Barbie Bar, came upon the puppies huddled in the ditch near a culvert. He galloped back to the farm and told the girls where to find the dogs. The pups had been without food for at least a week and could be sullen or even aggressive. However, when Lynn and Gail reached the shoulder of the road, four pups hurled themselves joyously upon them, whimpering, yapping and wagging their tails.

Josie helped pile the four pups into the front seat of the truck and drove them back to the barn. The dogs were about three months old, all males and of mixed breeds. They were half-starved and because of their shrunken stomachs we fed each one a small meal for starters. Then we put them in the high-fenced old tennis court until we decided what to do with them.

We were rereading "Gone With the Wind" at this time and decided to name the dogs Rhett, Brent, Ashley, and Stuart.

Rhett, the largest, black and white with a thick plumy tail, made a hit with Josie. He said he would like to take Rhett home with him. Brent, fawn colored and with a fine muzzle, was the smallest. Ashley, coal black with a dab of white on his chest, had border collie characteristics. Stuart was light tan and dark brown. A heart-shaped mask framed his wary brown eyes.

Three of the dogs scampered and played boisterously with the children while I sat on the entrance step to the court, watching them. Stuart stood off to one side, wagging his tail wistfully. Suddenly, he turned from the fracas and ran to me. He sat down next to my right leg and pressed his body against my knee and looked up into my face. He had chosen me. Not only was he my dog but I was his person.

Ida Mae agreed it was alright for Josie to bring Rhett home with him and one of the boarders took Brent. I decided to keep Ashley, as well as Stuart. They had a strong bond between them. Daily, they rough-toughed in between house and barn, running sideways, their muzzles in each other's mouth in the way of wild wolves' strange communication. They slept on the enclosed back porch in the summer and in the winter I let them into the house.

We nicknamed them "the boys" and often Josie would say, "Me and the boys are going to get the mares from the field." Someone overhearing that comment might think he had some hired hands, but it was always the dogs who accompanied Josie. They took their job seriously too, following closely behind, never nipping at the horses' ankles and keeping an eye on the giddy colts who often scampered ahead of their placid mothers.

Ashley was gregarious. He made up to almost everyone. Stuart, though affable, was more selective. Muttering ominous growls, he circled newcomers. There were those he liked and never forgot, and many close family friends he would never warm up to. Sometimes he embarrassed me by being so ultra suspicious of my friends.

In the barns, Stuart had an affinity for the foals. He touched noses with them gingerly, arching his neck, rolling his eyes in rapture. He knew which stalls held the newborns and their mothers. Whenever I watered and fed them he dashed ahead of me to greet them. The foals knew him, too. They extended their necks and recoiled at the touch of Stuart's cold nose on their muzzles. Eventually, the foals themselves waited at the front of their stalls looking for the dog.

One morning Stuart and I had a frightening experience. We had gone to the north pasture to bring in a couple of school horses. A few days before, I had added Peaches, a new boarder's horse, to the herd. A gold and white spotted mare, she adapted readily and the other horses accepted her. I had no idea Peaches hated dogs.

Stuart and I were more than halfway across the field, a long way from the gate. I located the two horses I wanted and started leading them out of the pasture. All of a sudden, a horse broke from the herd bearing down on me at a full run, ears plastered against her head, teeth bared. It was Peaches. I panicked momentarily, and jumped between my two school horses. Peaches passed me at a full gallop, her target, the small brown dog who had followed me into the field.

Stuart knew it too. He whirled and headed for the fence, pouring on all the speed he could muster. It was not an equal contest. I watched, horrified. My throat parched with fear as the horse closed the gap between herself and the dog. Her vise-like teeth were bared, inches from Stu's back. I could not pull my eyes away from certain tragedy.

With a sudden desperate burst of speed, Stuart miraculously reached the fence in time and scooted under the bottom strand of wire. I heard Peach's jaws snap shut, a split second later. The frustrated horse pawed and snorted on her side of the fence.

Thereafter, Stuart was reluctant to accompany me into the pasture. He waited at the gate and I could see the conflict in his eyes between wanting to come with me and remembering his narrow escape. Peaches was eventually sold, and in time, Stuart and I resumed catching horses together.

Stuart loved to ride in the old farm truck. The vehicle no longer passed a safety test, but it was still serviceable and handy for farm chores. I could throw a dozen bales of hay on its flat bed and drive to the school horses at feeding time.

The old truck was faster to use then coupling up a tractor and wagon. It had no muffler and started up with the roar of a jet. That noise brought Stuart tearing toward the truck. He'd leap up onto the worn leather seat next to me, his eyes pleading as if asking me to wait for Ashley. Seconds later, when his panting brother settled between us, Stuart sat erect looking straight ahead through the cracked windshield, a satisfied look on his face. I often laughed at the way he dominated me, making me wait for Ashley.

Sometimes, I just took them for a ride in the old truck, with their muddy feet, burrs and all, to see the progress of the hay fields, or to get the mail.

One evening, after all chores were done, and the children and I were in the house getting ready for bed, I suddenly missed Stuart. Ashley was curled up on the porch alone. This was strange because the brothers were never far apart. I whistled and called Stu's name, but he did not appear. I made a check of the barns and granary, then remembered he had been with me when I fed the roughers.

I ran to where I had parked the old truck behind the corn crib. There he was, sitting patiently on the old leather seat with its protruding steel springs. He was deliriously happy to see me and none the worse for his experience. If I ever mentioned the word "truck" he dashed ahead of me, waiting for me to open the squeaking door with its grating hinges.

Stuart became known as "Mother's dog" and for eleven years he shared the responsibilities of the farm as my constant companion. Hot summer days found him lying on the barn aisle's cool cement, one eye on me as I cleaned stalls. In winter he leaped ahead over four-foot snow drifts always looking around at me to be sure I was following him. Even in drenching, chilling rains, he trotted along beside me. Through the years there were many small animals in our life which were hard to forget. Stuart was one of these. I have never had a more faithful friend.

Chapter 11

Wildee Comes Through

One fall, during haying, Lester Rowe walked toward the house, his jaw set grimly. He had a burlap bag in his right hand. I met him on the back porch. "Damn it!" he blurted out. It was the first time I had ever heard him swear. "Damn it!" he reiterated, opening the neck of the bag. I bent forward and peered inside, horrified to see Melanie, Gail's orange tom cat, his head severed from his body.

"He was in the hay field, and I caught him with the sickle bar. I'll get a shovel and bury him," Lester said, visibly shaken.

"Let me get something to wrap him in," I said.

Upstairs in Gail's room, I sat down on the end of her bed, trying to compose myself. How should I tell her about the horrible accident?

The children loved their cats, many of them the offspring of an untamed, feral female they had named Wildee. They were never able to touch her. As wild as any predator can be, Wildee lived in our cellar for over five years, gaining access through an un-used dryer vent. She had litter after litter, most sired by an itinerant tom the children named James Bond. Few kittens survived. Wildee was not a good mother.

I saw her often when I did laundry in the cellar. From her refuge, a hole in the basement ceiling, she would peer down at me with her baleful green eyes, wide set in her multi-colored head. Gail fed her every day.

The children were always too eager to name the kittens before their sex was accurately established. For many years we had male cats with feminine names: Marilyn, Scarlett, Melanie. The tortoise cat, Marilyn, belonged to Whitney: Scarlett and Melanie to Lynn and Gail.

Before the orange toms came on the scene, Marilyn was in great demand at bedtime, the children arguing whose turn it was to have him sleep with them. Whitney marked the calendar so it would be fair, but I knew more then once he gave up his own turn to one of his sisters, who had already hidden the patient cat under her covers.

When full grown, Melanie became special to Gail. Not only was he handsome with his thick burnt-orange coat, four white paws and amber eyes, but his stirling disposition endeared him to her. He followed her everywhere.

I couldn't delay telling Gail any longer. I snatched her blue quilted bathrobe from the foot of her bed and hurried downstairs. Outside, Lester was digging a hole near the lilac bushes on the south side of the house.

I laid the robe with its tiny sprigs of spring flowers in the fabric, on the ground. Lester turned the burlap sack upside down. The decapitated cat, dirty and bloody, landed on Gail's robe. Looking away, I folded the material into a compact bundle. Lester picked it up and gently placed it in the hole. As I walked away, I heard the sound of Lester's shovel spreading the soft earth over poor Melanie.

The sound of children's voices led me to the three of them. Whitney had just nailed up the saddle rack he had made for Gail. Lynn was sweeping the equipment room.

"Hi! Mom," Whitney said, when he saw me. "How do you like this?" He pointed to the saddle rack. "I put it down low so she won't have to lift the saddle so. . ." He stopped talking, suddenly aware from my stricken expression that something awful had happened.

"It's a great saddle rack, Whit. You did a fine job," I said. "I. . .I need talk to speak to Gail a minute."

"What is it, Mom?" Gail's brown eyes searched my solemn face for an answer.

There was no way I could soften the hurtful news. I put my arm around her and took one of her hands in mine. "Gail, there's been an accident. Melanie got hurt in the hay field." I could not bring myself to describe the grisly details.

"Where is he?" Gail's eyes filled with tears. "Can I see him?" "Lester has taken care of him, he buried Melanie near the lilacs," I said.

Whitney broke in, "I would have done that. Why didn't you call me?" he asked.

"There wasn't time to call anyone," I replied.

Tears were streaming down Gail's face. Clutching her shoulders with crossed arms, she rocked her body back and forth, chanting. "Melanie, poor little Mel!"

Lynn ran to her, hugged her and with quavering voice said, "Don't cry, Gail. You can have Scarlett if you want. He likes you a lot."

We were all subdued at supper that evening. Lynn and Whitney tried to make conversation that distracted Gail from noticing Scarlett, eating from the cat's bowl, alone. Gail hardly touched her food. Her eyes were red and swollen.

After the dishes were washed and put away, Gail carried the cat food to the cellar as usual. A short time later she ran up the cellar stairs, clutching a tiny, bedraggled orange kitten in her arms. She was smiling. Wildee had come through, once again.

Chapter 12
Here, Here, You Pickle

The first time I saw the veterinarian, Dr. Prince, he was standing next to Chase Harper's Barbie Bar. Both his hands were high inside the mare's mouth. His dark green corduroy Tyrolean hat was pushed back on his head.

"Morning," he said. "I'm Thad Prince. Just checking this little gal's teeth. I've taken care of her since Mr. Harper bought her, three years ago."

I found it hard to believe this agreeable young man, looking like a college boy in his perky hat, had a degree in equine veterinary medicine. After meeting him, and because we had so many horses to take care of, I began to use him as our vet when I couldn't reach Jeff Roper. I soon developed respect for his diagnostic ability and surgical skill.

Thad had a genuine interest in all his four-footed patients. He had a fine memory for their individual case histories, and preferred to treat the horses without resorting to severe methods such as a chain twitch, or twisting ears. I often saw him take a very long time with an apprehensive patient, stroking the horse's jaws, talking to him quietly, while he gently inserted the end of a stomach tube into a quivering nostril. His stern but low key "Here! Here, you pickle" had more authority in it than loud, profane commands I had heard used with far less effect.

At first, Thad Prince conducted his practice from the back of a station wagon. In time he developed a wonderfully equipped conversion vehicle with cabinets and drawers mounted on the side of a truck bed where he kept his medicines and instruments. He had the blessing of hot water from a tank attached to the underbelly of the truck.

Once a house call was completed he sprayed a stream of hot water from a short hose over his boots and scrubbed them down with a long handled brush. This also gave me a minute or two to set up another appointment. Dr. Prince used this period to answer our endless questions, or to tell us an anecdote about one of his other patients.

"I've got a story for you, today," he said, while washing his boots. We gathered round so as not to miss a word. "You should have been with me last week when I made a house call in Killington. It was a vast estate with several big barns and an indoor arena. I'd never been there before so I drove right up to the front door of the mansion.

"I rang the bell and after quite a few minutes a lady came to the door. She was wearing a flimsy house coat with what looked like a feather boa around her neck like Jean Harlow wore in one of her old movies.

"Well, this lady was holding the smallest French poodle I ever saw, and the darndest thing, that dog was wearing a little housecoat with feathers just like hers.

"I asked her why she'd called me. She pointed to the barns and said, 'My houseboy says there is something wrong with the polo pony.' Then she slammed the door in my face. There wasn't anything for me to do but head for the barns.

"When I pulled up to one of the stables, an oriental fellow was waiting for me, pacing up and down wringing his hands. He signaled for me to follow him. It was a huge barn. It could accomodate a hundred horses easily, but it was empty. The man stopped in front of a box stall and pointed."

We were hanging on the vet's every word. Dr. Prince's tales always had elements of the unexpected.

"What was in the stall?" Gail asked for all of us.

"Was it a sick horse?" Whitney ventured a guess.

Thad Prince slammed his medical chest lid shut. "It was a horse alright. He was stone dead and had been for at least a week. I gathered from the oriental's broken English that no one had explained to him he was supposed to feed the horse daily. Obviously the poor horse starved to death."

I shuddered. What a horrible story, I thought, and hoped I'd never hear its equal.

Throughout the years, when Dr. Prince arrived at the south door of the big barn, we recognized him by his unique silhouette against the daylight in the shadowy doorway. His perky Alpine hats were his trademark, usually a forest green corduroy but sometimes a beige, a burgundy, or plaid. All his hat bands were

stained by rain and sweat.

Dr. Prince generously shared his wealth of medical knowledge with us. He answered our questions patiently and explained follow-up care for the horses after surgery, pregnancy or illness.. He taught us how to bandage efficiently and to treat the incisions of surgical cases. We learned how to reduce the swelling in horse's knees and ankles. There was always something significant to learn each time he made a call. Like Jeff Roper, he gave me moral support and guidance, sometimes in the face of tragic events.

Chapter 13

My Role Model

There are many essential services necessary for running a horse facility smoothly. I was fortunate to have made good contacts. A hay and grain company that treated me fairly, a man who kept us supplied with wood shavings and saw dust; two competent equine veterinarians and several good horse-shoers. None of these important in that order, but all were essential.

The first blacksmith, by far the best one I ever had, was Giulio Borro. An independent, wiry man in his middle fifties. Giulio was five feet tall, an ideal height for a blacksmith.

Ordinarily, Giulio did not shoe horses in the suburbs, keeping to his well-established clientele in Chicago, the stables on the south side and around Lincoln Park. When Chase Harper moved Barbie Bar to our farm, he asked if he could use his own horse-shoer. The blacksmith turned out to be Giulio Borro. Once, I saw his excellent shoeing, I asked him if he would consider handling all the horses at the farm. He agreed.

Giulio was selective about his customers. He would not return to a barn where his work was constantly interrupted by traffic in the aisles or where the manager did not have his money ready for him when he folded up his leather apron at four-thirty.

The ceremonious folding of Giulio's worn, stained apron was the signal that shoeing was done for the day. However, he always remained a little while afterwards and visited with us.

Giulio arranged to come to us on alternate Thursdays each month. As our stable of horses grew, he came every Thursday. There were always many of our horses needing his services. Over a five year period I must have watched Giulio shoe or trim horses hundreds of times. I couldn't be with him every visit, of course, but when necessary, he patiently answered my questions and showed me how to judge a shoer's craft.

A quiet man, Giulio's authority over a horse was a silent communication. He had supreme confidence in himself and the horses trusted him. He seldom whopped them around, as later, I would see other impatient blacksmiths do. He exercised control and discipline with a single command, steadily pursuing his craft. He picked up and held the horse's hooves so firmly, they knew he was not going to let go. He remained calm with the tough horses, those who fired kicks at him with their hind feet, or those that tried to rear up with their front legs, attempting to crush the blacksmith's unprotected back.

Throughout the years that Giulio shod our horses, he had a tolerance for each horse's foibles. He was lenient without being indulgent. Whenever I was close to losing my temper with an unruly horse, the rememberance of Giulio's patience came to my rescue.

Giulio was never like an arrogant trainer on an ego trip, nor a show-off for the owner's benefit. He was, without a doubt, the strongest influence that developed my attitude toward horses. I wanted to be like Giulio, self-confident, kind, patient, yet firm. From a different era and background, Giulio reminded me of Jim, the Adirondack guide who had helped take care of me when I was growing up. Jim, too, had raised the state of patience to a level of communion.

When Giulio first came to work for me, I went into great detail concerning all the shoeing problems he would encounter that day. He heard me out, standing quietly, sharpening his knife blade with a circular motion on an oval wet stone he always carried. After I described all the problem horses, those with short feet, or thin walls which would never hold a nail, or stressing problems I knew about, Giulio would grin, nod his head and use his stock phrase, "That's okay, I'll fix 'em up." And, of course, he always did.

Giulio had a singular, staccato beat to his hammer: four beats for each of the nails driven into the horse's hooves. His accuracy made certain that the animal was spared the agony of a misplaced nail.

He had learned his trade from an old blacksmith at the age of nine, as an apprentice. His first job was leading the big draft horses which pulled the garbage wagons in an earlier Chicago to the blacksmith shop on Morgan Street. When he grew older, he was permitted to pull off worn shoes, but it was a long time, he said, before he was allowed to nail shoes on the horses' hooves.

Early in his apprenticeship he learned the difference between good and bad shoeing. He maintained every horse should walk away the better, not the worse, from the shoer.

Ringling Brothers and Barnum and Bailey saved their toughest horses for him to shoe when they reached Chicago. Giulio showed us how to put the body rope on a resistant horse, one who fires with his hind feet and with lightning speed at the blacksmith or veterinarian.

First, Giulio placed the rope over the girth of the horse's body and across his chest: to this section of rope another shorter length was fastened. On the end of this length was a soft leather thong. He placed the thong around the rear ankle of a hind foot, the one he wished to trim, shoe or medicate. Next, he took the slack out of the rope and the horse's hoof was lifted six or eight inches off the ground. At that point, the horse was standing well-balanced on three legs, but if he kicked out he soon found himself pulling against his own chest and body. If he struggled and looked as though he was going to fall, a quick jerk on the slip knot loosened the body rope and the horse was standing on all four feet instantly. Giulio pointed out how holding a horse too high with a hind foot might cause even a gentle horse to fidget or pull away simply because the animal was in physical discomfort because of arthritis or some other ailment.

He loved cigars and that is what we always gave him for Christmas or when one of the mare's foaled. He never smoked in the barn, but constantly chewed on a cigar butt. It stuck out of a space in his upper left jaw where several teeth were missing. He always wore a tattered brown cap, a wool shirt to sop up perspiration and, of course, the leather apron of his trade. His high laced boots, like those worn in heavy construction mills, had steel toe plates.

I was the only woman owner-manager for whom Giulio shod horses. He often told me he thought I worked too hard. Many times he surprised me with a present when he came to the farm. It might be a banana whipped cream pie from his brother's bakery, or a loaf of freshly baked bread. Once he brought me two large blue and white agate kettles from the venders on Maxwell Street because, as he explained, "You like pots," his appreciation of my fondness for antiques.

I looked forward to Giulio's visits and made him my own role model of self-control and patience.

Chapter 14

A Real Cowboy

We had some of our acreage in a field crop, soy beans and cattle corn, and pasture for the forty boarding horses we usually handled. Once more, an ad in the local newspaper attracted my attention. "Pony Sweep - 5 ponies, $150". I didn't know what a Pony Sweep was and I told the children it might mean five little ponies who would keep the barn aisles swept. Of course, they didn't believe me, but they thought it was a good idea to check into it.

Following directions in the ad we reached the outskirts of a nearby village. There, in a woodsy setting, next to a small pond we came upon an authentic log cabin. A weathered unpainted barn and small corral spoke of another place and time.

Calvin Baker, seventy, tall and lean, a little stooped, met us at the cabin door. His pale blue eyes danced in his leathery face as he greeted us, "Come to buy ponies have you? Good for you."

Lynn tugged at my sleeve, whispering, "He's a real cowboy." Indeed, the affable old gentleman could have stepped out of a western movie. He was wearing an immaculate, lightly starched plaid shirt with pearl buttons; a red neckerchief, folded narrowly and knotted at his throat. A silver and turquoise belt buckle glittered at his waist. On his head was a ten gallon Stetson, weathered and stained from countless rainstorms.

I told him about my business and how I needed more income. He nodded his head and said, "Little lady you've come to the right place. I've been in the horse business more'n fifty years."

He led us into his small barn and we followed him along a short aisle. Cal Baker's description of each animal was fascinating. One or two horses from a recent auction were stabled in stalls in front of us. A new acquisition, a sorrel gelding was stalled with the smelliest male goat I had ever seen.

"So he don't jug up," Calvin pointed to the gelding and then spelled out the preventive measures old horsemen believe will ward off shipping fever. "Stall 'im with a goat. Keeps their glands soft," he explained.

Moving along to the other animals, he dipped his hands into deep cowhide pockets offering the horses handfuls of coffee-flavored lozenges. While the horses crunched the hard candy, he realized he had never had a better audience of greenhorns.

"Actually don't approve much of hand feeding horses or petting their noses either," he said. Our guide seemed to be doing a lot of both, but we listened, enthralled. "Hand feeding makes biters out of 'em. If they is already biters it makes the cusses worse. And don't always be poking at their noses." To illustrate he ran a calloused palm over Gail's nose and chin. She ducked away. He explained, "See, you don't like it at all. Horses are no different. They don't like it neither. Pat or rub them on the jaw or up on their foreheads, between the eyes, but leave their snoots alone."

When we reached the end of the barn aisle, there was a large box stall, the upper half fenced off with galvanized turkey wire.

"I got somethin' real special to show you here." Calvin Baker spoke with obvious pride and affection. There, before us, the light of a single bulb shining on his silvery hide stood a well- muscled, awesome Appaloosa stallion.

"This is Sammy, the finest stud horse you'll ever see. He's got it all, looks, disposition, manners. A real jim-dandy herd sire." Calvin opened the stallion's heavy door and stepped into the stall. "Come to Poppa, son," he said offering the stallion a handful of coffee treats.

While we moved around the barn, above our heads, looking down from the hay loft was a malemute dog. He never took his eyes off us, watching our every move with his inscrutable almond shaped eyes. Noticing my apprehension about the dog, Calvin assured me, "No way that old cuss can get down here. He's a good old boy. Turn him loose in the barn at night and no one will ever bother my horses." He laughed when he said this.

I reminded Calvin we had come to see ponies and he beckoned us to follow him into the yard. We passed two pens each holding a female malemute and a litter of pups. In the corral, eating hay together like a happy family were the ponies -- Rusty, Rickey, Sandy, Blackie, and Fritz.

Calvin showed us the "sweep". A merry-go-round wheel designed to give pony rides on live ponies. What a marvelous contraption and what adorable ponies, I concluded on the spot. Three of the ponies were brown and white pintos. One was a grey and the last was jet black.

I knew exactly what I would do with them. I would use them for birthday parties! We waited for Whitney to bring my purse and checkbook from the car as Cal filled the children's pockets with coffee candy. He admitted, "I could have sold the whole kit and caboodle to the Fair Grounds, but that's a hellava life for the little cusses."

He agreed to deliver the ponies and sweep the next day. On our way home the children and I decided where we would install the sweep. We agreed on placing it on the back lawn, near enough to the house for electricity. Lynn said, "Mom, you have to have music with a merry-go-round," And who could argue with that?

It was not our last visit to the cabin and Calvin Baker. We all loved to go there. The old man was full of horse stories, old horsemen's primitive remedies and lore. But, most of all, he was full of delightful conversation and warm fun.

Chapter 15

Coal and Cauliflower

By 1964 there were few wagon horses left in Chicago. Giulio shod the few that remained. He knew the old peddlers well, many of whom were Italian. I had asked him to keep his eye out for one of these horses and wagons, planning on using it for the birthday parties that had become so popular at Arcadia Farm.

One November, Giulio told me one of the old peddlers was retiring and would consider selling his horse and wagon. I made an appointment with Giulio in what he called "the old neighborhood", near Morgan Street in Chicago. There we met Mr. Mormino.

Antonio Mormino met us at the front door of his modest frame bungalow. He was a short, thick-set, swarthy man with muscular arms and broad shoulders. He was in his late sixties. An expansive smile on his weather-beaten face revealed a gold-capped tooth in the center of his upper jaw. He spoke no English. Giulio was our translator.

Mr. Mormino led us into the immaculate kitchen at the rear of the house. It was sparcely furnished with a table, gas stove and an ancient refrigerator. There was the aroma of freshly baked anise cookies.

Mrs. Mormino turned from the stove with a blue agate coffee pot in her hand. She gestured for us to sit down on worn wooden chairs drawn up to a table covered by a spotless, shiny, white oilcloth. Mrs. Mormino, a hospitable, tiny, frail woman, her blue-black hair pulled back in a bun at the back of her neck, poured each of us a cup of steaming fragrant coffee. She spoke a little English and communicated with me perfectly with her genuine smile, urging us to sample her abundant variety of Italian cookies. At one point she dunked a cookie in my coffee, and held it to my lips. It was my introduction to the real way to eat Italian cookies. Delicious!

Giulio and Mr. Mormino discussed the terms of the sale in Italian. Mrs. Mormino and I smiled at each other a lot. I nodded my head affirmatively whenever Giulio looked at me for approval.

We had dunked cookies for a half hour when Mr. Mormino rose to his feet and shook hands with Giulio. A satisfactory price had been reached. Then everyone shook hands. The sale price was three hundred and fifty dollars for an old wagon horse named Bill, his harness, rubber raincoat, rubberized blanket, feed bag, a halter and two red wagons with yellow wheels.

We went out in the alley to the garage to see Bill. For fifteen years, Bill and Mr. Mormino left here, daily, working on their route together, Mormino to sell and Bill to pull the loads. In winter they froze on icy streets with heavy wagonloads of coal; in summer they sweltered on fetid streets with heavy wagonloads of wilting vegetables.

The garage was really a tidy little barn right in the middle of a residential neighborhood. Against one wall, a small cast iron stove stood ready to take the chill off during harsh winter weather. In the corner were stocked half a dozen bales of hay, aromatic and fine as any we fed at the farm. There was a crude wooden chest, filled with plump, dustless oats. The vegetable wagon and the old milk wagon were parked side by side, shafts unhooked leaning against the wall. There too, in a straight stall with his head tied, his muscular rump toward us, munching on a mouthful of hay, stood Bill.

He was not a big horse, but he was powerfully built. A reddish bay with coal black mane and tail, his coat clean and glossy. The horse, hearing us behind him, turned his head. There was a white star between his eyes. His look was baleful as he rolled his eyes, not the mild mannered, gentle horse I had imagined. No matter. Innumerable handshakes and cookies had sealed the bargain. Bill was all mine.

Mr. Mormino spoke to Bill in Italian, walked into the stall and unhooked his head from the tether rope, then backed the horse slowly out of the stall. At this moment Mrs. Mormino began to talk excitedly. Giulio translated her concern that Bill would get his daily ration of "carrozze". I patted her arm and assured her he would.

Suddenly, a reporter and photographer from the Chicago Tribune arrived to take pictures. In a few days, a fine picture of Bill and Mr. Mormino appeared in the paper, with the caption, "Bill goes to greener pastures"! Mr. Mormino had capped his career with a bit of P.R.

Time to load Bill in Giulio's truck. Happily, he went right up the ramp. The two wagons were pushed up the short ramp of a low- boy trailer by the men, including the "trib" reporter and photographer. The wheels were chained down and blocked in place with huge wooden wedges, all in less than an hour. Bill was on the way to his last home.

I planned to put Bill in a large box stall. I thought this spacious accomodation would please the old-timer after he had stood so many years with his head tied.

He hated it, pacing round and round in the box stall, whinnying continuously. He quickly worked himself up into a nervous sweat, his chest and barrel wet and foamy with sticky perspiration. The whites around his eyes turned pink. I feared he was about to have a heart attack.

Trying to solve the problem, I asked Giulio to lead Bill across the yard to the annexes where the school horses were kept. He put him in the last small stall on the left. In semi-darkness, his head tied, Bill contentedly remained there all the years I had him.

We had many experiences with Bill, even some that are best forgotten. For his size he was extremely powerful. I wondered about his breeding. I had seen pictures of small, working horses from the British Isles. He had the height, conformation and strength of the Dale, or maybe he was from the sunny shores of Italy.

The language barrier presented a real handicap in the beginning. It was clear early on that we would have to learn to speak Italian or Bill would have to learn English!

Just harnessing Bill was more than irksome. He was so unruly, lunging back and forth, it took Josie, Whitney, and I to hitch him up. One person at his head, one lifting the shafts, so he could back between them, and a driver on the wagon seat, ready to pick up the lines.

How we came to respect Mr. Mormino's ability to do all this alone and deliver coal and vegetables besides! It must have been in record time for no sooner than we had Bill in harness, he was ready to go to work with a vengeance.

Eventually, our stern voices brought about harmony between Bill and us, but there were times, as Bill rolled his eyes and shook his head, that in sheer desperation I resorted to yelling in the best Italian accent I could muster. "Ahaaaaa Beel, cutta eet out! Behava youself!"

But it was Giulio who really got across to Bill. Soothingly, he'd say, "Comma on, Beel! Picka ups you feets, be agooda boy. Capisce?"

Giulio shod Bill with rubber shoes, iron shoes dipped in rubber coating. Such shoes break the concussion on the horse's legs as their feet strike hard surfaces, cushioning the impact on his old joints.

Whitney was anxious to drive the wagon horse. The first time we got a reservation for a birthday party after Bill's arrival, I told Whitney we would use him and his wagon. It was also the first time Whitney took him on the blacktop road.

The road in front of the farm was lightly traveled. It was a pretty ride with a wagon-load of birthday children over the old wooden bridge, across the creek where the huge bison used to water and up the long gradual hill past a handsome herd of Holstein milking cows in a neighbor's meadow.

Right off, Bill seemed to enjoy the outing. He jogged slowly, his curly black mane flying in the wind. The trip back, however, was something else. When Bill reached the top of the hill and Whitney turned him around to make his descent, Bill broke into a fast trot on the slick, smooth macadam incline.

Whitney had no experience with using the hand brakes to slow the wagon down. The best he could do was keep the horse's head steady as the vehicle swayed and listed. The children laughing, screeching, screaming and jostling one another, oblivious to the fact that they were behind a runaway horse.

Deep ditches on either side of the road made it impossible for Whitney to turn the horse into an open field. Bill kept right on trotting, head high, nostrils flaring. Miraculously, as the wagon approached the farm entrance, Bill slowed to a normal gait and Whitney had him under control again. Later, Whitney said we should never again call the horse "Old Bill." He had all the pep and vitality of a much younger horse. We never took him on the blacktop again, keeping to the lanes on the farm.

Bill and his wagons made it possible for us to fulfill unusual requests for a birthday party. A father wished to give his nine year old son an outing. The boy had Legge-Perthes disease of the hips. We put a mattress in the bottom of the wagon and the birthday boy lay on it, on his stomach. By raising himself on his elbows he could look past the driver and see the back of the willing Bill. His friends sat around him on the mattress, another group of nine-year-olds enjoying the thrill of a horse-drawn wagon.

Hard, long years on city streets had produced enlarged arthritic knees in Bill. Pulling a load requires a horse not only to strain with his chest and hind quarters but to dig in with his legs as well. It's especially strenuous when starting out from a standstill with a heavily loaded wagon.

The first few years Bill was with us he had no difficulty getting up or down in his straight stall. As years passed we found him more and more often, down in his stall, his swollen knees tucked under him, unable to bring them forward to get himself to a standing position.

Lying cramped through the night, Bill's legs became stiff and his immobility increased. We had to get him on his feet, restoring circulation not only to his legs, but to his lungs as well. By using a 2x12 timber post, a block and tackle, and the tractor, we managed to get him to his feet without hurting him, but this project involved the whole family.

First we wrapped several thicknesses of burlap around his hind legs, all the while talking to him, stroking his hind quarters, reassuring him. Then Josie ran a rope over this padding, around Bill's legs. From this rope, Whitney ran another piece of hemp through the block and tackle attached to the post and from there another rope to the tractor.

This enabled us to pull Bill several feet straight backwards. Slowly, with one foot poised above the brake, I eased the tractor forward while Josie and Whitney guided the ropes and kept the padding around Bill's legs. When the horse had cleared the necessary distance, I stopped the tractor and pulled the slip knot which held the rope around his hind legs. Then Bill was encouraged to lurch to a standing position by slapping him smartly on the rump. We coaxed and urged him, all three of us shouting in unison, "Up boy! Get up fella. Come on, Bill! Get up boy!"

Suddenly, there he was on all fours, already lowering his head to eat hay, though trembling.

As the situation occurred more frequently, clearly it was no kindness to put Bill through the mechanics of getting him on his feet every morning. He was then in his high twenties, a fair age for any horse, but Bill had lived a hard, rigorous life and the toll had caught up with him. Soon thereafter, and sadly, I asked Dr. Roper to come early one morning and administer a large dose of animal tranquillizer which ended Bill's life. We thought of Bill as going to the greenest of all pastures.

Chapter 16

Pony Rides and Birthday Cake

April through October we gave pony birthday parties for children of all ages, using a single horse for the ten year olds or Bill, the wagon horse. Some weekends we had as many as five or six groups.

I met the children in the parking lot as soon as the station wagons arrived. I had developed a short speech: Everyone would stay together. Each would pick a partner. There was to be no yelling or jostling in the barns. No child was to touch or feed any horse. For their cooperation, I promised to answer all questions and reward good behavior with pony rides and fruit-flavored pop.

The birthday celebrations began on the lawn. After I took the children on tour of the barns we ended up at the party room in the renovated machine shed where I kept many primitive antiques, an ox-yoke, side saddles and harnesses.

The party room walls were painted pale aqua blue, the windows curtained with short tie-backs of yellow dotted swiss. At low ten-foot tables, seated on small yellow, red or blue chairs with rush seats, the clamoring birthday children ate birthday cake and sipped pop.

The mothers brought paper tablecloths, plates, and favors and elaborately decorated cakes of ranches, complete with fencing and livestock, cowboys and Indians, clowns, even ballet dancers, all attesting to the creativity of the bakery and a mother's devotion.

For the most part, the tours were held without incident and when we had completed our rounds of the three barns the ponies awaited us on the lawn where Lynn, Gail or Whitney were waiting to supervise pony rides.

No child is ever completely satisfied with a set number of pony rides, but generally these children accepted the limit allowed. Once in awhile there might be a small tot who was afraid of the ponies, clinging desperately to his mother or father's neck. I discouraged forcing such a child to sit on a pony. Another year would make a big difference in their self-confidence. If we could encourage them to pat Rusty's mane or touch the red saddle, everyone was satisfied.

In addition to birthday parties, we had field trips and visits from day-care centers, the visually handicapped and with children having difficulties with coordination, balance and speech. Such children clutched the plush hides and wiry manes of the ponies in stiff inflexible fingers. One little girl, sightless from birth, pushed her nose into Rusty's coppery shoulder,crying out joyfully, "Smells good," discovering the distinctive odor of a healthy pony.

We always supervised the birthday parties and one more responsibility was to be sure our old cat, Googie, did not spoil the party. Our orange, black and brown "grand dame" had a sixth sense about party refreshment time.

Googie, a superb huntress, more than once brought a dead, dangling field mouse to the festivities, sending mothers into hysterics. Some of the children and their mothers were afraid of her, suffering from genuine catphobia.

Googie, her large amber eyes watching the pony rides from under the lilac bushes, followed the group to the party room. Occasionally, there would be a paper plate to lick, but generally, she was not welcome. I solved this by buying two chicken crates from my neighbor, Lester Rowe. After we scrubbed them down we left them to dry in the hot sun. These crates, with wooden spindles and hinged covers, were safe, airy places to confine Googie. We put one crate on the back lawn near the pony sweep and the other near the party room door. If the friendly cat, plumy tail erect, sauntered into the midst of refreshment time, one of us, on the alert, popped her into a chicken crate. In all the commotion, we sometimes forgot about Googie. Later, Lynn or Gail, remembering she was impounded, rushed to free her only to find Googie sound asleep, no doubt dreaming of birthday cake and dixie cups.

One day my persistent, curious cat lifted the lid of an unattended bakery box, leaving tiny imprints on the yellow icing. It was a scene of "Custer's last stand", with tiny cowboy and Indian figures. I had but minutes to whisk a knife from the nearby kitchen, removing the less than dime-size footprints of resourceful Googie from the gooey surface.

Chapter 17

Houdini

The puckish little pony called Fritz was one of the five bought from Calvin Baker along with the pony-sweep. A more fitting name for him would have been "Houdini". He had the talent of an escape artist. No pen, or paddock could hold him for long.

Fritz could decipher the most complicated gate mechanism, lift whole sections of woven stock wire with his neck and shoulders, drop to his knees and roll out of the enclosure. We saw him regularly step gingerly over strands of barbed wire without a scratch and joyfully trot off to graze on the front lawn.

One summer, tired of catching him daily, I decided to leave him loose. The little fey pony was happy in his freedom. He entertained himself by visiting the barns, filching hay with his tongue from under the stall doors of the stabled horses. He was able to shove aside the plywood water tank covers, drinking as much and as often as he wished. Fritz munched in the flower beds trailing tendrils of Lynn's prized petunias from his lips. The tartness of nasturtiums puckered his mouth, but he sampled them along with my pink geraniums, uprooting them from planters near the front door.

Every afternoon around three-thirty he could be found standing in the grotto, formed by four Colorado blue spruce, head bowed, fast asleep. His left hind foot cocked at an a angle to show complete relaxation.

When horse people say an animal is "put up well" they mean he is good looking and represents his breed to the best advantage. Such was the case with our Fritz.

He looked like a miniature horse with a good head and well-proportioned body. Gail and Lynn had such faith in his superior conformation that they took him to a horse show one July afternoon.

After a sudsy bath and elaborate combing and brushing of his full mane and tail, Fritz was buckled into a white cotton horse sheet. It looked like a nightgown on him, hanging down to his hooves. Then we faced the problem of transporting him to the pony classes. The show grounds were eight miles away. Our horse vans and trailers were already loaded with our boarders horses headed for the same show. Not an inch of room remained for a small pony in a white nightgown smelling of herbal shampoo!

My first customers, Carrie and Holly, offered to transport Fritz in the back seat of their old convertible. Once the top was down the tough pony tyke hopped right in. Gail held the lead rope, she and Lynn sitting on either side of him. No one seemed surprised at Fritz doing something unconventional.

Fritz's arrival at the show grounds caused a sensation. People thought he was a large dog standing on the back seat, until they realized he was a pinto pony.

In a class of eighteen ponies, most of the competitors having registered pedigrees, Fritz won a third place ribbon. Lynn and Gail were delighted.

Freedom to roam around our barnyard and lawns was not enough for Fritz. He began to leave the property, crossing the road to cornfields on the other side. I knew the priviledge of liberty for him would have to end. He was bound to be hit by a car. I kept postponing the decision to restrict him until one day as I was returning from marketing I was horrified to see Fritz walking up the middle of Allendale Road, a corn stalk hanging from his mouth. Cars were whizzing past him on both sides. Regretfully, I confined him to a stall with Sandy for company.

Whenever I felt myself weakening and considering putting Fritz back on the pasture I made myself remember the frequent sight of forty horses released from the pasture confines by Fritz's cleverness, jogging along the shoulder of the road, away from the farm, a small brown and white pony in the lead. Fritz seemed to be playing on an invisible pipe, "Come follow me, hey nonny nonny..."

Chapter 18

Would I Ever Know It All?

On another visit shortly after we bought the ponies from Calvin Baker, I asked him about school horses.

"I can let you have the pinto mare and chestnut gelding for fifty more'n I paid for 'em," Calvin said. "They're quiet and gentle. Kid safe."

The black and white mare had an oversized head. Her back was swayed from too many saddles and too little to eat. The gelding was in fair flesh. With some good feed and with their feet trimmed, I sensed the two would work out well as school horses.

While Whitney was riding the pinto and chestnut, I noticed another little horse standing way in the back of her stall, a grulla (grey) dun, according to Cal. When he tried to touch her she seemed to shrink into the wall.

"This one's a real spook. Fires up real easy. The boys rode her into the sales barn with spurs on," he said.

The grulla mare was the most timid horse I would ever see. Her liquid brown eyes had a haunted look. On her left flank were three ugly brands, each from a different ranch.

"Looks like she's got some miles on her. I bought her in a package, real cheap. Probably send her to the killers just to get my money out of her," he explained nonchalantly.

I shuddered at that obvious term used so casually by horsemen. The "killers" meant the dog food company. "I'll take the dun, too," I heard myself saying.

Calvin seemed dismayed. "Can't guarantee her," he said emphatically. "She's a firecracker. Won't do you at all in the busines,"

Out of the corner of my eye I noticed Gail patiently coaxing the grulla to come to the partition. The next time I looked Gail was scratching the mare's jaw.

Because of her kneehigh white stockings, we named the pinto mare Bobby Socks. Shortly after we got her home she acted very restless, stamping and kicking out with her hind feet while we were saddling her. Could she be another of our lemons?

It was Giulio who recognized the problem the first time he trimmed her hooves. "She'sa gotta lice in dem hinda legs," he stated flatly. "Lottsa lice."

I was horrified. "Ye Gods! Lice! Where did she get them?" I asked. I had never run into this before.

Giulio was grinning, enjoying my reaction. He explained that sometimes horses were stabled in old chicken coops which were contaminated by chicken lice.

"I fixa him up," he said reassuringly. He told me to get a bucket of hot water and add a bottle of household bleach. Using an old brush he scrubbed the mare's hind legs with the solution.

"You gotta do this coupla more times. Make it strong. Iffa you done wanna pick up his feets use a brush wid a handle." This had to be done discreetly so as not to incite panic among my horse boarders. Twice more, I overcame my revulsion, tying Bobby Socks to one of the fences, scrubbing her back legs with an old broom, its long handle providing distance between me and the abominable lice. The results were rewarding. The lice disappeared and Bobby had the whitest stockings on the farm.

Through these ordeals, I had learned another valuable lesson. Not only did I have to choose healthy, honest horses, but in addition I had to watch out for the kickers, biters and those with parasites. Would I ever know it all?

Chapter 19

A Lucky Little Girl

The early rising luminous harvest moon shone on the horses in the pasture. Soon it would be too cold to leave them out all night without shelter. Crisp fall nights were the time for hayrides behind the team, Dolly and Flory. Each weekend there were square dances and finally our Halloween party for the boarders. This gave me an opportunity to cluster armfuls of cornstalks around the base of the elms in the backyard together with pumpkins and gourds. In the hayloft, I tied dried stalks and sprays of artificial yellow and white chrysanthemums to the rugged purloins which supported the vast arch of the roof.

With Josie holding the ladder, I hung bunches of burgundy and yellow Indian corn from the stout beams which spanned the width of the loft. More pumpkins, sprays of dried goldenrod and purple wild asters were heaped in the old box sleigh.

We had an energetic square dance caller. He and his wife got everyone dancing, myself included. During the evening's festivities, out of breath, I needed to rest. Standing in the yard, I looked up through the loft door. I could see the shadows of the whirling dancers and hear the gaity in their voices above the nasal twang of the caller. To escape the strenuous "swing your partner, do si do" I sometimes retreated into the dark barn, turned on a light in the equipment room and watered the horses. I moved among the animals who remained quiet, content hearing my familiar voice as the ceiling vibrated to the rhythm of the dancers feet on the bare boards above.

Fall provided shorter working days and gave the family an opportunity to gather together in a special, personal way. Late October nights were cool enough to lay up a fire in the fireplace, the pungent odor of freshly cut ash and oak logs, corded near the back porch by Josie, The fire threw bone-warming heat to the dogs, Stuart and Ashley, as they lay on their sides by the granite hearth in the pine-paneled family room.

It was a time to roast marshmallows on the tips of green saplings which Whitney had cut or to pop corn in an antique brass chestnut roaster. The girls dried their hair near the fire as we talked over the day's events and made plans for the following day.

But it was most of all, a time for me to tell over and over again, stories of my own childhood, which they begged for, and never got tired of hearing. How, when I was eight, because of delicate health, my far-sighted, generous father hired Jim the Adirondack guide as my constant companion and nurse. Jim's responsibility was to teach me to swim, fish, handle a canoe and to see I came to no harm in the healthful out of door life which played such a major part in my recovery from infantile paralysis.

"Were you a tom-boy?" Gail asked one night. "Not really, but I learned to do many things that boys do," I replied, laughing. "I helped Jim slosh the bottom of the guide boat with pails of lake water after one of your grandfather's fishing trips, rinsing away bits of bait and other debris. He usually took me with him when he caught up on regular camp chores. I walked by his side as he strung yards of wet fishing line to dry between the white birches after a day's trolling. I helped him pile kindling in the woodbox on the back porch for the wood stove and fireplaces.

One summer, when I was nine, Jim rigged up an old guide boat, no longer seaworthy. He braced it underneath so it wouldn't roll over. He turned up a pair of lightweight oars and a short, scarred paddle. The dog and I rowed safely for miles and miles on top of a sandy ridge. The picture of me as a little girl, rowing for hours without going anywhere, always evoked laughter.

"If I had a boat like that I'd take Stuart with me," Lynn said.

"Ashley, too," Gail added, fondling the black and white sheepdog's head.

I paused, savoring the memory. Whitney stuck three marshmallows on the end of the green twig. "Why did grandpa choose Jim to take care of you?"

"Well, I was very frail after my long illness. Your grandfather knew the key to regaining my health was for me to spend as much time out of doors as possible with lots of physical activity. He wanted me to learn about nature, too.

"Jim and I did something different every day. Sometimes he had to carry me over the portage between the lakes and over steep, rocky trails. As I grew older and stronger, he and I often swam home from one side of Rainbow Lake to another. He shoved the canoe ahead of us through choppy water so I would have something to grab onto if I needed a rest. It took a strong man to do that."

"What did Jim look like?" Gail asked. I told them how straight, tall and strong he was, describing his deep blue eyes which almost closed when he laughed, and how he laughed a lot in a hearty way, his laughter echoing through the woods. I described his muscular arms and huge hands, calloused from years of swinging an axe and paddling a canoe.

"Jim was kindly toward me, and very, very patient. I often tried his patience. He knew when I had been swimming long enough in the icy mountain lake. Often, I wouldn't come out of the water when he told me to, even if my lips were blue."

The notion that I had been a naughty, disobedient little girl sent Lynn and Gail into uproarious laughter.

"You were lucky, Mom," Whitney interrupted.

"Yes, terribly lucky to have a childhood like that for although my parents encouraged me in all undertakings, it was Jim who taught me I had few limitations. I've carried that feeling all my life."

Rising to my feet, I straightened the firescreen against the fieldstone opening to prevent stray sparks from escaping from dying embers, and told the children, "I think that's enough story telling for one night. Off to bed with you. Tomorrow's a school day."

"I like hearing about Jim best," Whitney lingered in the doorway. "You really were lucky, Mom."

"Fortunate, Whitney, fortunate. I was much more than lucky." I knew that more every day. The contrast between my girlhood and my present life was more apparent. I understood how carefree my childhood had been. A life of privilege compared to the arduous life I had chosen.

The room was still except for the measured breathing of Stuart and Ashley and the sound of my pen scratching on the note pad as I made my list of chores for the next day. There were no more guide boats to slosh, but the task fitted well into the farm's routine. I wrote, "Have Whitney and Josie scrub and slosh the water troughs in the big barn."

Chapter 20

Another Place And Time

For me, Thanksgiving was like any other day, with no escape from chores and routine. Since 1951, there had been a shadow over what used to be my favorite holiday. On the 22nd of November 1951, my mother had been found dead from a coronary, slumped over her steering wheel at the Harmon New York train station. She had driven there to meet my brother.

The shock and desolation of this event stayed with me my entire life. I never had the same enthusiasm for Thanksgiving again. However, I made a special effort to make a traditional dinner each year for our family and I lost myself in the enjoyment of setting the holiday table.

First, I added three mellow pine extension leaves to the table. Then I spread an ivory damask cloth, an elegant background for the crystal goblets etched with wild flowers, weighty, solid silver forks and pearl handled knives which had been my mother's.

Whitney brought the barrel of Haviland china down from the attic, still almost a complete service for twelve, with a simple pattern of tiny green leaves and scrolls, and bordered on the rim with gold leaf. Five covered vegetable dishes and an enormous turkey platter were on the sideboard. Ivory candles in antique silver candlesticks, and a centerpiece of white mums completed the setting.

I lingered over the task, caressing the smoothness of the pearl handled knives and heavily embossed forks, reminding me once more of our dining room at

21 North Broadway in White Plains. The ten foot long refectory table, made to order for father, was oiled and polished to gleaming perfection. There were linen placemats and matching napkins edged with Battenberg lace at each place. My mother set her table with great care the night before the holiday, expressing the artistic touches that came so easily to her: small individual handpainted Limoge nut dishes, an elegant silver epergne with nosegays of fall flowers, the place cards in her elegant script; on the sideboard, handcarved wooden trays, heaped with dried raisins on the stem and pitted dates stuffed with blanched almonds and rolled in sugar.

Mother always planned a traditional Thanksgiving menu, as her mother had served in her own home in Philadelphia. There was a fruit compote of fresh grapefruit segments and pitted, sliced, Tokay grapes. Roast turkey and dressing with giblet gravy, white potatoes whipped to frothy mounds with farmer's cream and butter, creamed onions, french cut green beans with almond slices and a casserole of sweet potatoes topped with toasted marshmallows.

Our cook Ola's cranberry aspic salad,with celery and walnut bits was our own tradition, together with her light Parkerhouse rolls.

Dessert was always one of Ola's specialties. Chocolate, French vanilla, and strawberry ice-cream in turkey molds, as well as mince and pumpkin pie with whipped cream for father.

Mother took the preparation of the bird very seriously. To start with, the turkey had to be a fresh tom from the butcher. The night before the holiday, mother donned an apron and helped Ola prepare the turkey for roasting. Mother was very particular, removing every pin feather with a paring knife, singeing the fine hairs on the wings and the "Pope's nose" with long kitchen matches.

Then, there were last minute instructions to Delsey, our second girl, on how to serve the guests: keep the goblets filled with water, pass the side dishes without being reminded, and answer mother's bell promptly.

On Thanksgiving Day at the farm there was no amiable Delsey to serve, or Ola to cook, but mother's silver bell was by my place. I rang it briskly between courses heralding the special dessert carried into the dining room by Gail or Lynn.

Midwest Thanksgiving days were usually raw and windy. We did our chores as usual, moving from barn to barn helping each other finish up. The girls and I ending up in the main barn where Whitney had hayed and grained the horses. The three of us watered the horses while he brought in hay from the wagon for the evening feeding.

We looked forward to a precious hour and a half when we could sit down to dinner together. I put the turkey in the oven at eleven o'clock, planning on dinner at four. Then I dressed in a sweater and skirt, and because it was a rare occasion, clasped around my neck the string of pearls my father had given mother on their twenty-fifth anniversary.

Returning to the kitchen, already filled with the aroma of the roasting bird, I put on the blue and white checked Mother Hubbard apron Lynn had bought me at the Ladies Guild sale at old St. Martha's church that summer. As I began to peel potatoes, there was a sharp knock at the back door. It was Carrie. She looked surprised to see me dressed in anything but blue jeans. "Come on in," I said.

"No thanks, Mrs. K. I just stopped by to wish you and Bounty a happy Thanksgiving. I've got someone here I want you to meet. This is Paul."

Just behind her stood a young man, his shoulder-length, red hair bound by a leather band. A worn corduroy jacket barely covered his bony wrists. In spite of the raw November temperature, his feet were bare in worn leather thong sandals.

Carrie held out toward me a cardboard tube wrapped in white tissue paper. "Here's a little something for you. from Holly, me and Bounty." Then looking past me at the festive dining room table she exclaimed, "Wow! Far out! You guys are going to have a groovy time!"

"Not only groovy, but real mellow, with all the best vibrations," I replied, laughing at how easily I fell into using and understanding her vernacular.

When they had gone, I unwrapped the package. The little something was an Irish linen tea towel with the Lord's Prayer printed on it.

Chapter 21

Never Again

We had hardly spoken a word on the short drive. The three of us: Lester, Whitney and I crowded into the front seat of Lester's pickup truck. Behind us, in the blue, one-horse trailer, poor old Safari tried to keep his balance.

I thought of Cal Baker's advice about trailering horses. "Drive like you're hauling a bucket of water full to the rim and you don't want to spill a drop. Take it easy. Put your brakes on slow, turn corners slow, too." I always had that picture in my mind's eye, of a full pail of water sloshing around whenever we moved stock.

Safari loaded easily, trusting Whitney who enticed him up the trailer ramp with a scoop of oats. It was his last journey.

Both veterinarians and Giulio, as well, had given Safari's owner their opinions about the horse's condition.

After X-raying his front hooves, Dr. Roper said, "His coffin bone in both hooves had fallen." He had no doubt Safari was in a lot of pain.

Thad Prince agreed, adding, "Once a horse is that badly crippled there is nothing that can be done for him."

Giulio had shod him in leather pads but nothing helped. He had limped, all the time, in excruciating pain.

Safari's owner authorized me, in writing, to do what was "best" for the game little animal. I realized it was not best to prolong his suffering.

It was the first time I had to face terminating a horse's life. Several options were open to me. Since I had no experience, I followed Cal Baker's advice. "Take him to the 'killers'," he said, without batting an eye.

I could not even utter the hateful word used so loosely by so many horsemen. I called the business by it's company name, "Mid America Pet Food Products".

A weathered sign, it's letters worn away, marked the entrance to the packing house. Turning through massive chain link gates, Lester pulled the truck and trailer to one side of a long cement block building. On the loading ramp were cartons of dog food stacked one on top of each other. They were marked "Horse Meat" in red, block letters. I felt a slight queasiness in my stomach.

Across from the factory a ten foot unpainted board fence surrounded a small corral. Whitney backed Safari out of the trailer and stood feeding him handfuls of hay. I walked over to the enclosure. There were a few inches of space between the planks. I peered inside. There were seven or eight skinny horses milling about, each one in sorrier state than the other. Several hobbling on three legs, another with a gaping, open tumor on his withers, two obviously blind.

Immediately I regretted the decision to look behind the fence and I cringed with apprehension.

By the doorway of the processing plant, a burly figure wearing a bloodstained canvass apron stood watching us. I sent Whitney to ask him if there was an office. He pointed to the main building.

I handed Safari's lead rope to Lester, motioning Whitney to follow me.

The middle-aged woman behind the desk was detached, businesslike. Without looking up from her typewriter she said, "We're paying nine cents a pound for dog and mink food. The check will be mailed out to you in three or four days." Whitney winced at her blunt, off-hand manner.

I handed the secretary a slip of paper with Safari's owner's name and address on it, and went outside.

The employee in the bloody apron was talking to Lester. Seeing me, he said, "You want the horse turned out with the others?"

"No, I do not," I replied. "I was told when I called for an appointment, he'd be taken care of right away."

"Okay, let me check with the butcher. It takes an hour to dress out a horse, he may not have time this afternoon. He goes home at four-thirty."

I shuddered. The butcher! Once more I thought of calling the whole thing off. If I reloaded Safari, taking him back to the farm, Thad Prince could "put him down" that night.

The man was back in a few minutes. "Hurry up! We haven't got much time," he said impatiently. "Follow me."

We followed, Whitney leading and encouraging the limping Safari. Passing the open door of the processing plant, I glanced inside. Sawdust covered the floor. There were a number of steel-topped tables and counters. A man was hosing off one of them as blood and water ran onto the floor.

Again, I thought of calling the whole thing off. Hypnotized, I trailed our guide to the end of the cement block building, entering a small barn-like room. The man placed a loop of wire cable around Safari's neck. The cable ran up to an overhead conveyor belt. Then he led the horse into an area the size of a freight elevator with drains in the floor. He hooked two chain crossties on either side of the horse's halter and told us to step back.

My heart was pounding. I tried to tell the man I had changed my mind. My mouth was dry. Things were happening so fast I had no chance to reconsider what was best for Safari.

With a cigarette dangling from his lips, the man began to load a revolver with shells. Then he placed the weapon in a bracket attached to a stationary arm, aligning the muzzle of the gun against the white star on Safari's forehead. In a shattering moment I realized this man was "the killer" himself.

Suddenly, there was a dull thud, not the explosion I expected. Quickly, the man grasped a lever on the wall and shoved it downwards. The horse's limp carcass was drawn up to the conveyor belt, Safari moving slowly out the door into the cannery. A trickle of blood stained the white star on his forehead, dripped into his open, staring eyes.

Catching a glimpse of Whitney's ashen face as I pushed by him, I ran from the building. In a patch of weeds, in full view, I was violently sick to my stomach. There was no conversation on our way back to the farm. My stomach was still tied in knots.

At the end of this stressful day I took refuge among my mother's furnishings in the living room. I sat for some time in semi- darkness, shuddering from a chill that came from reliving the day's terrible episode. Speaking aloud to no one, I declared there must be a better way. I promised myself this would be the first and last time I would take any horse to Mid America Pet Food Products.

Chapter 22

Little Alice

Farming and the care of our livestock demanded versatility and organization, a fact I did not fully appreciate until I found myself doing day to day chores for more than a hundred horses. Whether it was scrubbing the horse's water pails with a long handled brush, a little task, or cleaning stalls, reliable equipment was needed. A dependable tractor was essential for pulling the manure spreader, moving wagons, and plowing snow.

I depended on, and even became attached to, our tractor. She was not the roaring smoke-belching International diesel, the giant of the field work, but rather a W.D. 45, Allis Chalmers. This piece of equipment fitted easily in the barn aisles. The children named the tractor, "Little Alice".

Although purchased second hand, she perked along faithfully for twenty years. I recognized her whir, which told me she was going to start right up and dreaded her whine that told me she wouldn't.

My neighbor, Lester Rowe, taught me to drive "Little Alice". The day he told me I was ready to back her into one end of the main barn was like graduation. Up to that time I had only driven on open fields. It took several more lessons for me to learn to back the tractor with the manure spreader attached. Finally, I learned to coordinate the steering wheel and the two back wheels of the spreader. Backing into the narrow aisle of the stallion barn was the hardest job of all.

When I mastered that skill I shared the news with anyone who visited the barn and would watch me do it.

I delighted in each trip I made out on the field with the equipment. In the fall, the diesel plowed under the manure and prepared the soil for next year's crops, but it was with "Little Alice" that I did daily farm chores.

Driving on the land in the summer gave me a deep, even tan, but in wintertime cheeks and fingertips became frostbitten. Winter driving was a challenge, with snow drifts sometimes impassible. I scanned ahead for less heavy accumulations of snow, trying to avoid patches of ice that made the tractor's wheels spin. On these days the children watched my progress from the shelter of the barn doorway.

Upon my return from the trip with the manure, my eyelashes tinged with icy particles, they would converge on me with hugs and glowing compliments.

"Good driving, Mom."

"You're the best driver in the whole world!" "You weren't afraid you'd get stuck were you, Mom?" Gail asked.

Whitney had the most confidence in me. He reassured his sisters, "She'll never get stuck, not with Alice." I prayed he was right.

The season I loved best was late summer for then I made my trips onto an unplowed strip along the west boundary of the farm. The front of the tractor, like the prow of a boat, broke through burgeoning scotch thistles and goldenrod, scattering clouds of orange and black Monarch butterflies. The undulating motion of the tractor felt as though I was riding choppy waves.

It was here I saw shy pheasant hens with their broods of scurrying chicks, the brilliant cock soaring from field stubble, calling attention to himself and away from his family. Here, too, the red-wing blackbird swooped from fence post to alder branch. Seeing the birds rekindled the memories of my Adirondack Mountain childhood. I could almost hear my father's whistle, calling the redwings to our feeder on the pine-covered ridge, almost see them flying up from the cranberry bog to be fed.

If "Brer Rabbit" had a laughing place, I had my thinking place out on the north forty. Driving on the fertile fields, I solved my problems and made decisions both the big ones like how to increase income, or the small ones, like what to cook for supper.

The farm dogs, Stuart and Ashley, always followed me to the fields. They trotted behind off to one side, exploring hedgerows, scaring up rabbits and other small game. When they saw me stop the tractor, put it in neutral gear and step down onto the tongue of the spreader, they knew the trip was over. After I compressed the levers, disengaging the mechanism, the dogs stood and watched me climb back on the tractor seat. Then, breaking into a dead run, they raced ahead of me back to the barns. No matter how many trips I made, or what the weather, they always went with me. They thought it was their responsibility to keep me company, I suppose.

During below zero winter nights we parked "Alice" in the big barn. The body warmth of the horses kept her oil flowing freely and her spark plugs warm. I made as many inquiries to Josie about her well-being as I did about the condition of the horses' health. If her engine labored or was missing, I bought a new set of points and plugs, often in place of a visit to the beauty parlor. There were many times I felt like patting Little Alice on the radiator cap as a reward for an honest day's work, and I often did.

Chapter 23

Sammy #3955

When Cal Baker called and asked if I would like to buy Sammy, I was surprised and happy he had thought of me. "I know you'll give him a good home," he said, his voice hoarse with emotion. "I've got to cut down on my stock. I hate to say it but it looks like I'm about all washed up in the horse business. Age is something I put off thinking about. Sammy's a permanent sire, certified way more'n the eighty percent colored foals to give him his permanent papers. You get yourself a few decent mares and he'll do a job for you."

I didn't need any urging. I had seen the stallion many times. His striking body color, beautiful head and the intelligent human eye of the Appaloosa made him memorable. Even with all this, the quality I would appreciate most about the stallion was his even tempered disposition. He passed this on to all his kids, as Cal called Sammy's offspring. I looked to the horse to help put the farm on its feet.

We spent a busy day making preparations for Sammy's arrival. We planned to put him in a large airy box stall with two windows and a fine view of our paddocks and barnyard. The children helped me get the accomodations ready. Whitney built a grain box in one corner of the stall. I bought a new galvanized water pail. The girls hung it, We made a nameplate of redwood with three inch aluminum letters: Sammy #3955, his Appaloosa Horse Club registration number.

We were very excited when, at last, Cal Baker's grey horse trailer turned up our driveway. Once in his new stall, Sammy inspected every corner. He looked out of the windows, rolled in his shavings, took a sip from his new bucket and began to nibble hay. From time to time he whinnied.

Lynn tried to count Sammy's Appaloosa spots over his rump. Calvin called them his "potatoes". She gave up after counting eighty- five.

I had the stallion's permanent papers recorded in my name. He had been bred in Mexia, Texas, by P.G. Osborne and I decided to write Mr. Osborne and let him know who owned his horse. Although I signed the letter Blanche Kloman, his reply on ruled paper, postmarked Coolidge, Texas read,

Dear Sir,

Will tell you about Sammy. He is a real good bred horse. His mother is a real good mare gentle, and well-mannered. I raised his daddy. Glad to hear from you and glad you own Sammy.

As ever your friend,
P.G. Osborne

"As ever your friend," touched me. All of us who had owned Sammy were automatically friends. According to Cal Baker, after Sammy left Texas, he was a herd sire in Southern Illinois until Cal bought him.

At Arcadia Farm, over a period of years, thousands of children stood outside Sammy's stall and heard the story of the American Plains Indian, the valor of the Nez Perce, the bravery of Chief Joseph. The children were attentive, asking me endless questions. I always enjoyed sharing horse talk and Indian lore with them.

After a tour, the grade-schoolers often wrote me letters. Ten to one, they read, "I liked Sammy best" or "Thank you for showing us Sammy." The birthday party children, those on field trips or class excursions, after completing a tour of the barns, usually asked, "Mrs. K, which is your favorite horse?"

It was always a hard question to answer, especially when it was asked in a barn full of horses, all of whom are up at the front bars of their stalls, watching you, waiting to hear a name mentioned. Happily, there was something positive or complimentary to be said about every boarding or school horse. The way he rode, the ribbons another had won, an especially long tail, the good mothers some were. No one was left out. The question about my favorite could be avoided. I hedged a little with, "It's impossible to choose one horse above the other. They're all different, but if I must . . . it has to be Sammy."

"Why?" a persistent child once pinned me down. "Because, Sammy has a beautiful disposition and he's always been a gentleman, never causing any trouble." Correcting myself, I added, "Hardly any trouble!" remembering the Sunday afternoon Sammy got loose on the farm.

That day there was a great deal of activity on the farm with boarders riding their horses, most of the school horses out on rental. It was after four-thirty, the horses almost due to return to the barns.

I was near the little barn which housed Sammy when I heard Josie hollering. "Mrs. K . . . Mrs. K, Help! Help! Sammy's gone!"

I rushed into the building. Sammy's stall was empty! I must find him. An aroused stallion's sharp teeth and flailing hooves can injure other mares or geldings and their riders.

Josie and I tore out of the west door of the barn. My eyes scanned the open fields leading to the riding trail. Loping purposefully across the field was Sammy! I felt frantic, helpless! Cupping my hands around my mouth, I screamed, "Sammy! Sammy!" over and over as Josie and I ran after him. It was impossible to catch him that way. I stopped running only because of a sharp pain in my chest.

With all the volume my aching lungs could summon, once again I cupped my hands around trembling lips and shouted, "Sam! Sam! Ho. Sam! Ho!"

This time, a miracle happened. The big Appaloosa stopped in his tracks, turning his head toward me.

"Come, Sam. Come." I entreated, walking toward him very slowly.

Sammy, as if thinking it over, looked toward the trail riders in the distance, and looked back at me. I repeated my appeal, "Come, Sam, Come!" After a last longing look toward the trail he took a step toward me.

Breathless, my heart pounding, I slipped my narrow western belt out of the loop of my blue jeans and ran it through the ring on Sammy's halter and led him back to his barn. The horse was steady and quiet in my hand, only his heaving flanks and dilated nostrils told how intense his purpose had been.

I put Sammy in his stall, double checking the iron hasp. Someone had left it open after watering him earlier in the day. The door, now barred, was secure.

Josie had followed me. Mopping his face with a blue bandana handkerchief he said, admiringly, "That was a hellava good job, Mrs. K. I thought we wuz gonners for sure, but you caught thet old bastard!"

I couldn't help laughing. The relief was tremendous. I knew I had come a long way in handling the horses of Arcadia Farm. My confidence rose to a high point.

Chapter 24

Dolly and Flory

I had lived near Prairie Grove several years when the children and I took a drive on a gravel road where we had never gone before. We came upon a team of horses raking hay in the late morning of a beautiful June day.

Beyond the hayfield where the team was working was a winding creek, shaded by willows and alders. In this pastoral setting a small herd of Holstein heifers grazed.

I stopped the car on the shoulder of the road and watched the team at work. They were a picture of faithful cooperation, pulling the spinning hayrake through fragrant, newly cut hay. The huge horses were strawberry roans, their hides auburn-red, grey and white hairs intermixed. They had iron-grey manes and tails.

Later, I learned from my neighbor, Lester Rowe, that the team belonged to his uncles, the Ruebner brothers, who farmed collectively. They helped one another on their four farms in the area. The brothers had many stories about their team, some of which I would hear from Jess Ruebner. The horses were Belgian mares. Dolly, affectionately called Big Doll, was the right-hand horse. The left-hand horse was Flory. By this time in their lives the mares were in their thirties. Their age restricted them to lighter field chores, raking hay, pulling the hay wagon or drawing the farm sledge loaded with cattle manure out on snow- covered fields when no tractor could cope with the drifted snow banks.

One day Lester told me his uncles were retiring from farming and the team was for sale. I thought about buying the Belgians for hayrides.

I went to see Mr. Harvey Ruebner. Everyone called him Uncle Harvey. It was the first time I had driven up the long, hilly lane to the homestead where the six Ruebner brothers had been born and raised. On the hilltop stood the immaculate, turn-of-the-century, white clapboard farmhouse with ornate gables and gingerbread millwork on the porch. The house was surrounded by an apple orchard, bursting with pink and white blossoms.

The barns and outbuildings were painted New England barn red, trimmed in white, not a board out of place or a shingle missing.

Uncle Harvey was standing at one of his huge diesel tractors, adding fuel to the gas tank. I could smell it as I walked toward him. He surveyed me with kindly eyes from behind gold-rimmed spectacles. I explained I had come to buy Dolly and Flory.

"What would you do with them, Missus, if I did sell 'em to you? The mares can't do heavy work anymore."

I replied that I would use them for birthday parties or hayrides.

Uncle Harvey seemed satisfied. He gestured to the barn behind him and said, "You know, Missus, we've owned the team better'n twenty years. First, they farmed for my brother, Jess, in Willow Grove. Then for Fred and me. They tilled all the land where you now see the village of Prairie Grove. As teams go, they were well known in our community, the only team you could drive right up to the threshing machine. I have a picture of them from the Chicago Daily News. There they stood, still as a board and all that noise and commotion around them, the thresher belching out steam and smoke."

He turned away and walked up on the porch, the screen door slamming behind him. In a few minutes he was back. In his hand he carried a faded newspaper. The clipping was of Dolly and Flory. The caption read, "Ruebner Brothers team of Belgians, steadiest at thresher in Prairie Grove".

Concluding our conversation in the barnyard, Uncle Harvey and I walked into the barn. The team was standing side by side in straight stalls. They were very large and muscular. They ignored us, continuing to munch their hay from a heavy wooden manger in front of them. The farmer and I talked further, arriving at a price for the team, including their harness, collars and hames, their bridles with red wool tassels and two fly sheets.

It was a glorious sight the day Uncle Harvey brought the team to the farm on a Sunday afternoon. We could see him coming a long way off, walking slowly behind them, lines in hand, their great heads bobbing with every step. As they came closer, we heard the chink-chank of small chains, straps and buckles, the rattle of ivory rings on their harness.

Each mare wore a headstall, crisscrossed on her forehead with narrow leather strips in the shape of a diamond. Flory had a bright red wool tassel hung at eye level on the left side of her bridle. Dolly wore her tassel on the right. The brass balls of the hames shone in the afternoon sunlight. The whole picture was one of strength and fidelity. I realized what the team must have meant to the brothers and why they had such genuine concern for their welfare. They would mean as much to me.

After the mares had rested and settled into their new home, Uncle Harvey showed Josie, Whitney and me how to harness the team. It was not an easy task. Each set of harness weighed over ninety pounds, made up of many parts. During the years I owned Dolly and Flory, two of us were needed to put on their collars and harness. We never attained the skill and agility of Uncle Harvey. He merely draped himself in the harness leathers and with a couple of hoists and heaves, had it all in place with little effort.

The team was remarkably schooled, you only had to pick up the lines and the huge creatures sidestepped over the wagon tongue, taking their places on either side of it, and backing themselves up to the whipple tree.

We had to learn to drive them, of course. The team set their shoulders into their collars and moved out willingly.

When Labor Day approached, the first holiday after I bought them, and since Dolly and Flory were the last team in the area and closely identified with Prairie Grove, we were invited to participate in the Village's parade. I invited Uncle Harvey Ruebner to drive them.

Giulio shod the Belgians with over-size rubber shoes, like the ones he ordered for Bill, to protect their feet while parading on cement or macadam pavements. He grasped their hairy fetlocks as he pulled up on their massive feet until he balanced the hoof between his knees or rested it on a kneecap. He had to put their hooves down more often than those of the riding horses. The mares weighed at least twenty-four hundred pounds each.

It was a beautiful autumn day for the parade. Our position was behind the mounted color guard and riders from the Arcadia farm. Uncle Harvey and his eldest brother -- frail, eighty year old Jess -- and I sat on the wagon seat. The wagon was gaily decorated with red, white and blue bunting and brimming full with my client's children, each holding a colorful balloon.

The team walked slowly down Creekside Road toward the street recently named Ruebner Boulevard, in the new part of the village. When Jess Ruebner noticed the street sign, he made a wide gesture with his arm and said, wistfully, "Missus, I farmed all this land with Doll and Flory. Over there was my wheat. Up on the hill was my corn. Down by the creek we planted soy beans." Following his gestures I saw rows of modest new houses.

Since it was Jess who had owned the team first, I knew he would be able to tell me special stories about them. As we rode toward the parade route in a leisurely fashion, I asked the old man where he had bought the team. He said the horses had been bought separately and at different times. Dolly at four, Flory at three, both at auctions. He thought he had paid a total of one hundred dollars for them. Harvey, gently corrected him, suggesting a much higher figure.

I asked Jess if he had trouble breaking Dolly to harness. "No, don't believe I did. Jest hitched her up with Oscar Pritz' old mare, Sheba, and she caught right on. Now that Flory, she was different. A might giddy, ye know." He cleared his throat and continued, "Yes sirree, that Flory...she was a pistol. Only three, ye know. Well, she kicked out the buckboard twice so I went in the shed and got her fly sheet. Put it on her, and that was the end of her fussin'." I loved to hear his stories, knowing however, that it took more than the application of a fly sheet to school a horse.

The old gentleman warmed up to the conversation and continued, "Let me tell you, Missus, about when we used to thresh the grain."

"She's already heard that one," interrupted Uncle Harvey.

Undismayed, Jess went on telling his favorite tale. "Well sir, we were the only boys who could drive our team right plumb along side of the thresher. We'd even fill our neighbors wagons for them, to save time. Many fellers wanted to buy our team but they was never for sale. Never . . ." His voice trailed off as he lapsed into silence, lost in thought.

I patted his arm assuringly. "Dolly and Flory will have a good home with me, I'm proud to own them." Jess wiped his tear-filled eyes with a shirt sleeve and smiled at me. "I'm sure of that, Harvey here tells me they're going to pull the kiddies around for birthday parties. Harv says you were the only one he'd let the team go to."

When we found ourselves at the parade, Uncle Harvey pulled the wagon to one side of the street and waited for the signal to fall in and join the marchers. From behind us came the martial music of the highschool band. They swung around us at the very moment the horns and trumpets blared and the cymbals crashed. The din of the cymbals blasted in the mares' ears and the team stepped back and forth in the traces jerking the wagon. Harvey held the lines steady but it was Jess who calmed the horses, murmuring almost inaudibly, "Easy Doll . . . steady Flory, old girl . . ." The soothing voice of the old man the horses had not heard in many years, calmed them instantly, restoring their confidence.

On we went, over the new bridge, the creek gushing beneath us, the horses looking neither to left or right, on to the end of the parade route, without mishap.

On our way back to the farm, I asked Uncle Harvey to let the lines go loose when we passed the lane leading to the Ruebner homestead. The team jogged along at a steady pace, passed the entrance to their old home, turned the corner onto Allendale Road and unguided, trotted briskly into the driveway of Arcadia Farm. They knew they were home!

That fall, after the corn-picker had harvested the crop, we took the team to the field with a box wagon. We drove down the rows, picking up fallen ears the machine had missed. Throwing corn into the wagon, five or six of us on either side, Whitney, Lynn and Gail and some of the boarders too. There was laughter and noisy competition. The team munched an occasional ear of corn, keeping their eyes on us and moving up by themselves without a driver, keeping abreast of us as we picked up the golden ears. Laughing children in warm sunlight doing easy work. It was happy retirement for Dolly and Flory. Who deserved it more?

Chapter 25

Haying Time

In late July or Early August haying time always came at the height of intense summer heat. After the field had been cut with the tractor and sicklebar, Josie or I coupled the docile team of Belgian mares to the old spinning hay rake and rolled the hay crop into rows to be baled.

We waited until the dew and morning moisture had burned off the fragrant grasses, and if there was a light breeze the hay was dry by noon. If by chance there was a sudden summer shower we would have to rake the field all over again.

My good neighbor, Lester Rowe, cautioned me often about baling wet hay, which he said could combust in the hay mow and destroy my barns and horses. As we unloaded a wagon onto the creaking conveyor at the barn, he showed me how to recognize the dead weight of "tough" bales, those with too much moisture. We threw these bales to one side, cut them open, spread them out to ventilate and fed them to the horses within a few days, but never stored them.

During harvest time we spent almost all day in the hay field. We took a hearty lunch and a large, blue pottery jug of milk. At noon Josie and Whitney unbridled the horses and led them to the creek for a long drink and left them unbridled so they could graze while we ate our lunch. The farm dogs, Stuart and Ashley, had been following us all morning and lay under the wagon bed in the shade.

We chose to eat our picnic at the far north boundary of the field where there was an old fieldstone foundation, the site of the original homestead of the farm. During haying we savored thick wedges of ham between slices of whole wheat bread, hard boiled eggs, fresh peaches and occasionally, chocolate brownies, if I'd found time to bake them.

Long ago, Lester and Josie had filled the old well pit near the homestead site with rocks and dirt and nailed planking over it so no one or no animal could fall into it, a nightmare I often had until it was sealed up.

The children often speculated about earlier settlers. Whitney wondered if they might have seen the buffalo grazing on the vast prairie and if they hunted them. He always hoped we would turn up a buffalo skull when we plowed the fields in the spring, but we never did. The little girls asked me endless questions about the pioneer children, what they wore and if they went to school and if there were other children with whom they played. I thought about the women farming here, two hundred years ago, women who didn't have a tractor and a willing team.

After we had eaten, there always was time for one or two of Josie's stories. "When I was jest a little shaver," he'd begin, or he'd say, "Somepin' about haying time bein' somepin' special." The children had favorites from the old man's reminiscences. "Like the time my daddy combined a nest of ground bees into a bale. Thet sure was a fracas. All them bees and my daddy swattin' and cussin." This was their favorite tale.

As the heat of the long afternoon intensified, Whitney brought a pail of cool water from the creek. Josie would stop from time to time and pour a dipper of water over the back of his sunburned neck letting its coolness run down between his shoulder blades where sweat had plastered his shirt his back. Whitney imitated him, soaking his own shirt front and back. I rung out the dark blue kerchiefs in the bucket and tied them around the girls' necks to ward off sunstroke. Even our wide brimmed straw hats did not adequately protect us from the relentless sun.

After the baler had gone through the fields and the hay bales were stacked nine tiers high, we followed up with Dolly and Flory and an empty wagon. We raked the field with the wooden hay rakes and forked the hay onto the wagon bed. When the load became too high for the children and me to reach, Josie pitched with the twelve foot hay fork which reached to the top of the load. It was light work and satisfying to know we had harvested every particle of precious hay in the field. The smell of the alfalfa-timothy-clover crop was one I never forgot.

On the way back to the barns Whitney boosted Lynn and Gail onto Dolly and Flory's broad backs where they held onto the gleaming brass balls on the hames, clinging with their short legs and bare heels to the sides of the placid mares.

Chapter 26

An Unexpected Visitor

One beautiful Indian summer day I had taken advantage of its crispness, hanging blankets on the lines in the back yard. My arms were heaped with winter blankets and afghans when I saw a frail wisp of a woman, silver-haired and stooped over, approaching my front door. When she saw me she raised a hand in greeting and with the other dabbed at her lips and forehead with her handkerchief. She appeared to be exhausted.

I told her to follow me into the kitchen. Throwing the laundry on one end of the old oak kitchen table, I pulled out a kitchen chair for each of us. We sat down across from each other.

My visitor was breathing with great difficulty, trying to catch her breath. I set a glass of water in front of her and asked, "What can I do for you?"

She fingered the satin binding on the edge of a blanket, smiled wanly, and replied, "Quite a lot, I think. I've come to talk to you about my mare, Beauty." She took a sip of water, wiped her brow and continued. "I've recently moved from Florida. My daughter wanted me to be nearer her because of my health problems." At that, she began to wheeze.

Her face became flushed and strained with paroxysms of coughing as she tried speaking in short, halting sentences. "I thought of putting Beauty down before I left the South, but just couldn't make myself do it. I've had her more than twenty-five years. She's over thirty now. I pretended we were going on a trip together." Again, she struggled to speak, wiping her face between coughs.

I had heated the tea kettle and put a cup of tea near her elbow. The hot beverage seemed to help as she continued speaking.

"I rented the horsetrailer and Beauty and I took our time coming north, more than ten days. I took her out of the trailer a couple of times every day so she could stretch her legs. She loads like a dream." My visitor's face lit up at the recollection of her mare's sensible behavior. "I believe Beauty enjoyed the trip. People were ever so kind to us at the horse motels along the way."

She sipped her tea slowly, asked for a second cup and said, "I'd like to pay you a couple months board. Your pasture looks pleasant. Beauty will like it here for awhile."

I realized what the woman was asking. She wanted me to have Beauty put down for her. I laid my hand on her shoulder, gently patted her and said, "I've very gentle horses in the front field, most of them old brood mares. Beauty should fit right in. Don't worry, I'll keep an eye on her."

We spoke a little longer and she wrote out a check. Then we walked out to the parking area where the old station wagon and horsetrailer were parked. The woman began to gasp for breath and I watched her helplessly.

Finally, she forced herself to speak. "I don't want to know. . . when. You take care of it, will you?"

I took the lead shank from her after she untied the mare's head and backed Beauty out of the horse trailer. The mare looked fit for her age. She was coal black with a little white snip on her forehead. Just like the original Black Beauty, I thought. She seemed very lame as I led her down the lane and turned her loose with my own mares.

Only once, thereafter, did I see Beauty's owner at the farm. She did not come to the house, but stood leaning on the fence feeding carrots to Beauty and the other mares. Then, one morning there was a phone call. It was Mrs. Parker's daughter. I could hear the tears in her voice as she explained. "Mother died early this morning. She told me she had made arrangements for Beauty with you. Mother left you a note. The letter came in the mail the next day.

Dear Mrs. K,

I knew when I left Beauty with you that I might not see her more than once or twice again. I felt relieved, knowing you would take care of the matter for me.

Thank you and God bless you.

Lorraine Parker

Tucked in the envelope was a faded snapshot of a smiling young girl. I recognized Lorraine Parker, holding the reins of a beautiful black horse.

On a weathered piece of paper folded in half, were these words, "0 my master, when my youthful strength is gone, take my life in the kindest way, and your God will reward you here and hereafter. I ask this in the name of Him who was born in a stable. Amen" Author Unknown.

After collecting my emotions, I dialed Dr. Roper and made an appointment with him to fulfill my responsibility to Beauty.

Chapter 27

Blue-eyed Wally

I bought a print titled "Winter Night" by Herring, an English artist, at an antique show held at the old Stevens Hotel in Chicago. The setting was an English barnyard in the eighteen fifties. I had it framed in wormy chestnut and the title covered by a dark chocolate brown mat. The framer stenciled the words, "Rough Board at Arcadia Farm" on the mat below the print.

The scene appealed to me very much. There is a thatched cottage, its roof covered with snow and a man and a young boy are feeding livestock. The man is pushing a wheelbarrow with wide wooden wheels heaped with cabbages and other vegetables for little piglets, scrambling all over the yard. There is a hay manger with a peaked thatched roof covered with snow. The color tones of the print are subdued shades of grey, black, and white except for the burgundy cabbage leaves in the wheelbarrow and the reddish chestnut horse eating from the manger. The chestnut horse is the image of my mare, Wally. I never look at the print that I do not remember her beautiful arched neck and rounded barrel.

There are five other horses in the picture and one pony, all sleek and fat. Uncannily, each of them are exact replicas of horses I have owned or boarded. The contour of their heads and body conformation, their poses, all indelibly stamped on my memory. Stonewall, ears up, and standing alone by a thatched cottage, watches the farmer. On his left, lying down, the mare,

Firestone; behind them, eating from a manger, heavy-set, blocky Frosty. He has one eye on the farmer. At the other snow-covered manger, a small black pony and a beautiful chestnut mare. Her perfectly proportioned body and luxurious satin hide, the only spot of color in the print. For me, a true likeness of my mare, Wally.

She was cross-bred with saddle horse predominating. I rode her under English or Western saddle. Wally had impeccable manners and a sweet, charming disposition. These qualities would have made her a joy to own, but she had another distinguishing feature which made her unique. She had blue eyes! Not the glass eye of the pinto or albino, sometimes called "walleyed". Wally's eyes were as blue as cornflowers with a dash of hyacinth and a hint of purple iris. I often wondered if there had ever been another horse with such beautiful eyes.

Whenever I took a group of birthday party children for a tour of the barns, I explained what we were going to see, always adding, ". . . and I have a special horse to show you. One with blue eyes, like mine." The children's expressions when they saw Wally confirmed what an addition she was to the tour. As they took turns patting her neck, I could trust her to stand perfectly still as they admired her remarkable eyes and four white stockings.

Wally always had her wits about her. Only once did she and I have an unsettling experience. On Labor Day, after all the riders had left for the parade, I found myself the last to leave, as usual. My morning had been spent helping my boarders wash their horses, find tack, and get organized for the parade. No matter how I tried to anticipate their needs, someone always arrived late and unprepared, expecting, nevertheless, to ride in the pageant. I'd pitch in and help the late-comers get their horses slicked up for the parade.

This particular year, I had splurged on a new turquoise, western outfit, bell-bottom jeans, a white ruffled shirt and turquoise vest. I tied a flowing turquoise chiffon scarf on my white straw western hat. Wally had a new hand-crocheted turquoise saddle blanket.

The night before, I had washed the mare's white hind stockings, grooming her thoroughly. All it took on Labor Day to get her ready were a few more strokes with a fine brush. After a rub with a piece of coarse toweling she looked more than presentable.

I left the farm a half hour after everyone else. Creekside Road, not paved in those days, was deserted and I took it easy. Wally had such a fast walk it was not necessary to canter more than a few times and we were at the crossroads. I was relaxed, enjoying my ride and the horse's company,

As we passed old St. Martha's Church, out of the double front oak doors burst the pastor, Father Mulvaney. His long black cassock whipped around his legs as he hurried across the road in front of Wally and me, toward the rectory.

Wally took one look at what seemed to be a phantom and reared straight up in the air. I was totally unprepared and lost my balance as she spun around. I fell over her right shoulder onto the roadside gravel. Father Mulvaney rushed to help me.

Fortunately, I held onto a length of Wally's reins or we would have been chasing the frightened horse down Creekside Road. Wally,snorted and pranced as the priest spoke soothingly, "Easy, easy, my beauty," he crooned. "Gently now, my pretty...that's a good girl you are... stand a minute...no one's going to hurt you...what frightened you, my pet?" Then, as he lifted me to my feet by an aching elbow, he asked, "Are you hurt, young lady?" Looking once more at Wally, the priest gasped in astonishment, "Holy mother of God! What eyes she's got. As blue as God's own heaven! Aren't they now?"

Shaken by my hard fall, I nodded. I must have looked a mess, my new outfit rumpled and dirty, a tender welt on my cheek where I hit the gravel.

Very much in charge, Father Mulvaney took Wally's reins from me. "Young lady, over to the rectory with you. Mrs. Brennan will have a cold towel for that cheek of yours." Admiring Wally, he added, "She's a fiery one. No question about that!" He led the mare as I limped toward the rear door of the red brick rectory. The priest called out, in a loud voice to someone in the kitchen, Whoo-whoo, Mrs. Brennan. Would you be comin' here a minute. There's a young lady who needs a bit of help. Whoo-whoo!"

Mrs. Brennan appeared at the screen door drying her hands on a red and white checked gingham apron. She surveyed me calmly, not taken aback at my dishevelled appearance.

"You should have seen it, Mary," Father said, gesturing toward Wally. "My saints she's a spirited one. A real beauty." Then, remembering me, he added,

"Can you bring a cold towel for the young lady's poor face?"

I never got to the parade. After the cold, wet towel, Mary Brennan brought me a cup of strong tea in a fine china tea cup. My arm was aching and I realized I must have chipped an elbow. My arm started to swell with pain shooting to my shoulder.

Father Mulvaney grazed Wally on his front lawn, humming to himself. The mare was cropping close to the Holy Name Society's garden, the priest holding her reins with a calm, experienced hand.

When Father proposed he ride Wally back to the farm for me while I follow them in his vintage car, I thought it a good idea. He was excited at the prospect but I wondered how many years it had been since he had ridden a horse. Although he inadvertently had caused the circumstances, I forgave him for he had been so kind.

He disappeared into the rectory and emerged shortly, wearing a pair of baggy, brown knickers, an old green sweater and his clerical collar.

On the trip back to the farm Wally walked or trotted slowly. I drove behind them until we reached the barns and after I put Wally in her stall we stood near Father's old vehicle a minute. I thanked him for his kindness.

"It's I should be thanking you," he said, a rougish twinkle in his eye. "What a grand morning I've had! All my life, ever since I was a boy, I've wanted to ride a horse. Now I've done it! It was wonderful! Just wonderful! She's a beauty, that one, and such eyes she has. As blue as the heavens above."

I was shocked, hearing the revelation. It never crossed my mind this was the first time he had ever ridden a horse! For years to come I would hear versions of the tale, retold by the pastor around the supper table. How many times the young assistant curate must have heard the story, with embellishments, Mrs. Brennan chiming in describing her contribution of the cold towel and steaming cup of tea.

Long afterwards, the rural mailman, George Dickerson, asked to see the horse with the blue eyes which had tossed Father Mulvaney over her head. I smiled at how the incident had grown.

Wally became known throughout the parish and eventually was described as Father Mulvaney's own spirited, blue-eyed mare.

Chapter 28

The Comedian

If the adjective *unique* can be applied to a horse it should have been to By Request. Handsome as the Palomino is supposed to be, with golden body and silver mane and tail, he was the glamour boy of our barn. Request's beautiful head with small ears set close together, gave him the appearance of a satyr. With his alert expression and watchful eyes he seemed to be looking for an opportunity to express his sense of humor.

His owners told us he had originally been called Trigger, the name for hundreds of other Palomino's. Since he had been purchased for all the Adkin family, they changed his name to By Request.

When we took him to the water trough to drink, Request often seized that moment as one of the children relaxed their hold on his halter, to jerk out of hand, tear out of the barn and go galloping down the driveway. At first, panic-stricken, we ran after him in a prolonged game of tag with the culprit. We quickly learned if we ignored him, Request would circle the barns several times at a fast clip and then walk quietly into the barn to his stall. The use of a lead rope fastened securely to his halter would have eliminated the game entirely. Once we knew it was a prank, we allowed him the luxury to play.

A light switch in his stall lit one end of the hayloft. Many nights I looked out of my window and saw the hayloft illuminated, and later saw it was dark again.

Our appreciation grew for By Request. To us, he was a free spirit living in a horse's hide.

At the end of our third year in business we discussed having open house for our customers in September. I sent out three hundred and fifty penny post card invitations. We planned varied entertainment. The polo team would play a short demonstration game. There would be several classes in English and Western riding. As a climax, we planned a Tableau of "El Cid". The movie had made an impact on us and inspired my family to recreate the pageantry of Medieval Spain.

Gail researched background information at the highschool library. Later, she told us that boys were trained from early childhood to handle the lance on horseback wearing full armor. By fourteen they were proficient. She assured me Whitney would be able to handle his horse, Buck, with all the accoutrements.

I called a theatrical costumer, rented two sets of armor, complete with mail, shoulder and breast plates, lances and shields. Lynn bought the stereo recording and sound track from "El Cid".

The hayloft door was directly above our outdoor riding area. I placed the record player there. At a musical climax and crescendo our two nobles on horseback, would enter the ring from opposite ends and engage in a mock joust for our customer's entertainment.

Gail had also said, "In Medieval times the knight was lowered onto his horse by a manservant because of the weight of the armor." Our armor was not that heavy. Our nobility could mount up unassisted.

But who had dressed a knight for combat in 1964? No one among us nor anyone else we consulted. We had two dress rehearsals with the cumbersome intricasies of the armor. It proved to be quite a ceremony.

First, Whitney and his friend Dennis stepped into their mail body suits, not unlike a baby's sleeper pajama with feet. It was made of closely woven mesh fabric dipped in aluminum paint by the costumer. Hoods of the same material covered their heads, fitting close to the boys perspiring faces.

We laid out other parts of the costumes in the order they were put on. Breast and back plates were buckled on their shoulders. Next, the shoulder armor, somewhat like aluminum football shoulder pads. Then came rigid sections which fit over the forearm, hinged at the elbow. Josie and I, kneeling on the ground in front of our nobles, helped them step into heavy leg and foot armor and buckled it behind their knees and over the instep. Last, the helmets with perforated visors, were placed on Whitney and Dennis' heads.

Dennis owned Mist, a grey gelding. He also owned a heavy bright blue quilted horse blanket, bought for the occasion. It covered Mist's body completely. I splurged at the saddle shop, buying one in red just like it for Buck. I convinced myself I could use the expensive blanket on one of my own horses during the winter, justifying it's cost in a budget where frugality was the watch word. I also bought quilted shipping hoods which fitted over the horse's heads and necks. Only their ears and eyes were visible.

We knew how long it took to dress the cavaliers but overlooked rehearsing with the horses. After I saw the two boys helmeted, shields and lances in hand, Lynn and I bounded up the hayloft stairs and she started the music. The turntable moved and El Cid's stirring music reverberated. Lynn played the music through once . . . twice. . . scanning the ring for the scarlet cavalier and his adversary, but no one appeared.

As Lynn played the recording a third time, I dashed down the hayloft stair to the barnyard. I saw one of the nobles in full armorial splendor astride Mist. The majesty of the visual effect surpassed my highest expectations. Out of the corner of my eye, however, to my dismay, I saw the figure of our crimson knight, Whitney, prostrate on the ground, on his back like a turtle unable to turn over. Gail, Josie and others were trying to raise him to his feet. Through Whit's visor came groans and harsh remarks directed at Buck.

Gail held Buck's bridle as the horse snorted and pranced, baffled by his master's appearance and unfamiliar odor. Buck had resisted Whitney's attempt to mount by whirling in circles, unloading him any number of times, on his aluminum backside.

I heard the music faintly in the distance the sixth or perhaps the seventh time as Josie relayed messages from the restless, disappointed audience. About the time I decided to send Dennis into the ring with an imaginary opponent, Mr. Adkins, who owned By Request, joined us as we deliberated in the yard.

"Request will do it," he volunteered, confidently. "I'll go get him." He came back with the Palomino in seconds. He transferred the red quilting and hood to By Request. Only his elfin ears and mischievious eyes showed. The horse stood perfectly still while being outfitted, then to our dismay, jerked himself free of Mr. Adkins and tore down the driveway.

"Damn that horse," Mr. Adkins exploded. "Why'd he do that?" Disappointed and chagrined, he stood helpless in front of us all.

"He'll be right back," Whitney explained calmly, adjusting the visor on his helmet so he could see the flash of scarlet now bearing down on us.

Request slowed down to a measured walk and came to a stop in front of Mr. Adkins.

In relief, Mr. Adkins cried, "Good boy. Good fella. Good Request!"

The Palomino stood like a statue as Whitney stepped from the flatbed wagon into the stirrups and settled himself in the saddle.

I hurried back to my post in the loft and Lynn started the El Cid theme again. Our cavaliers appeared to cheers from the spectators.

It was a stirring sight. Sunlight gleamed from their helmets and shields. Request's luxurious silver tail sweeping the ground, the music swelled in an increasing crescendo. By Request had saved the day. I still have happy memories of his unique personality.

Chapter 29

Five Good Ones

One winter afternoon in January, Justin Pike phoned from his Wisconsin farm. Whitney relayed the message. The Pikes had a new load of horses from North Platt, Nebraska. I could have "first pick".

Although the Pike brothers later built a small indoor riding ring to show their stock, at this time we had to work the horses out of doors, sometimes in the rain or biting cold.

"Can we go tonight?" begged Whitney, excited over the prospect of seeing the Pike's demonstrate the handiness of the new horses.

The promise of first pick was alluring. When the weather moderated, other buyers would flock to the Pike's to buy sound riding horses from the far Western states.

It was bitter cold when we arrived at the Pike's barn at twilight. I left the car motor running, keeping the heater on for Lynn and Gail. Their warm breath soon fogged the car windows.

Justin Pike, his ruddy face seared by the frigid wind, greeted us in the yard. "Got a real load to show you this time. Some dandies," he said. Droplets of moisture frosted his red mustache. He ran the back of his deerhide glove across his dripping nose and gestured toward one of the small buildings behind him. "Step inside the barn and take a look. Good broke horses, every one of them. Some of the best me and Jake ever had."

I knew from previous experience when Justin Pike said a horse was "good broke" and would "do me", it was as close to gospel as I would ever hear in the horse business. Dr. Roper knew what he was doing when he sent me to buy horses from them originally. The Pike brothers deserved their reputation for integrity as dealers.

In the small shed-like barn tied in straight stalls stood eight horses. Three were saddled. Jake Pike, taller than his brother, his weathered face reflecting the frigid cold, slipped a curb bit into the mouth of a horse nearest the door. He skillfully backed the chestnut mare into the narrow aisle.

"Classy, ain't she? Good rein on her too," he said, running his hand over the muscular shoulder of the Quarter horse mare.

Classy she was, from her intelligent head with its white stripe to her four, knee-high white stockings. I looked into her steady, mild eyes. We would later name her Honey Bee, a name that couldn't have been less apt. I then had no way of knowing that after re-selling her she would board with me fifteen years and we would find she was the fastest horse ever to set foot on our farm.

Whitney would borrow her twice, riding the mare in speed and action events, always winning the blue ribbon. Standing in the doorway of the little barn, I witnessed her amazing speed, Honey and her owner flying over the strip on our west boundary. Many challenged Honey, but no one beat her on the straightaway.

Now, in the yard at the Pike's farm, Jake swung up on the mare's back. He reined her abruptly to the right and loped her up a gentle rise toward the road, but a snowquall hid them from view. I was stamping my feet to keep them from freezing, but I could hear hoofbeats returning on the glassy surface.

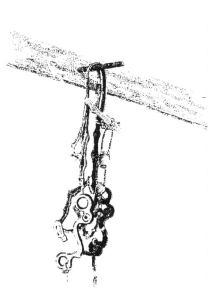

Grinning, Jake slid the mare to within inches from where I was standing. "She's a honey," he gasped, out of breath after the fast ride in the zero air.

I managed to say, through chattering teeth and stiffened jaw, "We'll take her, for sure."

By that time, Justin had another horse saddled. She too, was a deep red chestnut and rode equally sharp. In time we'd name her Firestone. Then, he showed us a black and white paint mare with such outstanding conformation she would become a halter and performance champion after I resold her. Next, Jake brought out a large Palomino mare from the Kansas City stock yards. "Broke to death" was the way he described her. Gold Medal became her name, a tribute to her burnished hide.

Never again would I buy such outstanding western horses in one package. All the time these transactions were going on, I glanced occasionally at a chunky quarter horse gelding tied with a piece of baling twine to the top rail of a fence behind us. He seemed unconcerned by the commotion around him. He stood with his rump tucked down against the polar wind, shifting his weight from time to time from one hind leg to another.

When I walked over to him, he looked like a Kodiak bear. His seal brown coat, four inches thick, covered with granular snow. I brushed the snow from his back and neck with my mittens and he turned and looked at me.

"What about this one?" I called to Justin. He shouted back through the driving snow, "Picked him up in Mandrake, North Dakota. He's a dandy!"

As Jake and Whitney were loading the other four horses in the stock trailer, I turned away from the brown horse. We were all frozen to our bone marrow. I put my hand on the car door handle, but looking over the roof of the station wagon I studied the horse again. He was almost obscurred by driving snow, his head was turned toward me. "Put him on the load too," I called to Jake.

"You won't be sorry, he'll do you good," he replied.

I named the stocky brown horse Dakotah and I kept him for myself. During the thirteen years I owned him, I had many opportunities to sell him. Jake or Justin often inquired, "You still got that little brown horse?" I always laughed and answered, "Sure do."

Dakotah, broke in Western ranch tradition, was good-looking, rugged, gentle and sensible. He was a great help to me in the business. I used him for older children's birthday parties as well as countless times for first riding lessons. Dakotah ground tied. I had only to drop his reins on the ground and he would stand in one place until I came back for him, no matter how long I left him.

He was probably born under the stars on the Western open range. At the farm he preferred being out of doors with the "roughers" and seldom went into the loafing barn for shelter. He and Big Boy were unchallenged bosses of the herd.

The very first summer I owned Dakotah, all the roughers broke out of their paddock during a dense,soupy fog. I awakened to the piercing squeals of the ponies, signaling the entire herd was loose. By the time I got dressed and aroused Whitney, forty horses had moved out of hearing onto the eighty acres north of the barns. I had used Dakotah that afternoon for a lesson and he was still in a straight stall. I saddled him quickly, mounted, letting the reins hang loose and headed him north toward the open fields.

The fog was so thick I could not see Dakotah's ears. I could feel his powerful, compact body, moving beneath me. The murkiness of the fog provided an eerie feeling as if I was suspended above the earth. It seemed Dakotah and I were parting a dense curtain.

I was very frightened and didn't know where I was or what was in front of me. From time to time I whispered, "Ho, boy," gently reining him to a halt as I strained my ears, listening for the loose herd. I couldn't hear anything except my own breathing. The fog's clammy mist surrounded us.

When Dakotah came to a dead stop on his own, I heard munching and chomping of grazing horses ahead of us. We were right among them. The hulk of Big Boy appeared on my right side. I leaned from the saddle and hooked a lead rope to his halter ring. Turning around, I completely lost my bearings and once more dropped the reins on Dakotah's neck, uttering an intense, silent prayer that he would bring us back to the safety of the barnyard and hopefully, that all the horses and ponies would follow Big Boy.

The return trip seemed endless. Big Boy fought me all the way, lowering his head and stout neck to graze. My arm ached from jerking his head up from the lush pasture. I scolded him whenever he balked, but finally we were in the barnyard area.

Whitney stood under the yard light, his blue and white striped pajamas tucked in the top of his boots. The corral gate was open and he had already repaired the broken fence. I rode deep into the paddock, towing Big Boy as the entire herd followed.

Locking the gate behind them, Whitney burst out jubilantly, "That old Dakotah horse! He'll sure 'do us', won't he, Mom?" Sliding from the saddle, weary but relieved I replied, "He sure will, son. He sure will."

Chapter 30

A Slender Thread

It was the twenty-first of December, 1964. It was after ten o'clock at night and we were on our second hayride. I felt frozen to my bone marrow, unable to unclasp my fingers from the tractor's steering wheel. Whitney had driven the first one at eight-thirty, up the shoulder of Allendale Road to Lester Rowe's turn-about and back to our farm. There was far too much snow drifting on our fields to chance getting stuck in below zero weather.

With Christmas a few days away, we needed every penny of income we could muster. December and January were notorious for the slowness with which customers paid their horse's board.

I had put a deposit on ice skates for the children. The fifty dollars earned that night would complete the transaction and buy our Christmas groceries.

Behind me, twenty nuns snuggled in the deep straw of the box wagon, covered by blankets and shawls. They were singing hymns and Christmas carols, one of them playing her guitar above the Allis Chalmer's tractor motor. Their music and laughter helped me forget my discomfort.

Snow squalls, driven by cutting wind, obscured my view of Allendale Road.

Sister Mary Agnes, seated in the back of the wagon, held an electric lantern with a red flasher. I turned one of the tractor's lights so its beam was shining behind us. There was no traffic on the road that night. Blowing snow flurries made it impossible to see the shoulder of the road and I worried about losing my bearings and sliding into the ditch, together with my wagonload of sisters from St. Martha's.

Dimly, the yard light of Lester's farm shone in the distance. As we passed the farmhouse, I saw Lester and his sister silhouetted in the doorway, watching us pass. The soft light of their old farm kitchen looked warm and inviting. For a moment, I felt like Hans Christian Andersen's "Little Match Girl", frozen, hungry, catching a glimpse of a neighbor's cozy hearth.

The return trip went well and a sigh of relief filled my chest as we approached the entrance to Arcadia Farm. The county snowplow had piled huge banks of snow at the driveway and I swung wide, making a smooth turn, careful not to bind the wagon tongue against the tractor wheel. Misjudging the distance, I slid into a drainage ditch with both front wheels, the tractor hung up on an icy snowbank.

There was no way for me to back out, although I tried reverse gear. My left foot slipped on the ice-coated clutch pedal, almost pinning my foot under it. I knew I had better leave well enough alone. It would take a tow truck to pull Alice from the snowbank.

When I turned around to the nuns behind me, they were singing, oblivious of my difficulties. I called out, "Sisters, we're stuck. Can you help me push the wagon out of the way so it won't block the driveway?"

I pulled the pin from the coupling and tugged on the wagon tongue, steering it, as twenty hilarious nuns pushed the wagon into a clearing near the mailboxes. I led the way up the long driveway, my legs buckling from lack of circulation as the sisters giggled and pelted one another with snowballs.

As we approached the farmyard, a light from the barn's open door shone on the snowdrifts. There stood Jeff Roper's familiar carry- all van parked nearby. The veterinarian and Chase Harper were standing in the doorway. "Had to call Jeff. Barbie had a mild colic," Chase explained. "She's okay now, though," he added.

"What in hell are you doing out on a night like this?" boomed Jeff Roper, shaking his head in disbelief.

My jaws were so stiff with cold I could hardly answer him. What was I doing? Only I knew how tight finances were, how I needed every dollar. I also knew the fifty dollars earned that night would pay the fee for a tow truck, a big one with a winch, to snake out the tractor from the ditch.

Tears welled up and ran down my frozen cheeks at the precise moment Chase stepped into the light and pressed an envelope into my icy mitten. "Merry Christmas from Barbie," he said, smiling broadly. He was paying Barbie's board two weeks early and had included an extra twenty dollar bill. Tears stung my eyes as I ushered the nuns into the family room. Gail was serving hot cocoa and cookies before the fireplace.

To the two men standing in the barn doorway I called, "Come on in, fellas. Join us for a hot drink. What are you doing out on a night like this, anyway?" They followed us into the house, laughing.

It came home to me, again, how our very existence hung by a slender thread. No matter how I planned ahead, no matter how many hours I worked or under what conditions, we were unable to get ahead. I told myself we needed a new venture, something bold, something daring and dramatic to insure more income. But what could that be? I tried to think of something, throughout another fretful, sleepless night.

Chapter 31
The Last Frontier

One winter day after medical rounds, as Dr. Roper left the farm, he looked out across the wide expanse of open fields and said, "This would be a great place for a rodeo. Have you ever considered it?"

Up to that moment the thought of a huge, public event had never crossed my mind. I knew the veterinarian's hobby was calf roping. He was a fine horseman in addition to his skill as an equine specialist. Each season he traveled to several international competitions among them, one of the most well-known in Cheyenne, Wyoming. One year he won the trophy buckle with his big grey roping horse, Mighty Mouse.

"I'd be interested if I thought it could make some money," I replied, the ever present spector of insufficient funds, not even making ends meet, always before me. Escalating feed costs, equipment repairs, seed, fuel, the mortgage, the overhead I struggled to master, in spite of a sixteen hour day, every day. The children had their own needs. Two were now in highschool, their tuition, clothing, medical and dental care all costing more.

The pre-second-world-war furnace, converted from coal to oil, labored, rattled and clanked in the cellar, too small for the two story house. It gave off infrequent, blasts of tepid air through the heating vents. Long underwear, wool shirts and sweaters hardly kept us comfortable on below zero days. We needed to replace the boiler. Years ago, the children had named it "Balky Bessie".

Through the years the water table had dropped and the old submersible pump often pumped air. It had to be replaced, too, and additional pipe added to reach the underground aquafer. The roof, as old as the furnace, brittle and worn out, leaked over Whitney's room. There was more damage to the ceilings after each rain. Estimates for these improvements, all necessities, totaled over five thousand dollars.

The rodeo was worth a gamble. If it could help me afford these improvements, the tremendous effort would be worthwhile.

We gathered in the family room after supper. Whitney at seventeen, so tall he had to duck his head below the door frame as he entered the room. How had I missed the passage of time? Gail and Lynn, fifteen and thirteen, were growing up too. We had been making decisions together from the beginning but this one about the rodeo was one of the most important. I knew I could depend on their mature judgement and support.

I lit the kindling in the fireplace setting a log on the stout fire-dogs and sat down in my wing chair. The children seated on the floor facing me with expectant faces. I told them Dr. Roper's suggestion about a rodeo.

Whitney was enthusiastic. A new goal always attractive to him. "Its a great idea, Mom," he said. "That old furnace has got to go and every time it rains water drips on my bed." Gail, her brow wrinkled above her serious brown eyes, was cautious. "It seems like a big undertaking. We don't have an arena. And you'll be so busy, who'll teach the day camps?"

She was right, of course. The camps were our best source of summer income. I thought a minute. "You girls will have to handle it and Whitney, too."

"We can do it," Lynn said. "We help mom with the classes as it is."

"Who'll be in charge?" Gail asked.

"You can be, Gail," I told her. The day-camp children and the horses will be your responsibility." With that, it was settled.

I dialed Dr. Roper's number, my confidence, supported by the children, at a high point. I asked him, "How will we go about this rodeo of yours?"

He laughed and said, "I'll have someone get in touch with you."

In February, I heard from an established rodeo producer, Mark Lathrop. We arranged an appointment and he came to the farm.

Mr. Lathrop, a handsome man, over six feet tall, was in his late thirties. Standing just outside my front door, he tipped the brim of his Stetson and smiled, saying, "Jeff Roper says you're thinking of sponsoring a rodeo!"

On his first visit to the farm Lathrop wore a chocolate brown gabardine suit, the lapels trimmed with darker brown silk braid; a pristine, white ruffled shirt with tiny pearl buttons; silver spur cufflinks, alligator cowboy boots, and a pearl grey Stetson.

Lathrop's manner was affable, direct and knowledgeable. The producer's great love was rodeo, "the last frontier" as he called it. His goal was how to produce the sport humanely with all its color and rugged flamboyance.

We talked at length and Mark agreed with Jeff Roper, our location was ideal, near a metropolitan area, in a rural setting. Lathrop explained about the cowboy's association which supports rodeo across the country and in Canada. He offered to rent me a portable arena and knew of a company from whom I could rent bleachers.

Comparing the costs, I decided to build our own arena as it would be available to us for horseshows and public events in the future. The long mid-west winters, often severe, cut down on my boarders riding time. In the fall, many of the customers moved their horses to barns with indoor riding facilities. Some said they would come back to Arcadia in the spring, but they seldom did. For Arcadia to offer all boarding services and preserve income, an indoor riding ring was essential. I decided to build that too.

None of these grandiose schemes would come to fruition unless I could get new and adequate financing. Once more I made an appointment with the banker, Henry Borchardt, of the Prairie Grassland Bank.

Seated across from the granite-faced banker, I presented my case. "You have considerable balance on the original loan, and your monthly payments have been late, several times, he said, gruffly, sorting through the documents in my file.

I felt my heart pounding. I realized at that moment how intensely I had set my mind on building the two arenas. Sitting erect, I tried to preserve the self confidence I felt eroding under Borchardt's penetrating gaze. I said, with all the assurance I could muster, "I am sure the two arenas will boost income considerably. I'm competing with businesses that offer these facilities."

The banker turned his swivel chair, looking out the window. He did not speak for a minute or two. Then, he whirled around until he was facing me across his desk.

"No question, you have the equity. I'll increase the mortgage, but I'll have to raise the interest, of course, but I want to emphasize, I do not think it a good idea for you to encumber yourself with a mortgage of this size. But then, I don't know anything about the horse business."

Driving home, I felt drained, my optimisn deflated by the conference with the banker. However, once back at the farm my spirits lifted. It was there the challenge had to be met. I resolved to give it my best effort. As Jim, who raised me, was fond of saying, "When the going gets tough, the tough get going."

Lathrop drew sketches for complete rodeo facilities, concentrating on the calf pens. Later, by mail, he sent blueprints, specifications and diagrams.

The next order of business was to find a carpenter to build it. My neighbor, Bud Riley, was not afraid to tackle anything as specialized as a rodeo arena. Most of it would be straight, rough carpentry, except for the seven foot high chain link fence to be installed by a fence company. Bud had already done a lot of building for me, improvements to the main barn, and the twelve stall ranch barn and loafing shed. There was no job too small or too big for Bud. He was a bachelor, a husky, sincere man in his early fifties with a generous mustache that he said he had been growing since he was seventeen.

The other members of his carpenter crew were Hank and Jerry, both in their early sixties. Hank was as short as Bud was tall. Jerry, lean and muscular, was the one who fearlessly walked the framing on top of the announcer's stand.

All three were crackerjack carpenters. They looked the part with their blue and white striped overalls and canvass aprons, their pockets filled with nails of all sizes. Jerry and Hank wore caps like locomotive engineers. Bud, as boss, wore an old rain-stained fedora.

Hank had a booming laugh and a love for practical jokes. . . like putting a grasshopper in Bud's coke, or bringing a piece of artificial chocolate cake for Bud, who loved sweets.

The carpenters brought their lunches in black metal lunch boxes with rounded, hinged covers. When the noon whistle sounded from the distant fire station in Prairie Grove, the three men stopped working for an hour. They sat with their backs against the arena fencing and shared chocolate, angel food cake or brownies from each other's lunch pails. Whitney rarely missed lunch time with the carpenters for they all shared with him. They also brought dog biscuits for Stuart and Ashley.

The hammering started at eight-thirty and kept up all day until four-thirty except for a coffee break in the morning and the lunch hour. They began work in April and hammered the last nail in August, two days before the first rodeo performance.

Chapter 32

Two Rascals

They did not belong to me, but I had responsibility for their care and welfare for ten years. Andy, the most rugged Shetland pony I had ever seen, was in his thirties, Stonewall, a handsome dark bay, in his twenties. They were nomads. I gave them the freedom of the farm, unrestricted until at nightfall we caught them and put them in a box stall, together.

All day, the two old cronies grazed on the lawns around the barns, appearing out of nowhere if they heard the sliding door to the grain room being opened. If, by chance the door was left open a crack, Andy could open it by moving his shaggy head against the door until he made an opening the width of his humped nose. Then, with his strong jaws, powerful neck and shoulders, he enlarged the opening to accomodate his whole body and Stonewall's too.

If they got into the grain room, what havoc! The horse and pony went from bag to bag of oats or sweet feed, trampling one, sampling another. Fortunately, they were usually discovered early, and a good yell, "Stonewall and Andy! Get out of there!" and loud hand clapping, sent them scurrying. Penning them up would have eliminated all the trouble they caused, but I couldn't keep them confined for long.

Andy and the inseparable Stonewall, visited the barns often during the day. The pony with his aplomb for moving objects always slid back the cover of the water trough so his chum, Stonewall, could drink. They sauntered down the barn aisle, filching packages of carrots left near the box stalls by the boarders. They licked the salt blocks and took naps in other horse's stalls while the occupant was being ridden on the trail.

Their daily routine included a trip to the indoor riding ring. There they raided the haypile and disrupted the riding. classes. In their retirement years, the old characters made countless friends. They often greeted our customers in the parking lot, hoping for a handout. Andy loved mentholated cough drops, his breath reeking an aromatic aroma after someone had given him a Vicks or Halls. Stonewall preferred a piece of coffee cake or sweet roll. Every day the two old reprobates walked up the sidewalk to my front door. They stood, patiently, blowing through their nostrils until I opened the screen door and gave them each a piece of toast or a heel of bread.

One August morning, I was sitting with a lady reporter at the wrought iron table on the front lawn. We were going over the press releases for the rodeo and enjoying pretzels and Coke. Out of nowhere, around the corner of the house, fresh from a scavenger trip to the orchard, came Andy and Stonewall. I saw them, barrelling down on us, pretzels in sight. Catherine Donovan's back was toward the animals. Before I could warn her, Stonewall and Andy had both their noses in the pretzel bowl and were slobbering with their old teeth all over Catherine's pink, shantung suit. They tipped over one of the glasses of coke, and the sticky liquid dripped into the reporter's lap.

I jumped up to catch Stonewall, but he eluded my grasp and took off at a brisk trot toward the indoor riding ring. Gail, on one side of the ring and Lynn on the other, were conducting riding classes. The record player was blaring martial music and the children on horseback were drilling at a walk, two by two, up one side of the arena and down the middle.

By the time the reporter and I reached the doorway, Gail was beside herself with frustration as she tried to round up the confused school horses and students. She stamped her foot and clapped her hands together, yelling, "Stonewall! Andy! Darn you guys! Get out of here! Get going!" Lynn, reduced to hysterical laughter, leaned against Bobby Socks for support as Andy and Stonewall ambled slowly out of the riding ring, ignoring the chaos they had created.

"It surely would be easier on all of you if your mother would keep those old reprobates locked up," Catherine Donovan said, dabbing with her handkerchief at her stained pink suit. Gail, now completely in control of the class, laughed. "Oh, we couldn't do that. They would hate it. We just put up with them."

With the rodeo so near, I couldn't allow Stonewall and Andy to roam any more, at will. They were too disruptive. They were found, several times, stealing treats from the cowboy's unattended vans and campers. Brad Bronson, the arena director, discovered Andy in hot water. He was trying to nudge the bar-lock which confined the Brahmas behind the "safe" fence, with his nose. "Wouldn't that have been something!" the cowboy reported, shaking his head in disbelief. There was no choice, I had to confine the two rascals to a box stall in the Ranch barn.

Chapter 33

Bad Apples

Clouds of dust and gravel followed the red sports car tearing up our long driveway. It narrowly missed Andy and Stonewall who had chosen that moment to cross the drive from the orchard to my front lawn. By the time I reached the parking lot to scold my visitors, they were standing by the Corvette in heated argument. The woman's voice was shrill. I smelled alcohol on her breath as she contradicted her companion. "Keep still!" she screamed. "I'll do the talking." The paunchy man, his florid face flushed with embarrassment, nodded his balding head. "Yes, dearie," he said, meekly.

The woman turned to me, shaking her henna-tinted, bouffant hairdo and yelled, "What's your boarding rate?"

Before I could answer, the pudgy man spoke. "Have you a special rate for two horses?"

The garish woman snarled at her spouse, jabbing him in the ribs with a red stiletto fingernail. "I told you, I'll do the talking." She glared at her husband, then lit a cigarette, dangling it between her too orchid lips. Modulating her voice a bit, she said, "We've got two precious horses. They're our babies."

Horses considered by their owners as "their babies" usually turned out to be spoiled and ill-mannered, sometimes even dangerous. I ignored this clue and quoted all the options open to the couple. I emphasized there was no special rate for two or more horses. I thought from their prosperous appearance, the fancy "Western" attire and red sports car, the Gardiners would choose box stalls. I was wrong. They selected two straight stalls in the annex. Pearl Gardiner wrote out a check for one month's board. I gave them a receipt and a copy of our Xerox sheet listing our business hours for the week and on weekends and holidays and listing the farm's simple rules: No smoking in the barns. Lights must be turned off by the last person to leave the facility. Please wear shoes or boots.

Whitney had been standing quietly, listening to our conversation. He was not thrilled with the new boarders. Later, at supper, I pointed out to him the additional income would insure the continuation of his flying lessons. He already had his private pilot's license and was accumulating hours toward his commercial license. Proudly, he told me his instructor said he was a "natural" flyer. He was not yet eighteen.

The Gardiner's horses arrived the next weekend, quite ordinary animals. A pinto mare and a dark chestnut gelding, an old polo pony with huge ankles from too many inaccurate blows with a polo mallet. It took less than a day to discover the mare was a fiendish kicker. The Gardiners arrived shortly after their horses. "Tell the barn boy to put our saddles in the tack room," Pearl Gardiner ordered. It was the only time anyone had called Whitney a barn boy and I should have set her straight, but her board was earmarked Prescott Aviation, so I bit my tongue.

Boarders in the annexes brought their horses across the yard and hooked them on crossties in the main barn, to groom and saddle, Pearl Gardiner was defiant about the "No Smoking!" rule. I found the butts of hastily extinguished cigarettes on the cement aisle many times.

One Sunday afternoon, Josie, Whitney, and other boarders ran with buckets of water to extinquish a brush fire in a patch of parched meadow grass. The Gardiners probably were the culprits as they had been riding in the meadow just before the fire began.

A water hose left running made a large puddle in front of the barn door. Muddy water seeped down the barn aisle and ran into the first two box stalls. The Gardiners were the last ones to use the hose. Josie confronted me with several empty vodka bottles found in the tack room.

"He's got Baby Doll's feet too big," Pearl Gardiner complained the first time Giulio shod the feisty little mare. "And he's got her tied up, too," she said angrily. Giulio kept hammering, an inscrutable smile on his lips as he chewed on a cigar butt. He had the body rope on Baby Doll who was trying, unsuccessfully, to kick him with a hind foot.

There were criticisms of Dr. Roper's modest medical fees, the quality and quantity of our feeding program. Every time I saw Pearl Gardiner there was another unfair complaint. From the beginning of the encounter, I had been getting, as Carrie called them, bad vibrations. With the preparations for the rodeo there was plenty to occupy my thoughts. I put the difficulties with the Gardiners out of my mind although too many disruptive things were going on to ignore them completely.

Chapter 34

The Misfits

A week before the rodeo, I awakened at two o'clock in the morning. Someone was pounding on the front door. Stuart and Ashley were barking in rising, threatening crescendo. I slipped hastily into a robe and went to the door where the two dogs were lunging. I turned on the outside light and opened the door an inch, the chain still on the latch. There, on the sidewalk, hat in hand. stood a cowboy. "Scuse me, ma'am, 'sturbin' you at this hour in the mornin'. I'm Jason Thatcher, yore featured performer in this here rodeo. Drove right through from Deeetroit. If y'all will tell me where to park my rig, won't trouble you a bit."

Scanning the cowboy from his curly black hair to his boots with hand-carved red and gold American eagles, I recognized him from his publicity stills. It was Jason Thatcher, in all his glory!

"You wait a minute, Mr. Thatcher. I'll be right out and show you where to park."

I dressed hurriedly. Taking the dogs with me, I crossed the back yard. In the semi-darkness, Thatcher's apple green pickup and camper were lit by amber safety lights on all four corners. Hitched to the camper was a long double horse trailer. No cowboy traveled without his horse and Jason Thatcher was no exception.

Cowboys and contestants were supposed to park over at the rodeo site. This early arrival in the middle of the night, changed that plan. I always had a stall, which could be pressed into service. I told Thatcher to follow me to the barn. I turned on all the lights, walked to the north door and opened it. There, outside the building, in a fine drizzle, stood an unforgettable picture. Standing before me was a small, olive-skinned man about the height and weight of a jockey. He wore a tan raincoat which dragged on the ground. Its sleeves covered his hands completely. His black hair was plastered to his head, trickles of water running down his smiling face. In the small fellow's left hand he held a leash attached to a pure white Samoyed dog. In his right, he had a lead rope fastened to the halter of a beautiful Palomino horse.

"This here's Benny," said Jason. "This here's Ben, Nugget and Frosty." Then, he shouted at the little man, "Where in hell you got Albert?"

"He's right here, boss, like you tolt me." The little gnome jerked his body forward and I saw still another rope tied around his middle, like a belt. "He's right here, boss."

Through the door stepped the trio, followed by the biggest Brahma bull I'd ever seen. This giant of the bovine world was Albert!

"Any little ole spot will do just fine for Al," drawled the cowboy. "Any little ole corner, he's used to sleepin' with Ben, here."

For a moment I stared at the entourage. The bull was half again the size of a horse. No stall would accomodate him. However, I still had the old bull pen, a carryover from the days when the farm had been a dairy operation. With its iron bars and outside run, it was ideal for Albert. That's where Benny put him.

Thatcher gave Benny his orders. "Get that horse watered and fed before you go to bed. I'm taking Frosty to the camper with me." Then, more civilly, Thatcher said, "Do thank you, ma'am for yore hospitality. 'Preciate it, no end. Mor'n I can tell you."

It seemed totally unreal to me, all these characters living, and traveling together from rodeo to rodeo: the performer, his valet, the horse, bull and dog. I showed Benny where to find bedding and hay for Albert and cautioning him not to smoke in the barn, went back to bed.

Daylight showed Thatcher's rig to be a compact trailer with dressing room, and a place for Benny to sleep not far from his responsibilities, Nugget and Albert.

Preparations for the rodeo continued at a fast pace. We saw a lot of Jason, Benny and Albert. The animals, stabled in our main barn, always attracted attention when Benny shampooed the big bull each day. The little man sat on the bull's back as he scrubbed him with a brush. There was always a crowd of boarders watching the bull's bath. The frail, little waif of a man ate some of his meals with us, not entering into the conversation, but enjoying the laughter and joking. If Jason Thatcher's name came up or if Whitney mimicked Thatcher's courtly manner of speech, Benny's eyes danced, but he never spoke. Any leisure time Benny had was spent reading comic books.

For all his temperament, Jason Thatcher was a top performer. He opened his act gorgeously attired in sequins and black satin, galloping into the arena on the golden Palomino horse. They went through intricate rope tricks, Jason standing on the saddle, the horse motionless.

At night, Jason performed his routine under the black lights. Benny's responsibility was to follow Jason's fluorescent figure around the arena with a spotlight, from an eighteen foot tower.

The dog, Frosty, jumped rope with Thatcher and led the horse out of the ring by his reins. Then, at a fanfare, Benny led Albert into the ring. The cowboy put the Brahma through an amazing routine of tricks.

First he rode him, jumping over low obstacles. He coaxed him up on a wooden tub, all four feet close together. The huge creature lowered his head in the traditional pose, usually reserved for horses "end of the trail" act. Jason waved his sequined hat and the crowd cheered. The climax to the act was Albert jumping through a flaming hoop.

All through the performance, Benny scurried around, providing the right prop for each part of the exhibition. I saw only bits and pieces of the rodeo, a little of one performance, five minutes of another, but there was no doubt Jason Thatcher was an artist with a rope and livestock. A star entertainer!

Chapter 35

The Roundup

We knew thousands of strangers would come to the farm for the rodeo, creating traffic and parking problems. We needed police reserve officers from Prairie Grove to handle the public and a man on duty, every night, around my house.

The first performance was scheduled for Friday night, August 19th. On Wednesday, all the stock had arrived. Fifty head of bucking horses, forty steers and calves and twenty-five Brahma bulls. The stock producer unloaded the animals into holding pens, broke bales of hay for all of the stock and filled their water troughs with hoses run from my barns.

After milling around the restless way of animals in a new environment, they settled down, adjusting to their new surroundings with the pacifying routine of feeding time.

Under the announcer's stand, behind a nine-foot safe fence of 2X10 timbers, were the great Brahma bulls with names like Black Jack, Scarface, Widow Maker and Old No Time. Between the bulls and the arena were eight portable bucking chutes, with access aisles to channel the bucking horses from the pens to the chutes.

Most of Wednesday was spent waiting for the huge stock trucks to arrive. The cowboys had been arriving since Monday. They were not only members of a cowboy association or ranch hands, but men who worked all week at various jobs. Some drove cement trucks or sold insurance. On the weekends, they were drawing for bucking horses or bulls, risking their necks for prize money and a silver trophy buckle.

The rodeo secretary took registration in her trailer on the rodeo grounds. The cowboys were drawing for the animals they would ride. Campers and trailers were lined up, row after row, west of the arena. There were sleek, well-muscled quarter horses tied to the vehicles. The license plates read Oklahoma, Texas, New Mexico. Manitoba, Saskatchawan. The contestants had come from thirty-eight states and Canada as our advanced publicity had promised. Specialty acts were there, too, including Jason Thatcher.

Beautiful young women trick-riders galloped across the arena, practicing, one leg over their special saddles, their long hair sweeping the ground in feats of skill and balance. They also practiced standing on their heads while their handsome horses faultlessly executed their routines.

Wednesday night there was a complete rehearsal for all the contract performers, including our drill team and Jason Thatcher and Albert. At eleven o'clock, after cheerful goodnights, Lynn, Gail, Whitney and I turned in, exhausted from the day's excitement.

I was awakened for the second time in a week by the sound of someone pounding on the front door. I recognized the voice of our night security guard. I opened the front door. There, in his blue uniform and powder blue brimmed Mountie's hat stood Officer Harland, his face flushed and beads of perspiration running down his cheeks. Wiping his face with a large handkerchief, he gasped, "Don't you set foot outside the door, Mrs. K. Those damn bulls are out. The boys are trying to round them up."

Through the open door I saw the full impact of the battery of arena lights. The area was as bright as day at three o'clock in the morning. I could hear the "Yah... yah...yahee" of the cowboys as they tried to round up the Brahmas. No one had to tell me twice not to go outside.

The noise and furor had awakened everyone in the house. We gathered in the kitchen, the girls in their nightgowns and Whitney in jeans and bare feet. Whitney was full of negatives about the night's events. "I knew we'd have trouble with those bulls the minute I saw them. What if they never catch them? If those bulls get onto the golf course it's going to cost us thousands!"

As a distraction, Whitney began spreading peanut butter and jelly, making sandwiches. He offered me one, but I couldn't swallow a bite. The prospect of paying to resod a golf course fairway was most depressing.

About four o'clock officer Harland returned. He tapped on the door, calling out, "All's clear." Since we were all awake, I asked him to join us for coffee. He gave us a full report on the night's happenings as we sat around the kitchen table. He began, "Well,... it was this way. I was walking around your house, on the hour like I always do, shining my flashlight here and there. I heard a kind of crunchy noise, like a horse grazing. I shone my flash through the pines along the driveway and my beam picked up four hairy legs. I thought it was a horse, one of those old ones you let roam around...until I raised my light further and further up its shoulder and then, Jeez, there was that hump and huge head with those long floppy ears, like a gigantic hound dog. Officer Harland sipped some coffee and continued. We were spellbound! "Well, seeing the bull, I took off at a dead run for the stock contractor's trailer. The lights were on, and what do you think those guys were doing?"

"What?" we said, in unison.

"I banged on the door and when one of the cowboys opened it, there were six or eight of them sitting, drinking beer and playing cards. Just like in a western movie. Seeing me, one of them said, 'Come on in boy, take a hand . . . I told 'em, hell, your bulls are loose. That's why I'm here! 'Bulls? Can't be . . . What they look like?" one of the cowboys drawled.

"I told them they're a lot bigger than steers and they got humps between their shoulders! You never saw a bunch of guys move so fast. They kicked over their chairs and took off at a run to saddle up their horses.

"We found right away how they got out. The arena gate was left open after that little trick-rider gal from Kansas got done practicing."

"Where were you while they were rounding up the bulls?" I asked Stan Harland.

"I was over at the arena gate. They told me to swing it wide when they started to drive the bulls toward it. The Brahmas were all bunched up, a big black one right up front, kind of like their leader. He was pawing and snorting and they all came charging toward the gate. The cowboys on their horses right behind them, hollering, slapping their legs with their hats and yelling.

"Well . . . I had the gate pretty wide open, I thought. I was up on top of it, watching those old bulls coming toward me. Well, this old bull wasn't about to be caught. He ducked around behind the gate right under my feet. He nudged my boot sole with the top of his head. I thought he'd try to knock me off so I hollered at him and waved my hat at him. He turned around as pleasant as can be and walked right into the arena."

It was fortunate we had a crop of soy beans on the farm. It slowed the bulls down as they lingered to munch the succulent leaves. It gave the cowboys time to saddle their horses, round up the Brahmas, count them, all except old No Time. He was somewhere between the arena and my house and the cowboys tore up my back lawn cutting him back and forth with their horses until they got him back to the safe fence. There were many heros of the rodeo, but none eclipsed our security officer, Stan!

It was Whitney who capsulized the evening's excitement by saying, "From now on, Mom, I'm going to check on those bulls every night, myself." Then putting his arm around Stan's shoulder, he added, "Me and Stan will, together."

I thanked my judgment that Andy and Stonewall were locked safely in the barn, no matter how reprovingly they looked at me every time I passed their stall.

Chapter 36

One More Worry

Mark Lathrop visited the farm periodically to see how the work was progressing. On his visits we tried to cover a lot of ground -- the plans for newspaper and radio publicity and many other details.

Our head carpenter, Bud, had planned for everything. He ordered a crane to lift the telephone poles which supported the structure of the announcer's stand, and to set the long poles for the lighting fixtures.

Bud and the other two carpenters now put all their effort into the construction of the arena. Each day was a milestone. I hired two laborers to dig the post holes for Bud, and to pull the wire with the tractor for pens to hold the bucking horses, steers and calves. Then they went to work painting the 2xlOs on both ends of the arena. I could hear Jerry yelling at them. "Hey, you guys. Give us a chance to nail a board down. Pretty soon you'll be painting Hank and me." Another time he yelled, "Say, you guys, was you ever in the Army? Is that where you learned to paint a moving object?" A good laugh helped lighten the pressure.

Over on the farmside, Lynn, Gail and Whitney were teaching riding to the day camps. We used sixteen horses in two classes every day, morning and afternoon. It helped meet the payroll. Carrie and Holly came every day, keeping my personal household running smoothly. They shopped for groceries, made simple meals and washed dishes. I needed and appreciated their caring, cheerful helpfulness.

The morning Bud and Hank nailed the sign, painted in threefoot black letters, ARCADIA FARM RODEO ARENA across the front of the announcer's stand was a high point. Jerry stood on the ground, directing. "A little more to the left. A hair up on the right corner. That's good, boys. Right there!"

The bleacher rental company had men setting up the framework. The electricians were wiring and hanging the light fixtures. The largest Country Western radio station broadcast our commercials. Occasionally I heard one on the barn radio. First, there was band music, then the roar of applause, tapering down. Mark Lathrop's voice followed, declaring forcefully, "And now, from chute number six, Widow Maker, with a daring cowboy aboard." Additional dialogue explained when and where to see the rodeo and gave the ticket prices.

Daily, we had a stream of people coming to the office, the sun- porch, for advance tickets. The mail too, had ticket orders. Advance sales showed people were eagerly anticipating the event.

August was a soggy, wet month. Three semi-loads of sand were spread to give the bucking horses and bulls better footing.

Everything seemed aimed at the initial performance. There had been no time for any personal needs. Suddenly, I realized I had no suitable western clothes for the rodeo. Carrie and Holly volunteered to shop for me and I sent them off to the saddle shop with my correct sizes and a blank check. They came back with three outfits, twice more than I would have paid, but all three very smart and the height of western fashion. The girls had chosen light blue bellbottom jeans, a matching blue shirt with green and white butterflies and small pearl buttons. Another costume, old rose pants, a pink shirt with a narrow border of lace at the collar. For the final performance, a light gold shirt, embroidered with gold and silver wheels above the pockets and gold jeans. All the outfits to be worn with black silk tie and pearlescent-grey boots with black wing tips. Those little boots were the best fit I ever had and every time I looked down at them their wing tips gave me a lift. I was exhibiting the syndrome, the spectacle that is rodeo.

New red, white, and blue bunting came from the specialty company. Once hung from the announcer's stand, and out to the lighting fixture poles, they flew in the breeze spectacularly. When the flags went up I had a feeling of pride and satisfaction and so did all the crew.

We appeared to be ready. The construction was finished. The chain link fence installed, the bleachers had been inspected by the fire chief. Fourteen chemical toilets were placed in the spectator area. Mobile food and soft drink concessions were located near power outlets. The public address system was in working order. The rodeo stock was on the grounds. More than one hundred fifty cowboys were registered for six events, steer wrestling, bull riding, bareback bronc, calf roping and girl's barrel racing.

All had been going along pretty well on the farm side under Whitney's supervision. I looked for him to report on the rodeo's progress and found him sitting on the edge of the bath tub. He held an eye cup in his hand. He was squinting, his right eye, partially closed.

"My God! What's happened to you?" I asked with a sinking feeling. Grimacing with pain he described the accident. "I was feeding the annexes. Right after I put Baby Doll's hay in front of her she plastered the partition toward Colonette, splintering the 2x4. I've got a wood splinter in my eye."

Not wasting a minute, I draped a clean bath towel around his head, told him to keep his eyes closed and led him to the car. Ignoring all caution, we were soon speeding to the ophthalmologist.

The office nurse said the specialist would see us right away. The doctor anasthetized Whitney's eye and deftly removed the splinter. "A close call," she said, but assured us there should be no problem. "Use the drops. Keep the eye covered. I want to see him in a week," she said. Then she put a pair of dark glasses over the eye bandage.

Looking in the office mirror, Whitney grinned. "I look like I've had a 'wreck'. That is what the cowboys call it when they've had a run-in with a bull or bucking horse."

I decided I was going to tell the Gardiners we could put up with Baby Doll no longer. Lynn and Gail, dismayed at Whitney's patched eye, agreed. Baby Doll had to go and the sooner the better. Lynn said she would take the responsibility for putting eye drops in Whit's eye four times daily.

By that time, dress rehearsal had started. I could hear the music. The contract performers were running through their acts. The girl's drill team, made up from the boarders was practicing. An electrician was adjusting the spotlights.

Lathrop, members of the rodeo committee, Lynn, Gail, Whitney and I sat on the first row of bleachers watching. As darkness fell Lathrop called for the arena lights. Suddenly, there was brilliance beyond imagination. Mark Lathrop jumped to his feet shouting, "Oh, my God! This is awful! Look at the glare on that fencing!"

My brand new, shining steel fence, erected to the tune of thousands of dollars was a disaster. It reflected a blinding glare. Spectators in the bleachers could not see into the arena: those in box seats could not see to their left or right. The higher we climbed in the bleachers, the worse the view into the arena became.

Sick with disappointment, I managed to stammer, "What are we going to do?"

"Don't know! Don't know, right off," Lathrop said, shaking his head. But one thing for sure, we've got to get someone up on those poles adjusting the angle of the light fixtures. They're overshooting the arena by a mile."

The whole north hayfield, where the cowboys parked, was as bright as day, while the arena had areas of shadow and total darkness.

The electricians stayed in the basket-crane, adjusting the fixtures for two hours but nothing helped. The glare remained. The fence, a safety feature no bucking horse or Brahma bull could scale, also meant no one could see the rodeo events through it.

When I saw Lathrop walking toward me, he didn't look as worried. Pointing at the fence he said, "We have to paint the darn thing. I'll get some of the boys in the morning. We'll roll a coat of latex on the whole shebang," he said cheerfully.

I felt heartsick. The fencing looked so shiny, impenetrable, safe and new. It made the arena. Now, we were going to paint it. It had been a stressful day but the priority was Whitney's accident. I went to the telephone and called Pearl Gardiner, owner of the bad actor, Baby Doll, who had caused the injury.

A fine drizzle had started. It continued all night, turning into a determined rain.

Chapter 37

Must the Show Go On?

The next morning Mark had rounded up thirty gallons of pale blue paint, rollers and the help of twenty cowboys, to paint the fence. Some of these painters were the top cowboys in America. They sloshed around in the mud in great, good humor. They rolled the insipid blue paint on my beautiful, shiny, seven-foot high, three hundred-foot long, chain link fence.

The all-night rain had soaked the ground in the box seat section. At least four inches of water puddled the ground where the spectators would sit. Things looked pretty grim.

I asked the producer and arena director to come to my office. They brought the three rodeo judges and the stock contractor with them.

"Mark," I began, "I'm going to cancel Thursday night's opening performance." He looked aghast. "You can't! It's never done. You know the old adage, the show must go on."

I was insistent. "I know that as well as you do, but I can't allow people who've paid box seat prices to sit with their feet in water."

Lathrop explained, "We can't cancel! Even if we threw in an extra performance and honored Friday's tickets, it would be a mess getting the cowboys re-registered. Let's go look at the arena."

Slowly, we walked together through the oozing mud to the rodeo site. The calves and steers were huddled in one corner of their pen. The bucking horses stood drenched, their heads lowered, hind quarters against the fence and driving rain. The stock contractor, reading my mind, said, "Fed 'em extra heavy tonight, Miss. Their bellies are full." I was glad to hear that.

As we walked along, I looked up at the limp flags. Lathrop's eyes caught mine. Very softly he said, "Okay, if you want we'll try and cancel Thursday night. We'll try. What do you say boys?"

I felt sorry for the producer. He had to face the old "hell-bent- for-leather" attitude of one hundred and fifty cowboys!

All day Thursday, we heard the spot announcements on the radio canceling the performance. We hoped we'd reached our rodeo enthusiasts. Thursday evening came, and it was evident we had not. Cars stretched for two miles north and south of the farm. The police reserve were briefed on what to say to the people. They patiently explained our predicament to carload after carload.

Lathrop, the arena director and a half dozen cowboys placed themselves at strategic spots along the road, some on horseback, chatting with disappointed spectators, urging them to return for Saturday's extra matinee and evening performance.

Only one man asked for a refund. He wasn't put out, he explained. He was going out of town. I thought that quite remarkable. We felt that most of the spectators would understand and come back for the delayed opening performance, so we continued preparations.

Friday morning, the rain had stopped. There was bright sunshine and many last minute jobs to be completed.

I found Mark Lathrop by one of the sheds, painting a four by eight sheet of plywood. He stood there in faded jeans and a blue and white striped shirt, his hands smeared with black lettering paint. He had just completed the word "Rodeo" in large block letters. He smiled broadly when he saw me and said, laughing, "Thought we'd better have another sign down at the intersection. Folks coming from the north just might miss us."

Together we lifted the wet sign onto the back of Lester Rowe's pickup truck and drove to the main intersection north of the farm. There, with me supporting the sign from the bottom, Lathrop nailed it to a telegraph pole. From that moment I felt everything would work out. I had justified confidence in the producer.

When I returned to the farm, Pearl and Harry Gardiner were there. We stood by the annex, Lynn, Gail, Whitney and I. I tried to keep control of the situation and explained about Whitney's accident with Baby Doll.

I handed Pearl a half month's refund. "I'm sorry, but your horse is a trouble maker. You'll have to move her."

Pearl Gardiner's reaction was predictable. She was furious. Swearing, she flounced off. Harry followed, looking sheepish.

As the red sports car tore down the driveway, I breathed a sigh of relief.

Whitney's good eye was dancing.

Chapter 38

Everybody Rides

When the rain had finally stopped, the sun making an effort to dry up the mud and water, Lathrop and I walked over to the arena site for a conference. The flags hung limp, the box seats still had a stretch of water the full length of the preferred seating.

"What could we put down to mop up some of the water?" I asked. The producer replied, "I'm sending some of the boys over to the lumber yard for a dozen rolls of resin paper. That'll do the trick. We'll roll it out lengthwise in front of the first row of box seats. The spectators can put their feet on it."

Brad Bronson, the arena director, volunteered to drive into town to the lumber yard. The carpenters, on hand for last minute jobs, kept busy. Henry brought bags of shavings and sawdust and sprinkled them in front of the calf and bucking chutes to dry up some of the mud. A light breeze picked up the flags and they began to snap and blow, their brilliant red, blue and white colors coming to life. Thanks to the wind, by noon the soggy arena looked promising.

The day before the soft drink company had delivered the mobile food concessions. The police auxiliary committee were ready to vend pop, coffee and hot dogs. It looked as though we had covered everything on the master list.

Willing hands helped spruce up the arena. Some raked, others rolled the trash barrels to strategic spots near the food concessions. I checked the chemical toilets for extra paper supplies. We met at noon in my office to go over last minute ticket sales and Lathrop called a final meeting of the cowboy contestants over the public address system. The same cowboys who had painted the chain link fence, mingled in small groups, conjecturing which bucking horse or Brahma bull they or their buddies would draw. Everyone was smiling and joking.

There was going to be a rodeo that night for sure. Lathrop sat on the top rail of a bucking horse chute, describing the details of the Grand Entry. I could hear him over the public address system, "Everyone rides! everybody! You boys and girls get over to the secretary's trailer pronto, and get your flags. This Grand Entry is going to be something the audience will remember for a long time. Remember, everyone rides!"

As he was speaking, one of the cowboys elbowed his way close to the producer, interrupting him. "Just a minute, Mark," he drawled. "Ye know Brad? He's hurt pretty bad. Took off his radiator cap and scalded his face turrible!"

At this, Lathrop and the cowboys scattered at a dead run toward the highway. We could see the red pickup truck with its hood up. Brad Bronson, his wife and eleven year old son were standing by the truck. The cowboy's face had been seared beef-red from the radiator's steam and was blistering badly.

Chase Harper volunteered to drive Brad and his family to the emergency room. Escorted by a police car, lights flashing, they sped off. We were very sober walking back to the show grounds. I was comforted there would be an ambulance on hand once the rodeo was underway.

Brad's buddies were very solicitous. "Wonder if he'll ride them bulls tonight," a burly Texan asked.

"Ole Brad, he's been piling up the points," another muttered. "He'd sure be in the runnin' for a National Championship, derndest luck."

I was sure Brad Bronson would not be in the competition that night.

When seven o'clock arrived, show time was on us and we all took our places.. Spectators by the hundreds were streaming in the gates. The boy scouts sold programs: reserve police parked the cars: the ladies auxiliary was on the job at the food concessions. Giulio hammered the last nail in a new set of shoes for Jason Thatcher's golden Palomino.

The rodeo bucking horses channeled smoothly through narrow fenced aisles for the first event, bareback bronc riding. The overture to the Grand Entry and the parade of states filled the night. The National Anthem, recorded on tape by the Mormon Tabernacle Choir and Philadelphia Symphony Orchestra followed.

Lathrop, from his vantage point high in the announcer's stand coaxed stragglers to hurry. "Ladies and gentlemen, step it up. Show's about to start. Don't miss a minute of the world's roughest sport here under the open sky, just like your grandaddy saw it in the old west. Hurry! Hurry! Hurry!

Finally, things were under control and I made a last swing around the east end of the arena. I nodded to the officer from the Anti-Cruelty Society at his post by the bucking chutes.

As I passed one of the concessions I heard someone calling my name. "Mrs. K!" one of the women called. "We've got a problem with our mobile unit. It isn't near enough to the telephone pole for electricity. We can't start the steam table for hot dogs and everyone wants coffee."

She was right. The fully loaded food trailer was at least twenty feet from the pole. Fortunately, the little Alice tractor was parked outside the arena. I ran the length of the field across the back of the calf chutes. The baldfaced calves were bawling.

I started Alice up, shifted into gear and headed back toward the marooned food unit. The hitch on the trailer did not adapt well to the tractor's tow bar. The best we could do was rest one upon the other and hope the trailer wouldn't slip off.

The ladies stepped out of the concession stand to lighten it. Two cowboys who had been waiting for coffee lifted the hitch and rested it on the tow bar. They walked along beside the vehicle as I moved the tractor forward slowly.

At that crucial point, I heard one of the cowboys exclaim, jovially, "How you doin', boy? Glad to see you, you old wreck!" Glancing over my shoulder I saw the burly figure of Brad Bronson, his head and face, swathed in bandages, astride the tractor tow bar. His weight held the hitch together.

"My glory, Brad!" I called to him. "How are you doing?" Only his nose and chin showed beneath the bandages. He tipped back his head to see where he was going. "Gotta be gettin' set. So long for awhile."

"You're not going to ride the bulls, are you? You can't possibly see," I exclaimed.

He laughed, "I drawed old Death Trap! That bull and me has been fighting it out all season. Wouldn't want to disappoint 'im." He was grinning as he tapped me on the shoulder with a bandaged hand. "Take care now. See you later." He walked away toward the Brahmas, one of his pals guiding him by an elbow.

I made the connection between the electric pole and the food concession and the ladies began to serve the impatient crowd.

Nearby, the Mescalara Apaches from the American Indian center stood shivering in their scanty native costumes, their faces painted authentically with war paint. Black and yellow lines ran from the corners of their mouths and eyes. They looked fierce. The Indians were a color guard for Sammy, our Appaloosa stallion. Each Apache carried a five by seven American Flag.

As I heard the opening bars of the Grand Entry music, I looked through the bleachers and saw the horses' legs galloping around the arena. Lathrop's strong, confident voice, announced the Parade of States, Arizona . . . Utah . . . Oklahoma, the magical names continued, California . . . North Dakota . . . New Mexico. The spotlights played on the flamboyant spectacle of Sammy's silver-grey body with its Appaloosa spotted rump, and the Indian color guard.

In one of the front box seats, next to the press, sat Calvin Baker. When Sammy and the color guard passed, I noticed him wipe a tear from his eye.

The spectators rose to their feet. The thunderous applause was for the flag, the Mescalara Apaches and Sammy.

I found a seat on one of the first row bleachers, the reverses, disappointments, rain and mud all behind us. Near the calf chutes, I saw the figure of Jeff Roper astride his stout roping horse, Mighty Mouse. He whirled his lariat over his head in small loops. Seeing me, he tipped the brim of his grey Stetson and grinned broadly. He was the next contestant, full-time veterinarian, part-time calf roper.

I leaned forward to get a clearer view. The bawling calf ran diagonally across the arena. In spite of the speed of Mighty Mouse, both loops of the rope fell short. On his way back to the chutes for the second go-around, Jeff passed close to where I was sitting. He winked at me and called out, laughing, "Bad calf." He left the arena grinning.

Three days and six performances of the rodeo over, it was time to total the receipts. Each night, the money had been transported, by police escort, into the night depository of the Prairie Grassland Bank.

After midnight, we met in my office -- the producer, Lathrop; the arena director and secretary, Gail; Whitney, Lynn and myself. Outside the front door stood two Prairie Grove police officers with drawn revolvers.

Lathrop dumped the receipts from heavy canvas bags on my desk as thousands of dollars piled up and the count began. The rodeo secretary, Lathrop and I each kept separate tallies. Out of the corner of my eye I could see Gail making her own computation in a ruled notebook.

It was after three o'clock before all the money had been counted. My family cheered when it was evident, after the producer's fees, prize money, food concessions, sanitary facilities and bleacher rental were deducted, that the beautiful arena, a sturdy announcer's stand and perimeter lighting would be all paid off. There was also enough money left for the new furnace, and a substantial down payments for a new roof, but the old pump in the milk house would have to do its duty a while longer. As for the indoor riding ring, there was considerable balance due. The sixteen hour days would continue for several more years.

The rodeo secretary tabulating points in three "go arounds", reported Dr. Roper the winner in calf-roping. He had won the prize money and a solid silver trophy buckle. For all of us this may have been the best news of all.

Whitney told me after the rodeo was over and the contestants began to pack up and load their horses that Benny was going to stay with us! "He'll sleep in one of the sheds. I can fix him a little room. He's not used to much and he's real good with horses," he said.

I talked to Lathrop and told him, "Benny's going to remain with us after Jason moves on."

Lathrop shook his head, saying kindly, "Don't you believe it. Ben talks about leaving Jason after every rodeo. Sure, he's had a good time with you folks, but

Jason Thatcher is all the family he has and I doubt he will ever leave him."

I didn't see them to say goodbye. They left in the early hours of the morning, heading for Oklahoma. I thought of the frail little man hunched over his comic books, smiling his wistful, gentle grin. I wanted to believe he was happy with Frosty, Nugget and Albert wherever crowds gather and the announcer speaks, "And now, ladies and gentlemen, the top trick roper in rodeo, Jason Thatcher, his trick horse, Nugget, his educated dog, Frosty, and Albert, the only trained Brahma bull in the world." I wished with all my heart some announcer, somewhere, would add ". . . and his indispensable assistant, Benny."

Chapter 39

Losing An Ally

Our hayfield had been inadequate for a number of years. I had been buying a semi-load of hay every three weeks. We were feeding two hundred horses. The driver would drop the trailer in the parking lot, and we'd unload the hay onto flat bed wagons which were moved to the barns as needed.

The first time Giulio came to work after the rodeo, the temperature was 102o in the shade by the barn. I had just climbed down from the semi of hay, salty sweat running into my eyes. On the ground were fifty, ninety pound bales I had pitched from the hay load. Wiping my eyes with a frayed bandana, I sat down on a bale and read off to Giulio the list of horses that would need shoeing.

Looking at my unkempt appearance, he said, "You worka too hard, too much. Hava the men do that stuff."

I wanted to laugh. The men he referred to were a seventeen year old and a man in his early seventies.

"Resta few minutsa," he said, pouring me a cup of water from his battered thermos. He held out a small box. In it were eight pair of brand new ladies spats and an elegant ivory-handled button hook.

Later that day, I saw him grimacing with pain as he worked on the horses. He confided to me, "Hurts like hell when I fila de nail holes."

"Giulio, you must do something about that arm of yours," I urged him.

"Wonna dese days when I gotta time," was his response.

The following week he did not appear. He had gone to the clinic. His son called to say an examination had revealed a malignant tumor in Giulio's brain.

After an exploratory operation and the tumor's removal, Giulio was left paralyzed, without speech. It was staggering news to me.

When he was able to have visitors I went to see him. Lying on his white, enameled iron bed he appeared so small, shrunken and vulnerable. I took his right hand in mine and gently squeezed it. His eyes never left my face, but there was no sign of recognition in them. Quickly, I turned away and left the room so he would not see my tears. Several days later his son called on the phone. Guilio was dead.

Giulio's death brought many changes. There was an end to those times, after a day's shoeing, when Giulio and I sat around the kitchen table as he made out his bill and we shared a hasty cup of coffee. I had taken him for granted, not realizing what a support system he had been. I had lost an ally and a very special friend. No one else would show me the same concern.

The lessons he taught me were enduring. Authority over the horse without cruelty and the success of patience with horses.

The horses would miss him too. From now on the Grulla mare would have to be tranquilized to have her hooves trimmed. This meant one of the veterinarians had to be on hand to work with the horseshoer.

The horseshoe nail driven into the 2x10's in the barn aisle where Giulio hung his tan wool jacket remained. The nail served no purpose, but I never removed it.

Chapter 40

On the Nose

In 1967, I learned how animal feeds are proven in the field before marketing. One of my customers, an executive with a large national company, made the arrangements. The corporation was branching out into animal nutrition, offering a complete pelleted feed for horses. As a cooperator, my agreement specified I would feed the new product to my horses for three months. The animals were to receive no hay, whatsoever, for the period of the experiment. I chose two teams of eight horses from the school stock, mares and geldings. Each horse had his own chart. Each day I recorded his intake, hours of teaching, trail riding and other comments.

We fed the pellets twice daily, measured according to the horse's body weight, so many pounds of pellets per hundred pounds of horse. All the horses were weighed at the start of the program and every Friday, thereafter. These records had to be very accurate. The company sent their own chemist to help weigh the horses.

Harold Pritchard, the chemist, was a frail, bookish man in his mid-forties. His fine black hair, on his balding head, was plastered with shiny pomade. He wore gold wire-rimmed glasses with thick lenses and always was dressed in a business suit, white shirt and tie, even on the hottest days of July and August. Pritchard was unfamiliar with horses. He was afraid of them, standing far from the scale, keeping plenty of distance between him and the docile school horses. He peered over his glasses, yelling, "Next, next. Keep them moving," as if he was in charge. It was the children and I who kept the horses moving, hurrying them through the scale.

The chemist had learned the gentle horse's names, which added to his confidence. "Go get Sugarfoot! Bring Colonel!" he'd bellow. "What's taking you so long. I haven't got all day."

Usually, we had an audience. To an observer, Pritchard seemed to be in command, but I knew if a horse even breathed on him, he would wilt.

The horse scale, a rebuilt trailer, had numerals on one side. The animals stepped in, paused a moment, the scale registered their weight, and they walked out the other end. The school horses became so used to the procedure we seldom lost any time completing the weigh-in of sixteen head in half an hour. Many of the boarders asked to weigh their own horses and it became a craze. Some of the horses were bad loaders. We had several episodes which made me reluctant to accomodate the owner's curiosity.

Carrie and Holly were no exception. They were anxious to know Bounty's weight. Carrie described Bounty to Pritchard as one of the "peaceful" horses with good vibrations. She said, however, she didn't get good vibrations from Pritchard. "He doesn't like horses," Carrie whispered to me, leading Bounty through the scale.

One Friday afternoon, after weighing Colonel and Colonelette, one of the customers approached us, leading her horse. Desi, an unruly creature the children had renamed, Destructo. because he kept us busy repairing his stall. He was a strong-willed, undisciplined gelding. "Am I too late to weigh Desi?" his pretty owner inquired breathlessly. I hesitated before answering. I'd had the dubious pleasure of loading Destructo in a horse trailer.

Out of the corner of my eye I saw Josie shaking his head as if to say, "No!" Lynn and Gail did the same.

Whitney pinched his nose and rolled his eyes, indicating his opinion of Destructo. I glared at him. Whitney substitued the nose-holding gesture by covering his eyes. Destructo was not a favorite of Arcadia Farm.

Before I could speak, I heard Pritchard say, "Not at all, Miss. It's not too late. Bring him right along." He reached for Destructo's lead shank.

Not only had he conquered his fear of horses, he was to prove it in front of a pretty girl, as well. "Give him to me. I'll weigh him myself," he said. Then pointing at me, he roared, "You read the scale!"

At this, I came to life. "I don't think you had better try him, Mr. Pritchard." The words were hardly out of my mouth when the horse and the chemist reached the scale. The fidgeting horse put one foot tentatively on the floor of the scale, lunged backwards, spun around, sending Pritchard flying into the dust and gravel. He scrambled to his feet, glasses askew, a surprised look on his face. He grasped the lead rope and approached the scale again.

Josie advised him, disapprovingly, "Better you let me take thet cuss, 'Destroyer'.

I frowned at Josie's use of our family's name for the horse. "His name is Desi," I emphasized, firmly, "Desi!"

Pritchard straightened his glasses, tucked his rumpled shirt into his trousers and once more approached the scale with the horse. After all, hadn't he seen sixteen horses walk in and out of the scale like angels, weekly, for two months? Any horse would do it. Anyone could make them.

Josie tried again. "Don't believe he wants to get hisself weighed," he said.

"Why don't we guess at Desi's weight. Say eleven hundred pounds?" I suggested.

"Ridiculous!" Pritchard panted, ogling the horse's owner. "this young lady wants to know his weight, on the nose, don't you, Miss?"

On the nose it was, for at that instant, Destructo whirled, sending the chemist sailing into the dirt and gravel again.

I could see a serious accident looming. This time I spoke firmly, "Mr. Pritchard, forget it. It's time to do chores. We'll try another day."

Reluctantly, he handed the lead rope to Desi's owner, wiped his forehead with a spotless handkerchief, and said loudly, "Can't understand it. I've been weighing horses for six weeks. This is the first trouble I've had."

Josie turned away. I could see the grin on his face. Lynn was giggling in the annex behind me. She whispered loudly to Gail, "Why did he try to weigh that crazy horse? Destructo is a pain!"

Josie, misunderstanding, replied, "He sure is a pain, tryin' to weigh ole 'destroyer!" No one corrected Josie.

Chapter 41
Lengthening Shadows

He came to board with me, like so many others. A big buckskin horse, his hide shining like burnished brass with luxuriant, jet black mane and tail. Together with the black points of his legs, he possessed the arresting appearance of the true buckskin.

Although of considerable size, strong and willful in hand, he responded well to verbal sternness and rode well for his fragile, young owner. She was very fond of Sandman.

One morning shortly after the buckskin's arrival at Arcadia Farm, Marcia sat near me on the water trough cover, watching as I cleaned stalls. "I could die anytime, you know," she confided, her manner sincere, matter of fact. She was chewing on a carrot.

I stopped shoveling and leaned on the stall door frame for support.

My young boarder continued. "Really, I could. The family feels awful about it. It's my heart."

Taken by her frankness, I didn't know how to respond. In many ways she reminded me of Gail with the same striking brown eyes.

The next time I saw her father, I broached the subject of Marcia's health. He confirmed she did not have a normal life's expectancy.

Thereafter, when she was out on the trail with Sandman, I often walked where I could keep her in view. I began to share her father's anxiety.

In the fall, after Marcia returned to college, I decided to put Sandman down on the pasture with our herd. The autumn weather was clear and sunny. I couldn't see any difficulty. There was some scuffling among the herd as Sandman tried to appropriate several old mares for his own harem. Many geldings, even though castrated, show stallion characteristics, shepherding off a band of mares or even one or two milder geldings. They try to keep them away from the herd and the herd away from them.

There wasn't any open confrontation. Big Boy and Dakotah were acknowledged leaders and they controlled most of the mares. However, we had recently added a little bay mare to the herd purchased as a re-sale horse. I had bought her from a private party who told me she possibly was in foal. Sandman took an instant fancy to the quarter type mare and kept her off to one side of the pasture. Occasionally he charged at other horses or ponies that tried to join them.

At dusk everything seemed to be alright, but during the night I was awakened by squeals and the sound of horses' hooves pounding across the pasture. I knew what was happening. Sandman, not satisfied with taking over the bay mare was attempting to drive off some of Big Boy and Dakotah's group. The two challenged geldings were charging at Sandman in turns while Sandman stood up to them.

It was too dangerous for us to go into the field among the fighting horses in the dark with sixty of them racing about wildly. I had only teenagers to help me.

I was up, dressed and down to the field by five o'clock. There, silhouetted against the sunrise, stood

Sandman. At his feet, lying on her side was the bay mare, the rest of the horses grazing a long way off.

I opened the pasture gate and approached the two horses. Stuart was with me. Sandman turned his head and looked at me. His expression told me, "Stop where you are, or I will charge." He snorted and made short lunges toward me, returning to the mare each time.

I stood still, trying to sooth the horse. "Here, boy. Good boy. Come boy." I hoped to get a hand on him and lead him back to the barn so I could examine the mare. He would have none of my coaxing, but became more aggressive. Stuart, sensing Sandman's menacing attitude, circled the horse, barking. Sandman, turning his attention to the barking, agile dog, made it possible for me to retreat slowly toward the gate.

When Josie came to work I told him, "You'll have to go down to the pasture with me. Something is wrong with the little bay mare. Bring some oats, a lead rope and the wagon whip.

We unlatched the gate and entered the field together, knowing the rustle of oats would bring the entire herd down on us. I had a cup full in a soup can, just enough to get Sandman's attention.

"Watch him, Joe. I've got to get close enough to see what is wrong with the mare. If he charges, swing the whip over your head. Don't hit him with it unless he comes for us."

We inched closer and I could see the mare was in trouble. Her flanks were soaked from sweat, her lips drawn back from her teeth in pain. Her eyes were closed. The matted grass under her told me she had lain in that spot for hours.

Sandman, mistrustful of our intentions, suddenly charged. Josie waved the whip while both of us yelled at him as loudly as we could, "Ho! . . . Yaw! Yaw! Ho boy!" The startled horse veered off to one side, disconcerted by the noise, stopped and looked at us.

Unless we caught Sandman, no veterinarian would be able to help the mare. She appeared to be in the throes of a painful abortion. Josie was game to try.

I shook a soup can of oats. The rustling grain made Sandman prick up his ears. He looked at me as I poured a handful of oats into my palm. The dry, rattling sound horses know so well made him take a step toward me.

Stuart, interpreting the horse's movement as a threat, started barking, circling the horse. We lost Sandman's attention to the dog.

"Quit it, Stu! Lie down!" I hissed at the enthusiastic dog. I scolded him until he slunk down on his belly and stayed in one spot.

Again, I poured the grain into my hand and trickled it back into the can. Sandman walked toward me, snorting, concentrating on the grain. "Drop the whip on the ground, Josie," I whispered.

"Golly, do you think I should?"

"Drop it, drop it!" I spoke softly but with urgency. "If he comes at us, wave your arms and yell at the top of your voice." To myself, I thought, "Stuart, pay attention. I may need you."

Sandman approached suspiciously, his nostrils dilating as he snorted, his frame quivered from nervousness. I felt his warm breath on my hand and I let him take a mouthful of grain as I quickly snapped a lead rope to his halter ring. We had him.

Finding himself under restraint, Sandman lunged backwards and almost jerked me off my feet. Josie added his weight to the lead rope and that was the end of the struggle. Basically, Sandman was a good horse. Josie had no trouble leading him back to the barns.

I raced to the phone to call the veterinarian and was grateful Dr. Prince had a phone in his vehicle. In reconstructing what had happened, I was sure the mare had been caught between the flying hooves of the fighting geldings, taking a kick in the side, causing her to lose her foal.

When we went back in the field with the doctor, Josie broke several hay bales at the opposite end of the pasture. That drew the herd's attention and kept them from bothering us.

As Dr. Prince knelt by the little mare, I sat on the broad part of her neck although she showed no inclination to get up. Josie stood ready to hand Dr. Prince whatever he needed from his medical bag.

Putting on a long plastic glove reaching to his armpit, Dr. Prince inserted his hand into the mare's vagina and removed the dead foal from her uterus. It was so tiny. The size of a kitten, perfectly formed, hairless with its perfectly formed tiny hooves and little eyelashes.

The doctor administered antibiotics but he didn't hold out much hope for the mare to survive. Placing a hot water bottle under her elbow, against her heart, we covered her with blankets. One of us checked on her every half hour.

At noon I felt her clammy neck. Her legs were growing cold, too. Josie brought another blanket from the house and refilled the hot water bottle.

At one o'clock he came to the back door and said, woefully, "Mrs. K, she didn't make it."

He never mentioned to Marcia's family what had actually happened because shortly afterward, Marcia died.

The day of her funeral, her father called on the phone and asked me to put Sandman in the paddock next to the road. About two o'clock in the afternoon, as I was returning from the mailbox, I saw the entire funeral procession approach the farm.

When the hearse was opposite Sandman, he raised his head and walked parallel to the funeral car until it passed. He walked to the fence line and stood with his head over the top rail, watching the line of black vehicles disappear over the rise, across the bridge. Then Sandman walked to the pasture gate and stood there.

I ran down the lane and took hold of his halter. We walked back to the barns together, each busy with our own thoughts.

Chapter 42

Icebound

We always watched for the homecoming of the swallows as some people anticipate the return of robins in the spring. They built their nests under the barn eaves or on ledges within the barn. One friendly pair, raising families for years, on a sill over Chief's door.

The horses became used to them swooping over their heads, in and out of the barn door, as they added to the firmness of their mud nests. Colonies congregated on the telephone wires between the barns. They sat, shoulder to shoulder, like blue-black clothes pins, surveying our activities.

Often, during the summer, one of us, using a longhandled brush, scrubbed down the face of the redwood door, washing away the white streaks left by their droppings. One more chore, but we never considered removingthe clay nests.

Then, there came a day, just as suddenly as they appeared in the spring, when they were gone. I always felt a sense of loss on that day. Nothing marked the passing of time like the disappearance of the swallows. Ahead of us stretched the bleak, long winter.

At Arcadia Farm, how long had I observed the seasons changing? One or two? More like ten or twelve. Time had passed almost unnoticed.

The grasses of the familiar backyard were still luxuriant, as I walked across them. One fall day after the swallows departed, winter's fine mist of first snow gently touched my cheeks. Overhead, cardinals swooped and darted among the tall pines, keeping me company from barn to house as they had dozens of times before.

I decided it was time to fill the redwood feeder with succulent sunflower seeds, to scatter pulverized crumbs of stale whole wheat bread which I had been saving.

The birds, twittering in bare branches of old elms, flew low above my head and soared straight upwards against the leaden sky. Suddenly, dozens of birds were in flight above me, red wing blackbirds, sparrows and grackles among them. I had never seen such soaring and swooping, such arabesques and fluttering fandangos. Some of the performers hid themselves in the dense white pines. Snow-mist dusted my upturned face. Reluctant to go indoors, I picked up a handful of spruce cones and gathered an armload of fallen elm branches, to kindle the fireplace.

The grey cat had followed me across the wet grass, picking up each paw, shaking the moisture from it, lamenting with his tail twitching. I picked him up and tucked his damp body inside my fleece-lined coat. The hairs next to his skin were warm and dry.

I reminded him of cozy accomodations in the horse barn and said, "A barn cat should stay in the barn," I walked slowly back to the barn, glad for an excuse to cross the yard again. I could feel the season changing around me from autumn to winter.

We had begun preparing for winter in late September. We vowed, this year, every window in the main barn would be re- glazed and sashes painted before severe weather descended on us. Whitney took measurements and ordered the panes of glass, aluminum glazing points and putty at the hardware store.

The weather was dry and pleasant. We worked out of doors, on a big table near the milk house door. In an hour we replaced a dozen cracked or broken panes. Once the sashes had a coat of paint, matching the sagebrush green of the barn, the whole structure blended into the pines and spruce around it. Few jobs were as satisfying.

Earlier, we had made a master list, remembering the experiences which taught us those winter problems to avoid. We bought heating coils for water lines, a heater for the pump house, a large beam electric lantern, fifty feet of new rubber hose, a charger for the tractor battery, two snow shovels and salt crystals for the barn aisles. If water was spilled on the aisles in below zero temperatures, they iced up in a jiffy, a hazard to the horses.

We checked our snowmobile suits, face masks, gloves and boots. Surely, we would have some degree of comfort caring for the horses this winter!

The twelfth of January set a record, the warmest day in history at fifty-eight degrees. During the night, a storm moved in from the western plains, bringing high winds and freezing rain. Ice pellets, the size of chalk, hammered against the window panes. Rain beat relentlessly upon the out-buildings, flooding the ground. As the temperature fell it all turned to ice.

The storm came up at midnight. I awakened Whitney and we went out to the pony paddock. Most of the animals were in the loafing barn except for Mr. Tweed, Candy, and Fritz, who couldn't get into the shelter because Rickey's and Rusty's bulky bodies filled the doorway.

Earlier, we had made emergency provision for the more timid animals. By sliding a door in the adjacent stallion barn, four spacious box stalls were available. We doubled up the ponies and threw a couple of flakes of hay to the animals. In short order all were under cover. Extra box stalls in the main barn accomodated the remaining school horses. Everybody was safe from the vicious weather.

All through the night the wind increased in velocity. By morning the mercury was at zero with a wind chill factor of thirty degrees below. One of the main concerns was our indoor arena, a building sixty by one hundred sixty feet, even though it was designed to withstand heavy snowloads and high winds.

The winds approached tornado intensity. The steel building creaked and moaned as though in agony. We opened both doors at either end of the arena to prevent pressure from building and watched as our precious stockpile of golden shavings blew away.

Whitney, Josie and I worked in shifts for the next two days. The winds never abated: the temperature at zero. One of us hayed the horses while the others watered and grained them. We took a break to change wet gloves or eat a snack. However, conditions were bearable in comparison to the ice storm of 1966.

In February there had been another mild spell with warm rain, then an abrupt drop in temperature. We awakened to the crystalline horror of a violent ice storm. The trees were encrusted with thick ice, Norway maples along our long lane bent to the ground, obstructing the approach to the farm.

For five days, the ice was with us before the trees could straighten into a somewhat upright position. But the Norways sustained extensive damage.

We were without electric power and therefore, without heat or water. Telephone lines were down and there were minimal groceries on hand. Carrie and Holly lived in a neighboring community, not as badly hit as we were. They walked in from the main road bringing milk, bread and dog food for Stuart and Ashley.

Though they protested, I sent Lynn and Gail home with Carrie and Holly for warmth and regular meals.

Whitney and I then took stock of our problems. The ground was like an ice skating pond, glassy and treacherous. Over the barn entrances, huge icicles hung from the eaves. Their dagger points and weight could inflict injury falling on anyone below. Josie knocked them down with a long- handled hay fork.

With no power, we had no pump pressure to fill water tanks. Fortunately, the five tanks in the main barn and one in the annexes and stallion barn were filled to the rim. With no idea how long we would be without power, we decided to ration water to the horses immediately, one half pail,, a gallon per day for each horse. One hundred and sixty horses and eleven ponies were then on Arcadia Farm.

My greatest fear was fire. With the power lines down in the yard from the main transformer, anything could happen. As a possible fire precaution, I turned off the power sources at the fuse boxes in the barns and houses. I was afraid to move horses over ice to equally dangerous areas. No horse could keep his footing on such glazed surfaces. We took turns policing and patrolling, checking and rechecking the barns.

We fed the stock at seven-thirty, watered them at one o'clock. Having no lights, we repeated the procedure at three when we still had daylight. With a metal pail, I scooped up snow, adding it to water in the bottom of Sammy and Chief's water buckets to augment our water supply.

In the house there was a fireplace in the family room. We kept the door closed to contain the heat. We used an antique oil lamp and candles for light. I cooked hot dogs and baked potatoes in the fire's coals.

At the end of the exhausting day, I lay on the floor my head cradled on my arm and stared into the fire. The subdued candlelight flickering on the honey-pine walls of our family room made me think longingly of 21 North Broadway, my childhood home. There, the mellow light through antique parchment lampshades cast shadows on the beamed ceiling as the firelight danced on the brass chestnut roasters on either side of the fluted Georgian mantlepiece.

I thought of Ola's cooking. I could almost smell her succulent chicken and the aroma of her roast leg of lamb. All Ola's cooking was ambrosia! How distressed she would have been to think her baby, as she called me, was hungry.

On the third day there was a moderate thaw. We scurried to find extra pails, pans and kitchen utensils, anything that would hold water, and placed them under the dripping icicles. We added the melted water to the storage tanks and shared it with the horses that were the heaviest drinkers and those who were pregnant.

By the morning of the fifth day we were adding snow to all the horse's pails. The animals were beginning to look gaunt in their hind quarters. Without water to digest it, they were leaving their hay uneaten. I was tired to the bone and very discouraged. Surely the lack of power couldn't last much longer.

Around four-thirty the afternoon of the sixth day, as I shoveled snow onto the toboggan from drifts behind the barns, I heard Whitney yelling. "Mom! Mom! Public Service was just here. They've fixed the lines. We've got electricity!"

"Turn on the pump and spigots," I cried, joyfully. By the time I reached the big barn, the music of spitting valves and rushing water greeted me. I filled a pail and set it on the barn floor for Stuart and Ashley, for they had been rationed, too. Relieved, we joked and laughed, leading each one of the horses to the water tanks, watching them drink their fill. Finally, we filled all their water pails.

It was midnight before we were through chores. When we went back to the house, the furnace had begun to warm the frigid rooms. We took a hot bath, threw our clothes into the washing machine and fell into bed without supper, sick of living on hot dogs and potatoes.

Exhausted, and just about to fall asleep, I heard Whitney calling from his bedroom, "Mom, are you asleep? Hey, Mom! Can you hear me?"

I answered, "Yes."

"Mom? What would we have done if the power had not come back on? Could we go to the creek with barrels and a wagon? Huh, Mom?"

I struggled to stay awake long enough to answer. "True, son, there was always the creek, but Dolly and Flory would have a time with their footing on the frozen, icy bank. I think I would have called the fire department and asked them to come out with a tanker and fill our tanks. Son? Did you hear me?" There was no answer. Whitney was asleep.

Chapter 43

The Hardest Winter of My Life

Rigorous as the whole experience had been, it was nothing compared to the winter of 1964, a few years after we started the business. I still find it difficult to recapture all those impressions, perhaps, because remembering it at all was such a painful experience. Certainly it was the hardest winter of my life. I had sixty-five of our one hundred horses in various states of illness with the "strangles". Before the discovery of antibiotics, when a horse had this virus he literally strangled to death. The swollen glands in his throat and terrible, uncontrolled paroxysms of coughing brought him to a wretched end.

The virus was brought to the farm in November by a horse from Nebraska. He showed all the symptoms of strep throat and I placed him in isolation. As the horse recovered slowly, other horses began showing the same symptoms, refusing to eat or drink. Then came the hacking cough and lassitude. The animals stood in a stupor, heads hanging low. their eyes blank and staring.

Dr. Prince made recommendations for their care. If the horse went off feed, I took his temperature, and if the fever did not exceed one hundred and three degrees no antibiotics were administered. Dr. Prince warned using medication too early created complications. Mares swelled in their udders: stallions and geldings in their scrotum or testicles.

Some mornings I took the temperature of ten or fifteen horses, grateful that Dr. Prince had shown me how. I took the temperature rectally. My clinical thermometer had a round hole in one end of it. I tied a piece of string through this hole then tied a knot at the end of the string. I attached a clip clothespin to the end of the string just before the knot. I inserted the thermometer into the horse's rectum, then clipped the clothespin to a generous strand of the horse's tail. Horses will sometimes draw the thermometer into their rectum, or expel it with a stool. The string makes it possible to retrieve the thermometer and keep it from falling on the barn floor where the horse might step on it.

It was twenty degrees below zero and chores took all day. We were only able to work a half hour at a time as the raw cold was so penetrating. Since the horses needed constant care, we took shortcuts whenever possible. At best, winter in a barn is a strenuous, wearing time, but when horses become sick it is a nightmare. If the medical mask over my nose warmed the air I breathed, nothing warmed my numb fingers. Many treatments had to be administered with bare hands.

I wore a mechanic's coveralls to protect my clothes when I leaned in front of sick horses. You had to unhook their water pails, contaminated with excretions from their nose and throat. The pails were frozen and had to be thawed by pouring boiling water over their upturned bottoms, tapping gently on the side with a hammer to loosen the ice. Hunks of ice held huge globs of yellow discharge from the horses throats. I hated the job.

As the disease progressed, that winter of 1964, the horses' glands under their jaws filled with heavy pus. Sometimes the glands became hard as rock and the pressure had to be relieved with black tar drawing salve. Transferring the thick ointment from a jar carried in my tin, blueberry bucket from northern New York, I heated the salve to spreading consistency and applied it with a wooden tongue depressor to the horse's swollen glands. Josie, watching me once, observed, "Seems like a lot of trouble you're goin' to account of horses." The responsibility for the horse's survival weighed on me. Could anything be too much trouble? I didn't think so.

Josie said when he first came to work for me, he would do chores and farming, but wanted little to do with the horses themselves. However, when the epidemic hit us I pressed him into service, coaxing him to hold the horses on a leadshank while I took their temperatures or painted their glands. As a boy, sixty years earlier, Josie had seen a team of an uncle's die from the strangles, a common occurrence. "Just coughed themselves to death, they did," he mournfully told me.

The cheerless old man confronted me daily with equally depressing tales. Eventually, I tied my patient's heads with a lead rope to a ring in the barn wall, rather than cope with the bleakness of Josie and my dismal task as well. I ministered to the horses by myself. Alone, in the frigid barn, often exhausted and hungry, my hands red, cracked and swollen, I laid my head against the shoulder of a sick animal and cried tears of loneliness and frustration. Those were hard days, my responsibility toward the horses ever on my mind.

During that period, I considered giving up the business many times.

Taking a moment's respite, I sat down on the edge of the old rusted wheelbarrow. The sight of a child's blueberry bucket, once bright and shiny, now dented and out of shape, brought back a shattering moment of nostalgia. I closed my eyes and I was with Jim again, he, in the stern of the green canvas canoe. His paddle scarcely making a ripple on the water. My blueberry bucket heaped with plump berries, tucked for safekeeping in the bow of the "Old Town" canoe. I had scrambled up the steep rocky bank of Blueberry Point where the most lucious berries grew. The sandy gravel slipped away beneath me. I often slid backward toward the water, skinning my bare knees on sharp rocks and hardpan. My small, child's hands desperately grasping for alder bushes to break my fall down the embankment. But, always, there was Jim's voice, encouraging me as he reached out a warm, calloused hand to rescue me. "Thatta girl! Hang on! You can make it! Keep trying!"

The soft breath exhaled through the nostrils of the horse I was nursing, put an end to my momentary escape. I saw clearly, coping with reality. The small blueberry pail was smeared with black, sticky, Ichthamol ointment, beginning to congeal in the freezing barn.

The epidemic lasted eight weeks, but we had no fatalities or residual respiratory problems. A rare occurrence, considering the number of horses affected. Dr. Prince considered writing a paper on the episode for one of the veterinary publications. Interesting as it was, it took years for me to recognize the value of the whole experience.

Chapter 44

A Throw-away Horse

The man on the phone asked if I ever "laid up" Thoroughbred horses. "Laid up" is a horseman's term for rest, rehabilitation and full care for the animal after a hard season at the track or following injury or surgery. He explained his horse was at the Horse Surgical Hospital recovering from an operation to remove bone chips from his left knee.

My caller and I came to terms on boarding fees and I agreed he could send the horse to me.

Dr. Roper was one of the organizers of the horse hospital and I knew other veterinarians there. I made a call to get some background on my patient for I wanted to do justice to the Thoroughbred. I spoke to Dr. Wade about the animal's progress. He was surprised to hear from me and said, "You're going to see the most pathetic case I've ever encountered. Believe this, if you can. After the horse tore up his knee in a race, he was put back in a stall while the trainer and the owner argued over who would pay for his board and surgery."

The veterinarian, very irate about the incident, went on punctuating his remarks with, "Can you believe this? Those guys at the track didn't feed or water the horse for over a week. Such callousness. The horse was in awful shape when he came to us." Dr. Wade paused, waiting for my reaction.

"That's an unbelievable story, truly unbelievable," I said, adding, "What should we do for the horse when he gets to the farm?"

"Feed him!" was Dr. Wade's explosive answer. "In a couple of weeks turn him out in the smallest enclosure you have. I don't want him to move around too much on that knee. You'll get along with him fine. He's gentle for a Thoroughbred. A good fellow and no nut."

A few days later I was thunderstruck to see a groom, on foot, leading a big, black Thoroughbred gelding up my long, long driveway. Apparently, the handler didn't take the time to determine there was ample room to turn the horse-van around in the barn area. He unloaded the horse on the highway and made him hobble and limp to our barn. The Thoroughbred was a wraith of a horse, gaunt and sunken.

That weekend, his owner came to see me. He said the horse's name was Hardship Man. I thought it most fitting. The owner paid a month's board. I never saw, or heard from him again.

We shortened his name to Man. He was five years old, very gentle and equally easy to handle. I tried to groom him each day, myself. The improvement was very slow. We had to build flesh on the inside of his carcass before we could see recovery on his bony frame. We took care feeding him from the beginning, trying not to kill him with kindness by over-feeding.

The boarders showed great interest in Man's rehabilitation. There were willing hands to groom him and clean his feet. Jeff Roper never sent me a bill for medical care, worming, floating his teeth or for tetanus/encephalitis vaccines.

The month went by with no contact from the owner, and with no board money check for Hardship

Man. He seemed to support his weight on the damaged knee as he walked around our smallest horse pen. There was no lameness evident.

Another month went by. My letters, call-back messages and numerous phone calls to the owner were ignored. I called Dr. Wade to discuss the case and he told me the surgical fee at the horse hospital had not been paid either. Man's delinquent board approached eight hundred dollars, a fortune to me.

Dr. Roper thought it time to see how successful Man's knee operation had been. If he was sound on the leg, maybe I could find him a new owner, someone satisfied with light riding.

We all gathered in the indoor arena, Whitney, Lynn and Gail, Josie, Dr. Roper and me. Man was truly handsome by that time, well filled out in all the right places. His barrel, neck and rump were covered with supple flesh. The months of care had produced a classic aristocrat, if only his leg had healed.

Jeff Roper clipped the lunge line to a gleaming brass ring on Man's halter and encouraged him to walk off slowly. He clucked softly to the horse. The Thoroughbred trotted around him in an arc. Our disappointment was overwhelming.

Every time the horse's left foot hit the ground his head bobbed, even on the arena's soft surface. Each trotting step caused pain. Not even easy riding was the answer for poor Hardship Man.

There were those who would have bought him for his classic beauty and gentleness, but I feared the horse's disability would cause him to be sold and resold over and over again, a tragic prospect.

I did not sleep well that night. Man's future worried me. We had all grown fond of him. To keep him on my feed bill was a luxury. I already had too many very old horses in pastured retirement. I could not afford to carry him indefinately.

One night when I was searching for a realistic answer, it came to me how I might manage it. I hopped out of bed and found a sheet of bright yellow poster cardboard. I rummaged in my desk for a marking pencil.

After breakfast, I carried the poster, hammer and a handful of carpet tacks out to the barn. I nailed my yellow placard to the front of Man's stall door. In bold black letters it read, "Have a heart for Hardship Man's upkeep."

More than once, I saw Chase dropping a twenty dollar bill into the pail and Josie emptying his pockets of small change. Through everyone's generosity I was able to keep the horse five years. Of course I didn't know, after him paying only a month's board, I would never see Hardship Man's owner again. I had been sure he would turn out to be a good owner for the race horse. Another lesson in reading human nature.

Chapter 45

The Piperoo

I bought Diamond from Justin Pike along with two other horses. "She's a piperoo," Pike said. "Never will understand some folks getting rid of a good horse because they need a little extra care. This here gal's got a pile of trophies and blue ribbons." He patted the buckskin's shoulder. "When she come up lame after too many short turns around the barrels, this guy's buddies talked him into trading her off. He even suggested I should send her to a dude ranch out east. She's too good for that. Jake and I thought of you. I believe she'll do you real good."

The mare's coat was satin to the touch. She had long fine legs and was beautifully headed. There was a crease in her forehead the shape of a diamond. Her eyes were hazel. Cal Baker had told me more than once a gypsy superstition, "Never pass up a horse with hazel eyes."

The buckskin mare was a preferred mount, her gaits so smooth that everyone who rode her thought themselves better riders than they really were. Her jog was slow, her lope flowed effortlessly, -- hardly moving the rider in the saddle.

Diamond could go months without her right knee lighting up. It happened twice when I sent her out on rental. She came back ducking her head, stepping gingerly on her right leg. It never happened in class where I could keep an eye on her.

The first time she went lame, a sack of fluid accumulated in her knee cap. Dr. Roper showed me how to reduce the swelling. He painted a sweat-linament on the knee with a fine paint brush and then bandaged it. Then he cut a spider bandage from a piece of old sheeting and skillfully criss-crossed the cotton strips to keep the knee bandage from slipping down Diamond's leg.

I repeated the treatment for a week, kneeling on the cold cement, working on the quiet mare.

"Will the swelling go down?" Carrie asked, her face full of the concern she felt for all the horses.

"Dr. Roper tells me it will in a few days, but we'll have to repeat the treatment until it does," I explained.

"It's like a bad sprain, isn't it?" Holly asked, handing me a rolled bandage.

"Exactly!" I replied. "Diamond has some age on her. She's in foal so we won't be using her for anything but lessons."

The girls were delighted to hear of the buckskin's ' pregnancy. "Far out!" Carrie exclaimed. "We must keep the barns real peaceful for all the mothers."

I laughed. "That's true. I'll depend on you two for that. Let's have a mellow maternity section."

The weeks went by and Diamond's knee healed. I turned her out in the mare's field with the other prospective mothers. One morning, I saw a young man with fiery red hair leaning on the top rail of pasture fencing looking at the horses. When I walked up to him, he pointed at the buckskin mare in the field and asked, "That little mare there, is she for sale?"

"None of the horses in this pasture are for sale. They're our brood mares." I replied.

The young man pressed on. "I know that mare. She's a real jewel, well broke. You could ride her with a piece of baling twine around her neck. She'll turn on a dime and give you change. I knew the guy who used to own her. Her name is Texas Lady."

No one had to tell me this was Diamond's former owner. "I always have a hard time understanding how a person can sell a horse because of a disability when that horse has given good service. Seems to me you owe a good horse something," I said, looking the young man in the eye.

A crimson blush started below his collar and spread rapidly over his cheeks. "You guessed I used to own her?"

"Yes, I guessed that. You know a lot about the mare," I replied.

"Will you take my number and call me if you change your mind about selling her?" he held out a scrap of paper.

"No need to give me your number. Diamond or Texas Lady, as you call her, is not for sale."

"Never?" he looked back at the mare.

"Absolutely never," I replied, firmly and walked away briskly. I felt his eyes on me until I reached the barns.

I met Lynn at the barn door. "Why are you smiling, Mom?" she asked. I explained my encounter with the red headed young man. "It must have given you personal satisfaction to talk to that fellow." she said, smiling herself.

"You bet it did. I seldom meet people who have discarded excellent animals, horses that found their way to us."

Lynn laughed. "We're so lucky to have her."

The buckskin mare was a favorite. Josie, who seldom showed an interest in any of the horses, called her Diamond Lil and Carrie and Holly begged to share my vigil when Diamond was due to foal. After I noticed milk trickling down her leg from her udder, I kept close watch on her. On evening, after a final check of the barns, Lynn reported Diamond was showing signs of foaling. She was restless, getting up and down in her stall, biting at her flanks.

I called Carrie to alert them. Within a half hour they were at the farm to keep me company through the night vigil awaiting Diamond's foal. The two girls and I sat on the cold cement aisle, our backs against the stall planking, the dim ray of the night light illuminating Diamond's stall.

We whispered far into the night and talked of many things, our thoughts about God, how I came to own the farm. They were the only ones to ask me if I ever thought of marrying again, and were delighted when I said, "Of course I had." Both girls had an understanding for what brought me to seek a divorce. "He's got to love animals," was the perceptive way they described my hypothetical new husband. I agreed. Frequently thereafter, Carrie or Holly proposed candidates they considered worthy as a father to the children and a husband for me.

Carrie loved hearing about Rainbow Lake. In time they knew almost as much about me as my own children. I found myself sharing my innermost thoughts with them, my fears and self-doubts. They were supportive and never judgemental. Each time they came to the farm there were scraps for the cats from their jobs as waitresses, and carrots for the horses. For me, a new flavor of herbal tea or a fragrant potpourri they had concocted from wild flowers that grew in my meadow.

The girls also helped water the horses and enjoyed supervising the pony parties. On soft summer days they could be found sitting in the deep pasture grasses holding Bounty on a lead rope while they braided daisy chains. Any of the school horses or ponies they could catch wore garlands of daisies, Queen Anne's lace, and chicory around their necks. Bounty, their favorite, wore three or four.

Seeing me they would call, "Come on Mrs. K., come sit with us for awhile." They pretended not to understand my schedule did not make allowances for sitting in the pasture making daisy chains. They coaxed me to the orchard to observe a robin building her nest in a gnarled apple tree. Later that day, Josie reported he found them in tears after finding a dead bird drowned in the pasture water trough. He put a small log in the tank so it would not happen again.

Their personalities seemed wonderfully spiritual.

Chapter 46

Soft and Gentle Days of May

May's arrival always held special importance. We looked forward to turning the school horses out on the pastures. Every few days I walked the alfalfa and timothy clover fields checking on their growth. Our goal was the arrival of June tenth. By that date flourishing grasses could support a number of horses for three months.

I tried to find an extra hour to walk the full length of the pasture, slashing away with a hoe at the stubborn stalks of Scotch thistles. Uncut by fall they would be a great problem, getting entangled in the horse's manes and forelocks. Kono, the only horse that ate the green burrs, selected the spiny buds as though they were rare delicacies.

During such walks through the pasture, I searched for lost halters or horseshoes. Rusted horse shoe nails were a serious hazard to the horses. At this time of year, the perimeter wire was crimped and tightened by driving steel posts deeper into the soft earth. Josie did this with a sledge hammer. Gates and hinges were inspected, as we were always aware that Fritz, the pony, would be making his own survey.

Since we had so few of the old horses left, putting them on the grass was very meaningful. Another worming, their teeth floated and feet trimmed, the old timers were in good shape.

Some years we had as many as forty adult horses and eleven ponies to lead to the pasture. They always knew where they were going.

The quietest and most mannerly school horse could be a handful at such a time. They reared and cavorted, trying to break loose once inside the pasture gate.

There were many volunteers willing to help. However, the sight of less experienced people jerked around and horses let go with a lead rope whipping around their front legs, limited our helpers. Usually, it was the girls, and Whit and Chase Harper that made all those trips to the field.

Quiet horses like Sugarfoot, Diamond and Bobbysocks followed each other, Colonel never far from Navaho.

Once free, the horses circled the field at a full gallop and always bunched up. The herd bosses, Big Boy and Dakotah were always in the lead, with the ponies bringing up the rear, trying hard to match the longer strides of the plunging horses.

Suddenly, as if by cue, they all came to a sudden stop, lowered their heads into the luxuriant grass and started to graze. Only the ponies remained in motion. They nibbled mouthfuls of grass, and walked about looking for a congenial, tolerant horse with whom they could crop.

Summer thunderstorms and driving rains found the horses, rumps to the wind, heads lowered between their shoulders as rain pelted them. After the storm, the sunshine brought their newly washed coats to glistening sheen.

On hot, breathless days in July and August, the herd clustered in shade from oaks which cast long, sheltering shadows. The horses withstood the searing dry winds by standing with heads toward the center of a circle, using their tails to fan away the flies from each other's eyes.

When the grass thinned in September, one of us drove down the lane along the pasture with a flatbed wagon piled high with hay bales. We supplemented the grass as soon as it no longer provided sufficient nourishment.

I found myself, many evenings, from the vantage point of little Alice's tractor seat, looking down over the horse's broad backs. They ate their hay side by side, peacefully, their body colors contrasting like a rich oil painting. The sand duns with auburn mane and tail: splashy black and white pintos, silver and charcoal tails swishing at the flies: the burnished gold of the Palominos with their silver tails sweeping the ground: the colors of the chestnuts ranged from pale auburn to rich red mahogany: the bays with rich sable pelts and coal black mane and tail. In my imaginary mental canvas, the pure white horses, Frosty and Chrystal, contrasted to the deep colors of the horses around them. Off to one side, by herself, the only mouse-colored dun I would ever have, the Grulla mare, small, fine headed. Her black mane and tail a perfect contrast to her steel-grey body, happy in motherhood, a loud-colored Appaloosa colt, sired by Sammy, at her side.

In late October, when the night winds began to chill, we brought the horses back to the loafing barn. Everyone of them walked slowly, obediently, next to us as if they knew their days under the open sky had come to an end. For days, afterwards, looking out on the deserted field, I visualized the horses grazing, their palette of color contrasts blending like a harmonious landscape.

Chapter 47

Heartache For Us All

The evening before our annual Memorial Day horseshow I hooked up the Allis Chalmers tractor to a flatbed wagon loaded with flag standards, and pulled it to the arena. For several years I had made my own flags. I bought yardage and cut it into three by five foot pieces. Each flag a different color, bright blue, yellow, purple, turquoise and shades of pink and green. I tacked the folded edge of the fabric on a pine standard with carpet tacks. It was one of the preparations for the show I truly enjoyed. I needed help in nailing the standards to the fence while I stepped back and judged their alignment.

Carrie was helping me. Holly was riding Bounty and reined the stolid creature where we were cutting and tacking the fabrics. Holly, impatient to see the finished results, sat on the horse talking to us. Bounty was wearing a sprig of apple blossoms tucked in a lock of her mane.

"What time do you want us here, tomorrow?" Carrie asked, tapping the last tack on a length of shocking pink fabric.

"Halter is nine o'clock. Do you girls think you can be here by eight-thirty to make coffee?" I replied. The girls usually served hot coffee and sweet rolls from the food concession before early morning classes.

"We'll be there. Don't worry," Carrie said, laughing. "Holly, don't forget to set the alarm." She hopped up on the wagon and stretched her long leg across Bounty's broad back, settling herself behind

Holly. The three of them headed back to the barn,
their laughter filled the air until they were out of sight.

There were many last minute details the morning
of any show. At nine o'clock I took the cash box to the
food concession. Carrie and Holly were not there.
Punctuality was not one of their greatest assets. I
wasn't surprised they were late, they often were. I
looked for Whitney and asked him to man the coffee

concession until I could round up a replacement. Lynn and Gail were involved with horseshow registration.

By eleven o'clock Carrie and Holly still had not arrived and I became very apprehensive. I started toward the house to telephone their apartment.

Rounding the corner of the garage I met Paul, Carrie's friend, looking for me. The stricken look on his face told me something terrible had happened. He clung to me sobbing.

Carrie's mother had called the farm a few minutes earlier. On their way to the farm, the girls were involved in a catastrophic head-on collision on the expressway. Holly had been thrown through the windshield and killed instantly. Carrie was in intensive care with multiple internal injuries, a broken jaw, broken ribs and a fractured leg.

I was stunned, unable to cry, trying to absorb the massive shock. We went through the numbing day. I remember little about the show. When it was over, the family and some of the boarders went to the office and called the hospital. We reached Carrie's mother. She said Carrie's condition was critical, but she was going to live.

When she could have visitors, Gail, Lynn, Whitney and I went to see her. There were hideous scars on her lovely face. Her jaws were wired shut and she couldn't speak. We could only stay a few minutes, unable to hide our tears.

It was eight months before we saw Carrie at the farm. She was very pale and wan with a quality of deep sadness about her that made all of us heavy-hearted.

Christmas season was with us and Whitney brought Bounty in from the winter paddock. He had found a piece of red ribbon and tied it in Bounty's mane.

Carrie buried her face in the mare's shaggy neck, stifling her sobs. "Oh Holly, why did it have to be you?" she wept.

That September, Paul and Carrie made plans to join a commune near Carbondale. Paul expected to finish his degree at the University. They planned to take Bounty with them.

When their old van, a rented horse-trailer hitched behind, pulled into the yard, Lynn, Gail, Whit and I went out to help load Bounty. We watched silently as Carrie brushed the horse. She said she was depressed from the hassle over the trailer rental and the big security deposit required by the company, but there was no question, Bounty was going with them.

Paul stood in the barn in bare feet and thong sandals, a leather brow band on his shoulder length hair. When Carrie had finished brushing Bounty she covered her with a khaki army blanket. In one corner, stitched in bright blue yarn, were the words, Carrie and Holly, Peace!

There were no goodbyes. Once the tailgate was slammed behind the docile mare, Carrie turned her pinched, tearstained face away from the children and me and climbed into the van. The three of us stood motionless, arms entwined, watching the decrepit old vehicle and horse trailer disappear around a bend in the driveway.

There were a few letters, Thanksgiving and Christmas cards, but I never saw Carrie again.

In the spring, a neighbor of her mother's called me, her voice choking with emotion. Carrie had died in childbirth at the commune. A baby girl survived. Paul had named her Holly.

Many springs thereafter, when the pink and white apple blossom petals, blown by a gentle wind, drifted through the orchard, I felt deep sadness. I fancied sometimes I could see the figures of my flower children, their backs leaning against the apple tree's gnarled trunks, Bounty grazing nearby. The petals drifting down against their upturned faces. I could hear their laughter at the sight of Bounty covered with apple blossoms.

Chapter 48

Tragedy in the Barn

Each night it was part of the routine to brush down the pregnant mares, due to foal, before turning in myself. Soon, it would be my blue-eyed mare Wally's turn. We began to keep close watch over her. The mare was in the largest foaling stall at the south end of the barn. The partition, only five feet high, allowed the friendly mare to stick her head over it and visit with anyone in the aisle.

One evening in early March, I bedded her down with fresh straw, filled her water pail and gave her another flake of hay. She was two weeks overdue according to my records. Dr. Roper felt there was no reason for concern. He had seen her that morning. Her legs were not swollen. She had a strong heartbeat and the foal was very active.

Maternity chores completed, I walked away from Wally and reached for the light switch to snap on the night light. When I looked back at her, she had her head over the partition, watching me with her remarkable blue eyes. "Be a good girl," I said, as I flipped off the long line of ceiling lights.

The March night was heavy with penetrating, damp cold. I headed for the house, looking forward to an uninterrupted night's sleep. Maternity vigils in February, with other mares, Diamond, Colonelette. Sugarfoot and Star, had worn me out.

For some time I had noticed a change in my equilibrium, experiencing difficulty walking in a straight line. At times there was numbness in my legs and arms. I reasoned that I needed more rest.

Whitney was spending the night with his friend, Dennis. Gail and Lynn each had a girlfriend sleeping over. After telling the girls to turn down the Hi-Fi a bit, I slipped wearily into bed and drifted off to sleep at once.

I was jolted awake by the back door slamming and hysterical voices coming from the kitchen. I was already out of bed fishing for a slipper when Gail burst into my room, sobbing. "Mother, mother! Get up. It's Wally! Something terrible has happened to Wally!"

I grabbed a blanket, threw it over my shoulders, forgetting my slippers and ran across the soggy back lawn, the girls trailed behind me sobbing. The cement barn aisle was cold to my bare feet as I rushed to Wally's stall.

On the floor lay the mare. She looked as though she had been slaughtered. Crimson blood was everywhere, as high as five feet up the sidewalls.

Wally was dead, She had disemboweled herself trying to give birth. A dead sorrel colt lay at her feet, enmeshed in his mother's intestines. Stunned, I had not noticed I was standing in a pool of blood that oozed through my bare toes. I thought I was going to vomit.

As I got a grip on myself, I thought how tragic for the girls and their friends to have discovered this horror. Calmly, I guided them out of the barn and told them firmly to wait for me in the house. When I saw the kitchen door close behind them, I staggered back to the grim scene in the barn.

I sloshed a pail of frigid water over my bloody feet, then I dialed Jeff Roper. He said he would come over right away. Then, I called the rendering company.

Then it was time to deal with my own remorse. I had not checked on the mare after the ten o'clock visit. I usually looked in on the prospective mothers at three A.M. It was after six. I felt I would choke with grief. My chest ached and I had no strength. Through tears, I hunted for a large horse blanket, and covered the pathetic sight of the mare and her dead foal with it. His little feet stuck out and I covered them with a burlap sack. Then, exhausted, I sat down on the floor near the mare's head. As if she could hear me, I repeated over and over, the inadequate words, "Oh girl! I am so sorry!" I don't know how long I sat there, but finally I was able to collect myself. I knew I had to go back to the house and console Gail and Lynn.

I found them huddled around the kitchen table. Gail, her face swollen and puffy from crying, was explaining to Lynn how she had found the dead mare.

"I wanted to surprise mom by doing the morning feeding by myself. Mom's lost so much sleep. . ." Her voice broke. " Poor Wally. Why, Mom?"

I shook my head dumbly, unable to share my feelings of guilt and remorse. The one night I had not checked on the mare, disaster had struck. It would be years before I stopped reproaching myself, if indeed I ever did. "I don't know the answer, Gail. When Dr. Roper comes, maybe he can tell us something."

I leaned my aching head wearily against the kitchen door frame. No one spoke. It seemed an eternity until I heard Jeff Roper's van on the driveway. We crossed the yard together, neither of us speaking. Dr. Roper's face was grim as he turned from the bloody sight. He shook his head, redraping the blanket over Wally. He faced me and said, "From what I can tell, the foal must have kicked his foot through the wall of the uterus, entangling a foot in the mare's bowel. With his own struggle to be born and the mare's violent contractions, it was too much stress for both of them." Then, as if reading my thoughts, he added, "I doubt if I myself could have done anything to change the situation except relieve the mare's pain. Sometimes these terrible things happen. Don't reproach yourself," he said kindly.

Hearing Dr. Roper's explanation, and with my own understanding of Wally's agony, I broke down in sobs.

"Would you like me to stay with you until the truck comes for her?" Dr. Roper asked, gently.

I knew the veterinarian's long day was just beginning and he was needed elsewhere. I replied, "You go along on your rounds. I'll be alright, but thanks for the thought."

When I got back to the house, the scene in the kitchen was more organized. The girls were dressed. They had made french toast for me and a pot of coffee. There was little conversation. I could not eat a bite.

After a cup of coffee, gulped down in three swallows, I took a quick shower and dressed. Then I took a pail of hot water, bleach and naptha soap, mixed a sudsy solution and returned to the barn.

The 2x10 planking had to be pried loose across the back of Wally's stall so she could be removed directly into the yard rather than being dragged up the aisle.

I looked for a wrecking bar. The driver would have to help me remove the partition.

After what seemed hours, I heard the truck in the yard. The man from the rendering company had no trouble removing the partition. He backed the truck to the opening and lowered the ramp. The old motor, gears grinding, unwound the cable on the winch. I shuddered at the motor's ungreased whine. I had heard it many times before, metal grinding against metal, irrevocable, unrelenting.

"Please wait a minute," I asked the driver. The realization of what was happening overwhelmed me. "Just one more minute," I repeated, my voice hoarse from tears which kept welling up in my throat.

The man walked toward the front of the vehicle and leaned against it, lighting a cigarette.

I bent down over Wally and repeated the inadequate words one last time. "Girl, I am so sorry."

The driver lifted Wally's head and slipped the wire noose around her neck, unbuckling her blood soaked halter. He started the motor and slowly Wally's shattered body was drawn up the ramp into the truck.

Next we turned our attention to the foal, carrying him between us, laying him next to his mother. I was relieved the man had not wanted to winch him up by the neck. He looked so pathetic.

I watched the truck pull away, then mechanically scrubbed the bloodstained planking. I pulled the tractor and spreader near and cleaned the stall. My motions were unthinking and automatic. The sight of the empty stall was too painful and after I bedded it with fresh shavings I moved Lynn's Katie-Twist mare into it,

The effect on the girls from this traumatic experience worried me. I knew I would have to face their anguished tears and questions, to which I had few answers.

What would I say to Father Mulvaney? How would I break the news about his pet? For several years he had driven out to the farm on his Sunday afternoon off, sharing a hard roll or apple with the mare. He did no more riding, but took great pleasure in brushing her from head to hoof. What would I tell him?

With my disorganized thoughts, I retraced my steps toward the house, unaware that I was not following the familiar path until I felt the prickly spines of the blue spruce on my shoulder. I had veered off into the evergreens. Dismayed, I realized there was no doubt I could no longer physically control my direction. Never had I felt so dispirited and defeated.

Chapter 49

Discouraging Days

After describing my symptoms to Dr. Northrup's nurse, she worked me into his busy schedule that afternoon. The internist examined me thoroughly, his face sober. He recommended I see a specialist right away and made the appointment in my presence.

An hour later, I found myself describing my symptoms again to an eminent neurologist chosen by Dr. Northrup.

"My dear girl," he said solemnly, "I want you in the hospital, immediately. I'll make arrangements for a bed."

As I listened to the specialist, I kept thinking, what was so wrong that I would have to go into a hospital? True, I had a problem performing his neurological testing. I did have great difficulty walking in a straight line and couldn't walk backwards at all. I had known something was wrong, but what was it?

I left the doctor's office very depressed. I needed to organize my household, putting additional responsibility on Whitney and Josie. Lynn and Gail, in their teens, would keep the house in order, make beds and simple meals. I would ask Ida Mae, Josie's wife, to cook the evening meal, do the laundry and help the girls with the ironing. She and Josie could eat with the children.

Whitney would be in charge of the horses, more than 150 of them, with Josie to share the responsibility. Besides me, realistically, Whitney had more knowledge of and interest in the animals.

I packed a small bag, then, with some effort, walked through the main barn pointing out stalls which needed policing, an accumulation of baling twine here, cobwebs and other housekeeping chores there.

"That's alright, Mom," Whitney assured me. "Joe and I will get it all done. Don't you worry."

I kissed everyone goodbye, tearfully. "Call me every day," I told them as they gathered at the garage to see me off.

Josie drove me to St. Boniface Hospital, fifteen miles away. At the door of the facility, I took my bag from him and urged him to hurry back to the farm where he was needed.

My first night in the hospital I could not sleep. My roommate was in her eighties. The nurses had restrained her in a little garment they called a posy. It kept her from getting out of bed and wandering. She was disoriented.

About three o'clock in the morning I had a strong urge to go to the bathroom. I knew I did not have the equilibrium to do this alone. I rang the bell and an aide helped me. I shared with her that I had been getting up at that hour for months, checking on my pregnant mares. It had become a habit. From then on, she called me Mrs. Horse-lady.

Back in bed, I became very confused. There were no mares to check on, but I thought there were. As I relived the memory of the last few days, I buried my face in the pillow, sobbing, as I remembered Wally's death.

I was suffering from homesickness. Once again I was a fearful. delicate child, struggling with the effects of illness, facing the unknown. This time I was on my own, without devoted parents and supportive Jim.

My specialist came early the next morning. He completed his examination, drawing fluid from my spinal cord for analysis. Later in the day he came back to my room. His face was grave as he sat on the edge of my bed. Taking my hand in his, he began, "Dear young woman, you have an incidious virus in your spinal cord fluid. We call it Guillain-Barre Syndrome. Not much is known about the illness. It is also called ascending paralysis. It's going to take some time for the nerves to heal. You probably were much sicker a month ago. You'll have to stay here several more weeks. There are some treatments including physical therapy. We must build up those foot and leg muscles."

It was a long statement, but I listened to every word, trying to retain control of my emotions. A couple of weeks was impossible. He couldn't begin to know my responsibilities at home. I protested, trying to explain why I couldn't be absent that long.

The neurologist would hear none of my protests and pleadings. "You fail to understand, my girl, you already show a degree of paralysis. If you do not follow my guidance, I cannot say what the outcome will be. You could sustain permanent damage to your central nervous system".

The next day I began extensive physical therapy. The little old lady had been moved to another room when I returned from my first treatment in the Hubbard tank. In a chair by the window sat a familiar figure, Father Mulvaney.

He jumped to his feet grasped my two hands and helped me out of the wheel chair. "Child!" he exclaimed, his voice warm with compassion,"Your poor little hands are as cold as ice!" He turned to the nurse. "Sister, he ordered, "do be getting a hot cup of tea for the little dear". Then he sat down in the armchair next to my bed.

We waited for each one of us to start the conversation. Father Tim finally began. "I stopped at the farm. Lynn told me about you," he hesitated, then continued almost inaudibly. "And about the mare." He blew his nose loudly, wiping his eyes with his handkerchief. "I was just telling the Bishop about Wally the other day. His Eminence wanted to see her extraordinary eyes for himself." Father Mulvaney paused to wipe his glasses again.

"Wally would have liked that," I answered. "To see the Bishop, I mean."

"Yes, I believe she would have."

We sat quietly a few more minutes, neither of us speaking until the floor nurse came to announce the end of visiting hours.

Father paused at the door and looked back at me. "I wish," he began, pausing as if he had changed his mind.

"Yes? What do you wish?" I gently prodded him.

"I wish the Bishop could have seen her, and you riding the mare. It was a fine sight," he said wistfully.

As he disappeared down the hospital corridor I fought to hold back tears. In my fragile condition I wondered if I would ride any horse again.

I did not go home for three weeks, and when I did I walked with a pronounced limp. There was another big difference, my golden blonde hair was silvery white.

I was in frail shape most of the summer, but anxious to help run the farm in any way I could. Whitney brought Dakotah saddled, every morning, to a spot under the maple tree by the back door. He dropped his reins in the grass where the horse waited patiently until I needed him.

Dakotah made the difference for me to participate in the farm routine. If I could find someone to press the calf of my left leg against Dakotah's side as I put my foot in the stirrup, I could mount without too much difficulty. However, if I lost the stirrup I was unable to put my own foot back into it. Control of the foot muscles was a long time coming back.

The blocky stock horse and I covered every inch of the farm together those next months. I rode out to see the progress of our crops and hay field, down to the mailbox, over to the rodeo arena, where I sat in the saddle, teaching some of the riding classes.

More than once, slipping down from the saddle after an afternoon's teaching, I thought how lucky I was to have the bull-dog quarter horse, so steady, so reliable. "Do" us, indeed! Dakotah "did us" as Jake Pike said he would, for all the years I had him.

At my next checkup the neurologist was encouraged by my progress. "I believe we've got it whipped!" he said, referring to the virus which had partially paralyzed me. "That numbness in your chest will be the last symptom to leave you. I don't know how long it will last but you are making fine headway." He shook his finger at me. "With your past medical history in mind I urge you not to overdo. Don't lift hay bales."

In addition to my health, there was another anxiety. The war in southeast Asia was accelerating. Whitney had come home from college to run the farm during my illness. His draft number had come up, and his records showed he was not in school.

We planned a farewell family dinner party for him and Dennis, who also had enlisted. They left for Vietnam together in different companies of the 5th Army.

I kept my somber thoughts to myself as I carried on the farm's responsibilities. My usually optimistic attitude could not erase a sense of foreboding which cast a shadow on our lives.

Chapter 50

Stewball: He Only Drank Wine

One spring morning a young woman drove into the yard. She had with her, three little girls, and a baby. She got out of the dark green station wagon slinging the baby over one hip. The little girls followed her. Their ages were between six and nine. Brushing a strand of coppery hair from her round, pleasant face, she asked, "Do you board ponies?" I looked at the children. They were hanging on my answer.

"Yes, I certainly do board ponies." My reply brought instant smiles.

"We've just won a pony at the Folk Festival in Arkansas," explained the enthusiastic mother.

"How old is he?" I inquired.

"They told me he's about two. We don't know a thing about ponies. At first we weren't going to take him, but you know how kids are."

I knew well. What child would turn down a pony? I boarded a few ponies besides our own in small box stalls in the corn crib. A pony could turn around in them. Each stall had a gate, grain feeder and water bucket. The young mother chose a stall near the doorway and the oldest of the three little girls asked, "Can we put up a sign with his name?"

"Sure," I replied, What is his name?" The children chorused in one voice, "Stewball! His name is Stewball!"

"My goodness, where did he get a name like that?" I asked, laughing.

"It's from a song sung at the Folk Festival," they said, and proceeded to sing in chorus, their mother chiming in with harmony.

"Oh, Stewball was a race horse, and I wish he was mine. He never drank water, he always drank wine. His bridle was silver. His mane, it was gold; And the worth of his saddle has never been told."

Three weeks later a battered old station wagon pulled into the yard. There were two teenage boys in the front seat. Both of them wore ragged straw hats and loud-colored shirts.

"Yar he be," said the boy behind the wheel, grinning as he spoke, "Yar he be. Right yar. War you want we should dump him?"

I approached the ancient vehicle and saw a large, wooden packing case in the back of the wagon. I bent over to get a better look and saw there was a small, russet-colored pony jammed inside the crate. Stewball had arrived.

The two Arkansas mountain boys lifted the crate from the station wagon to the ground. Josie went off for a wrecking bar and claw hammer to extricate the pony from imprisonment.

"Tell me, boys," I tried to keep my tone calm, "did this little pony travel all the way from Arkansas in this crate?" "Yup, sure did," one of the boys answered proudly. "We jest pushed him right in, nailed it shut, an he were as snug as a tick on a goat."

No more prophetic words were ever uttered! Josie, muttering disapproval over the way Stewball had been shipped, removed the last board. I felt a rising anger at the obvious ignorance that had almost caused the

pony's destruction. I remembered something Dr.
Prince had said often. "Most cruelty to animals is
caused by ignorance." We had a classic example in our
back yard.

The two boys took off in their rattle trap car,
heading for Chicago "jest to take a peek" as one of
them confided to the disapproving Josie.

With all the framing removed, a light tug on his
rope halter brought Stewball out of his portable prison.
Lynn had called his owners on the phone as soon as
the pony arrived. By the time we had him out of the
crate, the three little girls and their mother arrived.

Stiff, weak from riding hundreds of miles without
food or water, little Stewball could hardly stand. One
look at him convinced me he would need special care.
His coat was matted and caked with mud. There were
bare spots on his hide, suggesting to me a fungus
infection, probably ring worm. Upon closer inspection,
I saw his skin was infested with Arkansas ticks. These
parasites fasten themselves on sheep, cattle, horses and
dogs, living off their blood. To compound the sad
situation, Stewball had been recently castrated in a
crude, incomplete manner.

My heart went out to the pony. He was a sorry
sight. I enumerated to his new owners all the things
afflicting the pony. One of the little girls began to cry.
"Is he going to die?" she sobbed, putting her cheek
against the pony's neck.

"Honey," I cautioned her, "don't hug him until we
get those ticks out of his hide." I realized my anger at
the pony's condition made the children think they were
to blame for his sorry predicament. I had to remedy

that. "Come on kids. Let's all take care of Stewball," I said. "There's lots to be done and everyone can help. First, we're going to give him a good drink and some hay so he can be eating while we get set for the next job."

They were delighted to learn they could help me. One filled the water pail and Stewball drank it down. Another brought a flake of tender alfalfa from the wheelbarrow. While the starved pony nibbled away, his new family admired the way he chewed and swallowed. He pulled the tender grasses into his mouth with a little pink tongue. There was nothing wrong with his appetite.

After Stewball had eaten for half an hour, it was time for the frontal assault on the woe-be-gone creature. First, Gail helped me clip the pony from head to tail, removing his entire coat and mane with the electric clippers.

Exhausted from his journey, Stewball stood quietly, enduring the clippers loud, buzzing noise. The pony's shaved body exposed the ticks embedded in his chest, neck and mane.

After I dabbed the hateful parasites with alcohol which made them wriggle, I took hold of their tails with my tweezers, pulling them from the pony's hide. It was one of the most nauseous tasks I had ever undertaken, but necessary. I dropped the squirming ticks in a coffee can of kerosene. Later, we burned the crate, ticks and all, in the burning pile.

After the session with the ticks and because the weather was warm enough, we gave Stewball a bath with a disinfectant, iodine shampoo.

The children helped, taking off their red gym shoes and paddling around in the wet grass. They helped me rinse the pony too. Then we stepped back to survey our handiwork. We had a naked pony, but he was immaculate.

The next morning Dr. Prince came to take a look at Stewball. He shook his head when he saw the raw wound in his scrotum. "Some bird who clamps hogs did this job," he said caustically. Then, he tranquilized the pony, scrubbed his genitals, injected a local anesthetic, trimmed the wound and finished gelding the animal properly.

I've always been amazed by the speed with which hair grows back on a clipped horse or pony. Stewball was no exception. It wasn't long before he had reddish fuzz over his entire body. In a month it was long and luxurious.

The children took turns brushing him in the sunshine. They formed a production line, turning out an immaculate pony in twenty minutes. I suggested they wait several months until Stewball developed physical proportion to carry their weight for short periods of time.

Summer turned to fall and time for our Labor Day Horse Show, an event almost as well-attended by the public as our rodeos. One of the classes was original costume. My customers and other contestants came up with marvelous, innovative costumes. In the past, we had the Headless Horseman, Raggedy Ann and Andy, Indians and Knights in armor among the many other entries. One of the most imaginative was devised by a family who borrowed my pure white school horse,

Crystal. They hung a huge gold key on her side with a surgical strap as if she was a mechanical toy horse. Crystal won the class that year.

Stewball's family entered into the spirit of the festivities although no one knew what they were planning. Lynn reported she had their registration for costume class with their pretty little pony.

I was up in the announcer's stand when that class was announced, a vantage point from which to watch the horse show. As the costume class contestants passed the spectators on their way up the south side of the arena, I heard loud applause and looked down to see the entourage approaching.

Stewball's family were all in Elizabethan costume, painstakingly created by their ingenious mother. First came Mimi, dressed as a herald, her blonde hair tucked up into a black velvet beret, a white ostrich feather plume curling against her cheek: she wore a long-sleeve white satin shirt, bright blue breeches, and long white silk stockings. In her right hand, Mimi carried a replica of a medieval horn which she kept pressed against her mouth. Next came Becky, the oldest, seated side-saddle on Stewball. A white chiffon veil billowed from the tip of a high pointed whipple headdress and draped over the shoulders of her pale blue velvet gown.

The chestnut palfrey, minced along, escorted by Lisa dressed as a page in royal purple velvet. One hand resting on Stewball's scalloped white and gold reins. Like everyone else, I gasped at the authenticity. After the group passed the judges and lined up in the middle of the ring, I waited anxiously for the judge's decision. Finally, I heard the announcer saying, "Ladies and gentlemen, I am pleased to announce that the winners of the costume class are the Zwich family and Stewball." A roar of cheers and applause greeted the judge's decision.

Since I was to present the trophy, I hurried down the stairway, through the gate and into the arena where the ribbon girl was standing. She handed me the striking, goldtone trophy and I walked toward the winners. The children's faces were shining with pride. I reached out and placed my hand on Stewball's forehead, saying, "Stewball, I am so proud of you today."

Many Saturdays and Sundays, thereafter, we saw the group returning from other horseshows, the children screaming with joy from the car windows, wavlng still another trophy. Loose, in the back of the station wagon, swaying on all fours. surrounded by his adoring family, the veteran traveler, "Stewball . . . the race horse, and I wish he were mine, he never drank water, he always drank wine . . . "

248

Chapter 51

Avoidable Accidents

"Kneel on the pony's neck," Thad Prince said as he set about suturing Stewball's lacerated eyelid. The pony's eyes were closed, his lips drawn back exposing his upper teeth and gums.

"It's my fault," I blurted out, feeling the need to confess my negligence to someone. "I've seen that water pail with the jagged rim for a week in his stall. It would have only taken a minute to replace it."

Dr. Prince nodded his head. I felt his empathy. He skillfully passed the sutures through the folds of pink and grey eyelid tissue. "I'm using a new tranquilizer. Works quick; doesn't keep them out too long. Hardly any after effects. Developed in Germany, I believe." He continued to stitch, pausing from time to time to swab the wound with a gauze pad.

I knelt on Stewball's muscular neck with one knee, pressing down with my right hand on the pony's muzzle. I felt sick with remorse. It was my responsibility to recognize hazards around the barns.

"This should close up well. Shouldn't even be a hairline scar," Dr. Prince said optimistically, stitching through a fold of eyelid skin. "There, we've got it now." He snipped the last suture. "Do believe he's coming round. You'd best get up. I'll let go of his head."

Indeed, Stewball was coming out of the anesthesia. No sooner I stood up, he scrambled to his feet, a bit wobbly but looking much like his usual self.

The veterinarian handed me a small tube. "Put some of this ointment on the incision a couple times daily. I'll be back in a few days to take out the stitches."

I led Stewball back to his stall in the corn crib and threw him a flake of hay, unhooked the damaged water pail and threw it in the garbage can. Next, I walked throughout all the barns checking the galvanized buckets. I found two with sharp edges and replaced them.

I still felt guilty and remorseful. The avoidable accident bothered me. Would I, I wondered, ever be on top of everything, with enough experience to handle all emergencies, those avoidable and those unavoidable?

I got in the habit of looking for damaged water pails as I conducted visitors on a tour of the barns.

"Would you like to see a real Indian pony?" I asked the attentive group of eight-year-old Brownies. We paused outside of Redwing's stall. "The American Plains Indian prized the flamboyant coat- pattern of the pinto horse highly," I said, sliding back the door to Redwing's stall. "Indians chose these sturdy horses because they are small enough for a warrior to vault onto, bareback."

Stepping inside the box stall, I reached my right hand for the colorful pinto's halter. Suddenly, I felt an excruciating pain in the left side of my neck and shoulder. Redwing, awakened from a sound sleep by my presence, without warning, had lunged defensively like lightning, clamping his vise-like jaw on my throat. Senseless with pain, I fell against the stall's rough planking, sliding to the floor, unmindful of the wood slivers piercing my gingham shirt.

Redwing, recognizing me, released his grip and stood trembling in the back of his stall. On the floor and partially hidden by the half open door, I pulled myself to my feet. Fortunately, the children had not seen the horse's assault on me. My high-collared western shirt hid the massive bruise already forming.

I could hardly swallow. I offered an excuse for leaving the barn and turned the rest of the tour over to Lynn who, at that moment, entered the barn.

Somehow I managed to walk through the row of busy boarders brushing their horses on crossties in the aisle and out into the sunshine, to the house.

Once in my bedroom, I unbuttoned my shirt and pulled it down over my shoulder. It felt as though there should be a gaping wound. An ugly, purple, mottled bruise was forming. It extended from my collar bone to under my left ear. The pain was excruciating. The shock and fright of the horse's brutal attack had left me weak and trembling.

There was the sound of footsteps in the hall. A horrified Gail stood in the doorway. "What happened, Mom? What happened!" She gasped at the sight of my shoulder.

Between sobs I told her, "Redwing bit me. He was asleep. I should have known better than to waken him suddenly. Pulling myself together, I asked her to drive me to the doctors. "It's a horse bite and that is nothing to ignore."

The internist's waiting room was full of patients. However, the nurse put me in an examining room immediately. The pain nauseated me. My arm throbbed from shoulder to wrist. Finally, our family doctor, Dr. Northrup, entered the room to examine me. "You're God damn lucky the horse didn't crush your windpipe," he said. That sobering thought made me cry again. He explained the nerves had been squeezed and crushed. He gave me a tetanus booster and applied a topical anesthetic ointment and gauze dressing to my neck.

For three weeks I literally sat up in bed at night, sleeping fitfully. It was two more weeks before I could turn my head from right to left.

Poor Redwing! The episode caused him to be ostracized and black- balled by our customers and this didn't change until they saw me riding him two months after the accident.

Shortly thereafter, I sold him to a lady with whom he had been very popular as a school horse and she moved him to another stable. Of course, I told her about my experience and she said, "It was your own fault." And, so it was.

In spite of this traumatic incident it proved not to be my last horse bite.

Chapter 52

A Dubious Distinction

It remained the only stall in the barn not fully enclosed. A seven-foot galvanized water tank stood in front of the 2X10 planks. Diamond and her filly were in the double-size foaling stall. The mare eating hay, her foal lipping green alfalfa leaves in between nursing. I stood watching them, my right arm resting full length on the sill.

Gail was approaching the tank with one of the school horses after giving a riding lesson. Sturdy Thunder lowered his head to drink, when, like a serpent striking, Diamond lunged toward him, protecting her offspring. The mare caught my little finger between her upper teeth and the 2X10s like a trap.

The pain was agonizing. I thought I would faint. Surely I had lost the finger! A second passed before I made myself look at my mutilated right hand.

Gail, horrified, reacted quickly. She clipped Thunder to a chain crosstie and rushed to put her arms around me. "Oh, Mom," she said, her compassionate brown eyes filling with tears. "Not again! Please, not again!"

Once more I found myself in Dr. Northrup's examining room. "Young woman! Those horses of yours are lethal," Dr. Northrup commented tersely as he surveyed my mangled finger. I turned my head away at the sight of the bloody, shapeless mass.

"We've got to get you to a surgeon, right away. Wouldn't surprise me if you lose the finger," the doctor stated glumly, shaking his head. He picked up the phone, dialing an associate and told him he was sending me right over, then he applied a temporary gauze bandage.

The orthopedic specialist stated flatly, "You'll lose your nail, for sure, and probably never grow another one. If we can't control infection you may lose the finger," He splinted and bandaged my lacerated pinky. "Stay out of those barns. Observe the utmost care re-dressing your hand. See me in a week, we'll know a lot more by then."

Stay out of the barns! How could I do that with so much work to do. I continued to feed and water but did not push my luck with cleaning stalls.

Lynn set up a tray of necessaries on the counter on the kitchen, hydrogen peroxide, bandages, scissors, all covered by a clean tea towel. Daily, she skillfully changed the dressing, flushing the wound with stinging, cleansing peroxide, then a liberal application of the miraculous healing salve, White's A and D ointment. She taped a splint over the gauze bandage. At my suggestion, she extended the splint three inches beyond the tip of the finger so I continued to work with some degree of protection every day. The only thing I could not do was drive the tractor. I tried, but the splint kept getting caught in the steering wheel.

Four weeks later the doctor removed the splint and bulky protective bandages. He replaced them with a small dressing over which I wore a soft goat's skin glove.

For a year, if I bumped my finger, pain shot all the way to my shoulder. In zero weather the finger throbbed and ached painfully.

I did not lose my finger, in itself some kind of a miracle. I had earned the dubious distinction of being an authority on horse bites.

Lynn began talking about entering nurse's training.

Chapter 53

Never, Never, Never Again

The overweight, balding young man ran breathlessly toward me in the parking area. He blurted out in short gasps, "Am I too late? Are the others gone? Have you a horse for me?"

Indeed, most of my horses were at the parade except for the ponies and Red, the blocky sorrel gelding I had bought from the Pikes that spring.

Jess Pike had told me what he knew about Red's background. He had belonged to a retired Chicago policeman and had a repertoire of circus tricks. A placid creature, he fit well in the school horse band.

"Were you here for the practice session with the rest of the village officials last week?" I asked the eager village trustee. I had given the officials a riding lesson, and showed them a few pointers on handling the horse's mouths.

"No, I wasn't, but I know how to ride," he replied, wiping his perspiring face.

"It's a very hot day. You'll have to take it easy with this horse," I said, as I beckoned him to follow me to the equipment room. I looped Red's headstall over my left shoulder and walked to the paddock.

The big red horse raised his head from the hay manger and looked me right in the eye long and steady. I felt a moment's hesitation as I slipped the bit into his mouth and raised the crown band over his alert ears. He submissively lowered his head. Because of my splinted finger I was clumsy and slow saddling him.

When I had Red saddled, I held the "off" stirrup so the pudgy rider would not loosen the saddle while mounting up.

Again, I admonished him not to run the horse in trying to catch up with other village officials and the parade.

The exertion of saddling Red with the cumbersome bandages and splint on my right hand had tired me out. I got a soft drink from the vending machine and sat down on the cover of the water trough. The barns were so quiet.

Refreshed, I swept the long barn aisle and raked dry bedding into the middle of some of the boarders empty stalls. It was one of those rare times when I was alone on the farm. I could luxuriate in three hours to myself before everyone returned from the parade. How I used the time was up to me.

As I passed the extension phone, it rang shrilly. I recognized the voice of one of the Village Police Reserve officers.

"Mrs. K," he stammered. "There's been an accident to one of your horses. He had a heart attack and dropped right in his tracks."

"Oh my God. Which one was it?" I asked fearfully.

"Don't know his name, he was the big reddish one at the end of the parade," he explained, still stammering.

"Oh no! Not poor old Red," I said, breaking into tears.

I hung up the receiver, turned and stared into Red's empty paddock. I felt the horse had been trying to tell me something that morning when I bridled him. How guilty I felt!

The rumble of a heavy vehicle on the gravel broke into my thoughts. I splashed a handful of water from the sill-cock by the barn, on my flushed face, wiped my tears with the tail of my cotton shirt and turned to meet the disposal truck as it swung into the back yard.

Poor Red was in the rear bin, his four feet sticking straight up in the air. I bit my lip to keep it from quivering in front of the burly scavengers.

"Where do you want him?" the brawny driver asked, a suggestion of amusement on his florid face.

I pointed to a grassy spot behind the indoor arena. The scavangers had brought extra manpower. I couldn't watch them unload Red.

When they drove away I walked over and looked at him. His massive frame seemed to be shrinking before my eyes. Swarms of horseflies were worrying his head and partially closed eyelids.

Sweating and straining with one hand, I dragged a waterstained tarp to the horse and covered him with it. It was Sunday. There was no chance the rendering company would come to pick up Red until sometime Monday.

That night I did not sleep. I kept visualizing the old horse lying out there in the darkness under the shabby tarpaulin. I remembered his reproachful look as I bridled him.

My suppressed anger was directed as much at myself as toward the paunchy rider who had literally run the horse into the ground. It was the last time I loaned my horses for any parade in Prairie Grove.

Chapter 54

The Phone Call

Whitney had been gone a month. Every time the phone rang, these days, my heart beat faster. This time, I was at the barn. I leaned the push broom against the front of Sammy's stall and hurried into the adjoining storage room and lifted the receiver.

A woman's voice asked, "Just where are you located anyhow? We've been trying to deliver a telegram to you since yesterday afternoon." I told her our address and how to get there. Almost as an afterthought I inquired, "Who is the wire from?"

She hesitated. "I'm not supposed to give you any information over the phone. It must be delivered to you in person." Then, she lowered her voice, as if someone might be listening. "It's about your son. The telegram is from the Adjutant General," she whispered.

"My God! Tell me!" I pleaded, "Is he dead?" The blood had rushed to my head. My heart was pounding as if I had been running up hill. I could hardly breath. I clutched the partition which held the wall phone. The voice on the other end of the phone spoke almost inaudibly, "He's been hurt," then, hurriedly she added, "I can't tell you anymore. We'll deliver the telegram right away."

I don't know how I got back to the house. My legs like rubber, I was stunned and unable to cry. Maybe there was a mistake I told myself, but when the man from Western Union handed me the telegram all the statistics were accurate. Whitney's full name and serial number were correct. There was no mistake.

The girls and I huddled together on the couch reading the message over and over through our tears. How little it told us.

"The Secretary of the Army has asked me to express his deep regret that your son, Whitney C. Kloman, was placed on the seriously ill list, in Vietnam on February 28th, 1969. As the result of a head injury. Exploration of right frontal scalp wound was performed. He was crew chief on a military aircraft, when aircraft crashed but did not burn. In the judgement of the attending physician his condition is of such severity that there is cause for concern."

"Isn't there someone we can call?" Gail was the first one to regain some degree of composure.

I tried to think. Possibly 5th Army Headquarters would have some information. Calling the base number, I got through to a Sergeant who gave me a toll free number in Washington where medical bulletins were posted regularly and the information was available to family members. It became our one contact with Whitney. The Army personnel who manned those phones must have spoken with thousands of mothers and fathers. They were always patient: often very kind.

I felt I had to get off by myself to think. I drove down the winding shortcut to old St. Martha's Church. There was no one there. I knelt in one of the worn pews in the back, the flickering vigil lights cast dim light on the lifesize marble replica of "La Pieta". The sight of the prostrate figure of the dead Christ in His mother's arms moved me to uncontrolled weeping.

I felt a hand on my shoulder. It was Father Mulvaney. I had not heard him walk up to me. His eyes were full of tears as he said very softly, "I'm saying a Mass for Whitney tomorrow morning at eight o'clock."

I don't know how long I sat there. It seemed to me I was seeing the interior of the church for the first time. My eyes traveled up the gothic arches to the stained glass windows, dedicated in memory of ancestors of families I knew so well, Ruebner, Rowe and so many other good people among whom I lived in this farming community. It was a comfort to be in the atmosphere where they worshipped. Many knew Whitney. He had helped Uncle Harvey Ruebner one summer when the old man was short-handed. Lester Rowe drove Whitney to school every day for six years. They all showed concern and kindness through the long days and nights Lynn, Gail and I waited for further news from Vietnam.

It was dusk by the time I passed through the vestibule of the old church. On my left was a small plaque and photograph of a boy who had lost his life in the second World War. The inscription, "In loving memory" cut deep into my heart. His sisters and I had such loving memories of Whitney.

A number of customers and friends attended the early Mass the next morning. When he came to the part in the service when the priest announces from the altar for whom the Mass is being said, Father Mulvaney, his hands clasped, head bowed, said aloud, "The services are offered for the recovery of General

Dwight David Eisenhower and Specialist 4th Class, Whitney C. Kloman."

Father Mulvaney was standing in the church doorway after Mass. He pressed my hand and said, "They are all equal in the sight of Almighty God." The thought was a comfort to me.

The daily routine of the farm was a blessing. Caring for the livestock was a distraction for all of us and helped to pass the days. Nights were a horror. Often I did not sleep at all. Lynn was working at the checkout register at the drug store, helping to pay for her Nurse's Training tuition. Gail was in her first year at the University.

Whenever they saw my light on, the girls brought a tray to my room with a sandwich or soup. None of us had any appetite. Meals were sketchy. All three of us sitting on my double bed, surrounded by the sympathetic cats, talking far into the night hours.

We wrote long letters to Whitney, not knowing if he would ever receive them. We hid our anxiety from each other, the constant fear that Whitney would not survive. To each other we spoke optimistically of the plans when he finally came home. Sometimes we just sat there in silence without speaking, in the semi-darkness. My little bedside lamp shone on the writing paper portfolio and the untouched sandwiches.

A week passed and then another wire came, telling us Whitney had been evacuated to a Military Hospital in Japan. There was some scrambling of Whitney's name and serial number, but with the help of the overseas operator I got through to the ward and spoke to a staff doctor. He said Whitney was still in a coma, but alive. Our hopes grew stronger.

Three more weeks passed when the word came that Whitney had been transferred by air to a military hospital a half hour from his home.

It was a cold, drizzling March day when the girls and I drove to the Naval Hospital. The wind off the choppy water blew sheets of rain against us as we walked from the parking lot to the main entrance. We didn't notice the rain drenching us. We were so elated that we were going to see Whitney.

The corpsman at the information desk directed us to the elevators. The ride up to the eighth floor seemed to take forever.

Finally, the elevator doors opened. Ahead of us a small sign which read Neurological ward 8 South. As we stepped out of the elevator. I could see wards stretching out in three directions. I was not prepared for row after row of beds, each with its casualty. There was a tiny American Flag at the head of each bed. A few steps further, we stood at the nurses station of Eight South. The head nurse pointed to the right side of the ward and said, "Sixth bed on the right."

I felt myself moving as if in a trance. My eyes took in the grim picture of boys on the left side of the ward, most of them motionless. These boys had been severely mortared. Few would ever move or speak again. I suppressed my tears as each of the girls took an elbow and hurried me around the partition dividing the ward. On that side of the ward, most of the boys were sleeping, a few reading, one or two playing cards.

Then I saw him! He was sitting on the edge of his hospital bed, his long legs barely covered by a skimpy blue and white striped seersucker hospital robe. His head shaven, he was completely bald. There was a large, spongy mass of swollen tissue, the size of a grapefruit, creased with a purple incision, on his forehead.

When he saw us he grinned, and raised a hand weakly in greeting. There was not a tooth in the front of his mouth.

We hugged and kissed him, bombarding him with questions. He didn't answer, but kept grinning and hugging us. Then, the boy in the next bed put down his comic book and said in a southern drawl, "Mam, he can't talk. Your son I mean. He understands what you all are saying, but he can't talk."

With a shattering realization, I suddenly knew why Whitney was in the neurological ward. He had suffered brain damage! He had lost his ability to speak and his memory was impaired. The black rings around his eyes, spreading down his cheeks, indicated the severity of internal hemorrhage in the frontal lobe of his brain. The hospital staff and fellow patients called him the "Panda".

In time we learned the details of the accident: how he had been pinned under the helicopter, that a tracheotomy was performed in the field by the medics, which saved his life, for he had vomited the contents of his stomach into his lungs. He had very little lung capacity for a long time. His right shoulder and hand were broken, but he was alive. We could see and touch him!

My first consultation with the doctors came before visiting hours were over. The neurologist looked me straight in the eye and said, at that moment there was no way of evaluating the degree of recovery we might expect. He said there would be surgery for the hand and shoulder, but above all,rest so the brain tissue could recover. He would require speech therapy. The neurologist also thought in a few weeks he would allow Whitney to come home from Friday afternoon to Monday morning. The doctor hoped his home environment might help him regain speech.

Lynn, Gail and I took turns during those eleven months, one of us at every visiting hour, day or evening, at the hospital. Improvement was very slow. Since he was six feet six inches tall, his height presented problems in coordination and balance. He moved with a staggering, shuffling gait.

In early May, he came home for his first weekend. The horses were down on the pasture. As we drove up the lane to the farm, Whitney put his hand on my arm, indicating he wanted to be driven closer to the horses.

I turned the car onto a strip of farm road which ran next to the pasture. Taking his arm, we walked toward the horses. Several of them came over to the fence and we patted their necks and I heard Whitney's voice. His speech was slurred and halting, but it was clear to me he asked, "Where's Big Boy?"

When I called the big bay to us, Whitney said his name over and over. The doctor had been right. Familiar sights had stimulated his ability to speak.

That first night home, Lynn, Gail and I tiptoed many times into Whitney's room and stood by his bed.

He was in a deep sleep, his shorn head against the floral pillowcase, lips parted, showing his missing teeth and the misshapen, swollen forehead. We bent over him, studying his shallow breathing, to be sure he was alive.

Although hospitalized almost a year, that first summer found him propped up on the hay wagon in the sunshine or sitting on the lawn with the dogs, Stuart and Ashley. As he grew stronger he was able to sit and run the spigots to fill the five water tanks in the main barn, watching them carefully, to see they did not overflow. Later, he took a lot of satisfaction in sweeping the long barn aisle clear of sawdust and hay particles. The effort tired him quickly and sent him back to the lawn chair for a long nap.

In time, there would be surgery for the useless arm and shoulder, ongoing speech therapy, always the threat of frequent, severe, debilitating headaches. Some tremor in the extremities would never leave him. His sisters and I everlastingly grateful, remembering those boys in the wards who were not so fortunate and those who would never come home from Vietnam.

Gradually, after he was discharged from the hospital, he began to help with lighter chores. He was comfortable with the livestock, his anxiety diminished. His dream of flying for a commercial airline set aside, forever.

Chapter 55

Sister Mary Bridget Mahoney

About three o'clock on a Monday afternoon when the farm was closed to the public, I saw a figure crossing the lawn toward me as I stood filling the bird feeder.

My visitor approached me briskly, her long black wool skirt and diaphanous veil billowing out behind her, the late afternoon sun rays glancing off the silver cross on her breast. Behind wireless glasses, merry blue eyes sparkled with delight.

Suddenly I found myself enveloped in a warm, tight hug as my visitor exclaimed in her musical Irish brogue, "Sure! and I've come to see your blessed horses!" Sister Mary Bridget Mahoney had arrived.

For all her seventy-eight years, I could hardly keep up with her as together we crossed the yard toward the barns, Sister moving with long energetic strides. As we stepped inside the main barn filled with horses, Sister Bridget grabbed my arm. Her face, framed by her white coif, glowed with anticipation. She peered into my face and whispered, "Sure, and isn't it the grandest smell in the world?"

Walking down the long aisle, we stopped in front of each stall. I was amazed at the nun's knowledge of horses. She pointed out to me the differences in each breed. The broad jaw. muscular chest and hindquarters of the quarter horses, the dished profile and short back of an Arabian, the slender legs, long neck and powerful hindquarters of a thoroughbred. Quite possibly Sister was the most informed individual ever to visit Arcadia Farm.

"This fellow's a rogue," she commented. The Appaloosa, rolling his human eye, tossed his head in defiance making a tangle of his sparse mane.

"I look deep in their eyes," Sister Bridget remarked. "He wants to have a good run."

She wanted to know each horse's name, their good points and to whom they belonged. Standing in front of a gray half-Arab mare, Sister became enthusiastic. "This one's a pet! See how she holds her head and looks you straight in the eye." Moving along the barn aisle, she praised the brood mare with the chestnut foal by her side. "What a love!" she cooed tenderly, stroking the usually shy filly under her jaw. The filly had come right up to Sister Bridget as she stood in the doorway. "Ah! You little darlin'," she murmured, kissing the white star on the filly's forehead.

The love the Irish express for the horse is considered to be a national characteristic along with their love of the land and music. This affinity is not easily described, but I understand it for I have Irish roots. My grandmother was a Doherty.

Near us, kneeling on the cement aisle, Whitney was flushing a small wound on a gelding's knee with hydrogen peroxide. Sister Bridget walked toward him, leaned over his shoulder to get a better look at the knee and placed her hand on Whitney's bowed head, saying, "Sure, and this fellow's a saint! Isn't he a grand one?" My son grinned at her unexpected praise, never having considered his ministrations to the horses qualified him for sainthood.

It was close to feeding time. Whitney began to break hay bales in the barn aisle. Sister Bridget insisted on helping. She enthused over the bright hay and plump oats which she scooped into each feeder. I watched her entranced, listening to her cajoling.

"Come here to Bridget, love. Don't be hangin' back," she said, coaxing a timid mare to the front of her stall. "That's a fine girl you are."

The nun was oblivious to the hay particles clinging to her veil and habit as she dragged her long skirt through accumulations of sawdust and shavings on the cement aisle. Feeding and watering in the main barn which ordinarily took thirty minutes took an hour, for Sister Bridget seemed lost in a special time, lingered by each stall, reluctant to close its door.

Later, passing the equipment room, she walked toward the row of saddles, stroking the bridles with her gnarled fingers and confessed, "I do so love the smell of harness leathers!"

Once back in my house after our tour of the barns, seated in rockers opposite each other in the family room, Sister Bridget regaled me with stories about the horses at the Mother House in Wisconsin. As a young novice, the horses had been her responsibility along with the hens and the kitchen garden. Her favorite was a horse she had named Buddy.

"He was a rambunctious one, that one was," she confided. "Kicked the very divil out of the box wagon when the other sisters drove him to the vegetable garden with plants or tools." She threw back her head laughing at the special memory.

"But he niver kicked when I had him in hand," she boasted. "That horse was a love, fairly a love. Twas I who saw the twinkle in his eyes. Bored to death he was, doin' simple chores, but I changed that, I can tell you. He and I would fairly gallop up and down the dirt road leading to the convent. I just let him be havin' his head. Horses got to run or they store up all that pep and mischief until it just explodes."

Sister Bridget sipped her tea and continued with what I recognized as a prized recollection.

"Reverend Mother thought for sure I'd be after gettin' me neck broke and worse, but the runnin' worked like a charm. Buddy settled down and hauled the bedding plants to the garden without anymore divilment."

One entertaining story followed another. She related how her enthusiasm for horses had found an outlet when she became involved with the Wild Horse Association." She told me she solicited everyone she met to send a check for the preservation of the wild horse bands.

I was fascinated to learn that Sister Bridget had made a trip to Nevada and stayed with Velma Johnston herself. Mrs. Johnston, best known as "Wild horse Annie". While in Nevada, Sister witnessed the birth of a foal in Annie's garage, the mare recovering from a leg injury. "Sat myself right down on the floor by the two of them," she said. "I held the little pet in me arms 'till she nursed, that old mare touchin' me veil ever so gently with her nose."

The nun's face alight with the special memory, she continued. "It was grand to see them, just grand. Annie named the filly, Bridget. Wasn't that lovely?"

I agreed it was. Captivated by my visitor's tale, I offered her another piece of pound cake and inquired, "Did you see the wild horse herds?"

"Did I see the horses?" Sister's face became pink with emotion. "I can tell you yes, indeed! I saw them twice. Annie took me up on the high ground, driving her old jeep. We drove about an hour, then I climbed over rocks to the rim of a canyon, and right there below us on the canyon floor was about forty of them!"

Sister Bridget became more animated. "I can tell you it was some sight, the thrill of me life to see 'im right before me own eyes. Sure and it was grand!"

Helping herself to another piece of pound cake, she leaned forward toward me as if to share a confidence and asked, "Did you know there are fifty or more places in the Bible that horses are mentioned?"

I hadn't known that and said so. Sister continued sipping her tea, and then inquired, "Have you ever read chapter thirty-nine in the Book of Job?" I shook my head. "Do you have a Bible?" she asked.

That I did have. I got up from my rocker and went to the book shelf and handed her the American Standard Edition. The nun set her teacup on the table and began to leaf through the pages.

She leaned back in her chair balancing the Bible on her knee, saying, "I'll be reading from chapter thirty-nine, verses nineteen through thirty." Then she began to laugh roguishly. "That Job! Didn't he have a nerve about him, questioning God Almighty?"

I was entranced by the richness and drama in her voice as she began to read in her expressive Irish brogue.

> *Do you give the horse his might?*
> *Do you cloth his neck with a mane?*
> *Do you make him leap like a locust?"*
> *His majestic snorting is terrible*
> *He paws in the valley and rejoices in his*
> *strength.*

Sister was no longer reading from the text, but was reciting the familiar verses by heart.

> *He laughs at fear and is not dismayed.*

"Ah, I love this part!" Sister exclaimed, sitting erect on the edge of the rocker, speaking faster, caught up in the imagery of a battlefield.

> *And he does not turn back from the sword.*
> *The quiver rattles against him.*

Sister Bridget drew a deep breath as though to fortify herself for the powerful verses to follow.

> *The flashing spear and javelin*
> *With shaking and rage he races over the*
> *ground;*
> *And he does not stand still at the voice of*
> *the trumpet.*
> *As often as the trumpet sounds he says*

Ha!
And he scents the battle from afar,
And thunder of the captains and the war
cry.

My visitor stopped speaking, set down the Bible and picked up her teacup which I had refilled. Her face was flushed with emotion.

"Isn't it grand poetry?" she asked. "Just grand! I love the part, 'he laughs at fear.' I be thinkin' of all the great calvary engagements like Balaclava and Gettysburg."

"And like Waterloo!" I chimed in.

"Yes, yes!" she nodded her head vigorously. "Like Waterloo."

A tap at the door signaled they had come to take her back to the residence. Sister rose to her feet and hugged me warmly, saying, "What a grand time I've had . . . just lovely. Besides seeing the Holy Father, me next choice would be to see some horses!"

During the next five years I visited Sister Bridget at the Order's convalescent home. She was always deeply involved in a project. If it wasn't the wild horses, it was making dozens of rosaries for the Missions.

She was wistful when I told her I had retired, sold the farm and moved into town.

Wiping tears from her eyes, she blew her nose loudly and consoled me with just the right words. "Sure and you must be fair heartbroken not to have your darlin' horses anymore." She understood as few did.

On a wintry day in March 1989 I attended Sister Mary Bridget's funeral. The frail assembly gathered in the simple chapel. There was a Mass and several familiar hymns. The priest spoke as though he had known Sister Bridget well, commenting on her keen wit, humanity and goodness. Then, best of all, as far as I was concerned, he spoke of her love for horses. Taking a few steps toward the altar rail, he opened a Bible and read aloud Sister's favorite passage from the thirty-ninth chapter, Book of Job. She would have been pleased.

After the service, driving home through icy snow squalls, I found myself thinking about the nun's first visit to the farm and how it had deepened my appreciation for the horses. That day, so long ago, I had learned through Sister Mary Bridget Mahoney, who indeed *had given the horse his courage, taught him to answer the call of the trumpet, and to laugh at fear!*

Chapter 56
The Long Night

It was early March 1970, at five-thirty in the morning. A dense fog enshrouded the entire farm. I could hear the measured split- splat from drops of moisture dripping from pine needles and limbs of the old elms. In addition to heavy fog, a smoky mist, caused by the warmth from the horse's bodies, rose from the roof of the barn. Twenty-two small windows on the east side of the barn cast their saffron light. The snow had melted after a night's continuous rain. Large patches of ice remained.

I picked my way carefully over the ice, through the fog, toward the dim outline of the barn. I recalled passing other farms when it was still dark, and thinking about farmers caring for their stock in dimly lit barns.

The families living in five hundred houses across the road were not there when I bought Arcadia Farm twenty years ago. At this early hour they were sleeping. The only visible light was at the door of the community well across the road. No one saw my lights or wondered why I was up at such an early hour. The fog was too thick and murky.

Worried, I was up checking on the chestnut mare, Ginger, a boarder. She had a freak accident the day before, shoving her tiny hoof between the stall door and sill. She had torn ligaments in her ankle. Following Dr. Roper's advice, we soaked her ankle in warm water and Epsom salts, and led her for short walks in the barn aisle, hoping to soon put her right. There was however, an eerie resemblance to past fog and circumstances. Misfortunes had happened before in the early hour fog, drizzle and silence.

There was tragedy in the barn again. I would never forget the horse Ralph, although I long since forgot the name of the teenager who owned him. We found the brown and white paint at morning feeding time, his head twisted against the stall planking in a tortured position. His eyes, though open, were glazed and expressionless. Blood-flecked foam oozed from his lips. Dr. Roper said his neck vertebra were probably ruptured.

How had this terrible thing happened? We had always tied Ralph's hay feeder far above where he could entangle his feet in it. His young, inexperienced owner had taken more hay later that evening, and rehung the rope feeder where Ralph could get his front hooves caught in it. The horse had fallen in his straight stall, injuring himself, critically.

It took Whitney, and Dr. Roper, with the help of Josie and Chase Harper, to move Ralph to a box stall. First, they took down a partition, making enough room to roll the horse's hindquarters onto a tarpaulin. Next, we pulled the tarp into a large foaling stall. Dr. Roper tried to make the horse comfortable by injecting him with a painkiller and a sedative.

He was not optimistic, telling us, "You folks will have to turn the poor fellow over, every hour, night and day, so his lungs won't fill with fluid."

"We'll do it, Doc," Whitney assured him.

It was a job, though two people could do it. Whitney and I grasped the horse's leg farthest away, rocking him back and forth with increased momentum, until he rolled over. We did it all day, the boy and his father anxiously watching with strained tense faces. Eventually they learned the technique and we took turns.

As the horse struggled to breath, bloody froth from the horse's dilated nostrils stained my bare forearm. The moist, March air in the barn was heavy with the rancid odor of urine and fecal matter seeping from the horse's prostrate carcass. I felt the heat of his feverish body through my clothes as I soberly attended to my responsibility, sitting on his shoulder to keep him from injuring himself further.

As the sedative wore off, the poor creature thrashed about and tried to gallop while lying on his side. This was a frightening thing to see. Keeping out of the way of his flying hooves, Whitney sat on his shoulder and I on his neck. We discovered when Ralph was on his left side he hardly moved at all, did no galloping or thrashing about. His brain injury was to that part that controlled the left side.

We rested while the horse lay still. Only his closed eyelids twitched. Great, deep sighs came from his shattered frame. The four of us stayed with Ralph all night, the teenager cradling the dying horse's head in his slender arms. Throughout the long vigil I walked up and down the aisle to stretch my legs. Passing Honey's stall I noticed the gray barn cat asleep on the mare's rump. The other horses were lying down sleeping.

At dawn there was a dense fog and fine drizzling rain. Dr. Roper arrived at five-thirty. He examined Ralph soberly, confirming his original diagnosis, the horse's condition was hopeless.

The boy sobbed uncontrollably. His father put his arms around him and led him from the barn. Heartbroken, the young owner buried his tearstained face against his father's shoulder. I heard his anguished, muffled sobs. "Oh Ralph! Poor Ralph!"

As Dr. Roper hunched over the horse I looked away. I was unable to watch him insert the needle into the animal's neck. When I looked again the doctor was returning the syringe to his medical bag. The struggle was over, but I felt a deep sadness.

Once again I asked myself, did you ever imagine owning a horse facility would plunge you into these traumas, over and over again? Nowhere had I read or heard of the frustration, anguish and tears which went hand in hand with caring for a large number of horses. The saying, "Horses are more prone to injury than illness," had become for me a viable truth and those who care for them are as prone to grief as to joy.

Chapter 57

Goodbye, Good Fella

Although the joys were many, my heartaches were never quite over. In 1974, Sammy, our Appaloosa stud, in his high twenties, showed signs that his health was failing. He seldom came to his door looking for the carrot I usually brought him. I would find him sleeping in the daytime as if he were dreaming of better days. Sammy was the sire of my sturdy colts and fillies. When the young horses were weanlings, yearlings or two-year-olds, I had been able to sell them and often make boarders out of them as well, adding to my monthly income. He surely contributed to our financial security.

The stallion was a dividend in other ways, too. There in the barn aisle in front of his stall, hundreds of times I told the school children on field trips, stories about the Appaloosa, the war horse of the Nez Perce. My attentive audiences were captivated by Sammy's size and colorful coat, but most of all by his presence and manners. The children understood when I described him as a gentleman. Having owned a horse like Sammy who contributed so much to our lives, it was sad to contemplate parting with him.

Dr. Roper examined him carefully, listening to his tired old heart with his stethoscope. "He is getting feeble," he said.

Dr. Prince, also examining him, shook his head. "He is not happy."

Together, we made the decision to put him down, that totally descriptive expression used to signify putting a horse to sleep.

I told Lynn and Gail the decision I had reached about Sammy. We talked about the kind of a day it should be. A perfect autumn day, one of warm sunshine and moderate temperature, a day to soften sadness. Lynn, by that time a registered nurse and married, drove to the farm with Gail, then in graduate school at the University.

I left them alone with the stallion. They found the same little chores to do for him as when they were little girls. One filled his water pail, the other raked dry shavings into the center of his stall. As I stood outside the stallion barn I heard them offer phrases of encouragement to him. "That's a good boy. Move over, good fellow." A short time afterwards they walked past me, brushing tears from their eyes, and drove away without looking back. Now, all the family had shared in the decision.

The day we chose was November 4th, 1974. Jeff Roper came early in the morning. I watched Whitney walk up the barn aisle to get Sammy. I remembered how young he had been when the stallion had first come to Arcadia Farm. Now, Whitney was a towering man with a full red beard. He walked down the barn aisle into the brilliant sunshine, his right arm draped over Sammy's neck as one might walk with an arm around the shoulder of a well-loved friend.

At the arena door, the two paused a moment, waiting for me. I could barely see Sammy through my tears. I reached up and straightened the blue nylon

halter on Sammy's broad jaw. Then, the two of them
passed through the arena door and out of sight. I knew
the veterinarian was waiting patiently, his medical kit
open and at his feet.

After Sammy was gone, although still filled with
horses, the barn never seemed quite the same to me. It
was months before I could pass Sammy's stall without
imagining I heard the silvery flute- like tone of his
whinny.

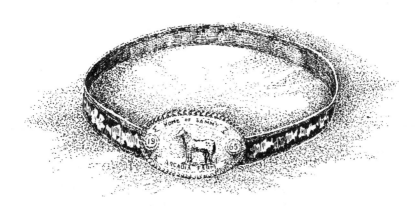

Chapter 58

A Scamp of a Horse

Justin Pike backed his four horse trailer to the big barn entrance. Jumping out of the pickup truck, he opened the trailer's steel doors with a loud clang.

I stroked the neck of the apprehensive horse, trembling as my hand touched him. "Good of you to help me out," I said to the lanky man with the red handlebar mustache I had grown to know so well.

Justin Pike reached out his hand, taking Chief's lead shank from me.

"No trouble at all little lady. I recollect the day you bought him from us as a yearlin'. Seems like a long time ago."

"Seems like ages to me, too. A lot of water has passed over the dam," I replied, getting into the pickup's front seat. Our project that morning was to transport Chief to the horse hospital. I wanted Dr. Wade to tell me why Chief was deteriorating. He seemed to be going downhill before my eyes. I found it hard to believe he was just aging. He was only eighteen. He had lost a lot of weight and muscle tone.

Dr. Roper had done blood work and catheterized the horse for a urine specimen. Nothing was conclusive. Chief's vague symptoms required we go a step further to the horse hospital where more sophisticated blood chemistry could be done.

Chief was Gail's horse, and though she rode him more infrequently because she was involved in graduate school, I knew she valued and appreciated him.

Whenever I thought of Gail and Chief, I pictured her sitting cross-legged on the family room floor. Her face set in a determined look I knew so well. She was pushing fly sheet strings through tiny openings in simulated bone and brass French trading beads, working on her Woman's American Plains Indian regalia. The tips of her fingers, stained with blue dye, were red and swollen from the tedious job.

It was Gail's second show season with the Appaloosa. She had bought the horse from me through her own labors. I gave her credit for every hour she spent on chores, recorded in a small, green notebook, hours spent teaching in hot summer sun, coping with young inexperienced children, classes, too, in winter's chill dampness in the indoor ring. She faithfully did day to day tasks of feeding and watering. All these work hours were credited to Chief's ownership. She had set her heart on the Appaloosa.

The summer before, after acquiring the regalia of a Plains Indian woman, the deerhide dress and horse trappings, Gail had been satisfied to tie baskets of artificial red poppies and wild mustard blooms along Chief's silver flanks. However, competition had become more keen. Contestants appeared with travois and intricately beaded baby boards, and other authentic props. She knew she must augment her regalia with more imaginative touches.

The cold water dye had taken evenly on the porous flysheet fabric. Once its fringes were beaded it would be the first part of the regalia put on Chief. When he moved, the gleaming brass beads swayed around his legs. After the blue fly sheet came the deer hides. I had pinned them securely to a bareback pad. On the breast collar of tiny red, white and blue seed beads, Gail had sewed mink tails and tiny brass bells.

Whitney drilled a small set of antlers from an Axis deer supplied by Chester Hayes. A straight-bar bit tied with latigo leather to the antler side-shanks gave Gail some control over the unpredictable, sometimes obstreperous Chief.

All winter, Gail labored over parts of her costuming. She was anxious over how to introduce feathers into her attire. The use of feathers for women's regalia was excluded in competition between men and women. The warriors had the edge in combined classes with their colorful feathered head dresses and brandishing coup sticks. Appaloosa Horse Club rules are very strict.

We decided to see a taxidermist. We asked him to secure a Marsh hawk, a bird native to the Prairie states. He called us in early spring to report he had one. Gail and I made another visit to his fascinating studio.

The taxidermist attached a leather wristlet to the bird's talons. Gail, reining Chief with her right hand, extended her other arm with the hawk, his wings outspread. It appeared the hawk had alighted on her extended wrist.

The visual effect of the Marsh hawk perched like a falcon on Gail's wrist was dramatic. She had introduced feathers without breaking the rules. She won the first-place trophy and blue ribbon in many classes that summer.

One sultry August night, Gail, Lynn and Whitney had gone to the movies. I decided to give all the horses in the barns another pail of water, although Gail had said she would rewater them when she got home. If Gail did the evening watering, there would always be water in the horses's buckets in the morning. She called her system tippy toppy. It meant she had to go back to each horse with the dipping pail at least three times as the animal drank down the first pailful.

When I opened Chief's stall door, he took several stiff, awkward steps toward his water bucket, as I filled it. I leaned in front of him, holding his halter with one hand and placed the palm of my right hand on the horn of his hoof. It was hot to the touch, the beginning of founder. Conditioning him for halter class, Gail had overfed him. The hot weather added to the problem. I knew if steps were not taken immediately to reduce the fever in Chief's hooves he would be permanently lame.

Dr. Roper came within a half hour and confirmed my worst fears. He gave Chief a shot of anti-inflammatory medication and pulled off his horseshoes. He said I would have to keep a cold hose running on Chief's hooves for several hours. Using his van's headlights, the veterinarian and I mounded sand and gravel in an area the size of a truck tire. He got the hose and the icy well water soon made a puddle.

I was on guard, for potential injury from Chief was always present. I did not look forward with pleasure to spending hours in the dark with him. It turned out that the darkness made it impossible to see the impish look in his Appaloosa eyes.

The horse and I had always had an up and down relationship. I was always a little afraid of him. I had a vivid recollection of seeing him clip Whitney in the head with his hoof. Chief had been gelded and Whitney knelt beside him washing dried blood from his hind legs. Suddenly Chief cross-kicked under his belly, catching Whitney's head with an unshod hoof. Whitney winced as I touched the wound in his scalp with a wad of cotton saturated with peroxide.

Ready to make excuses for the App, he said, "You'd kick too, Mom, after that surgery. Chief's no dummy."

Josie, unfamiliar with horse terminology, referred to Chief as the "gallion", a cross between the stallion he once was, and the gelding he had become. It was an appropriate name. The horse was one of a kind.

Three long hours passed in pitch blackness. I struggled to keep Chief's front hooves in the cold mud. He lipped my wrist and pushed against me with his muscular chest as the battle went on. I pushed him backward or pulled him forward, keeping his feet in the wet clay. There was no way around it. I had to do this.

I had plenty of time to remember how nondescript and homely he was when bought as a yearling from the Pikes. His wormy belly was swollen from neglect, and his front feet were splayed and cracked. No promise of the halter and performance horse he would become. He never lost the mischievous, rascally look in his Appaloosa eyes or the prankishness that went along with it. To bring him to maximum maturity, we left him a stallion until he was four years old. That proved to be a mistake for, gelding or not, he was always a handful. After Gail and I concluded the arrangements that made Chief hers, we sent him out for thirty days of professional training. Gail worked with him every day as time allowed.

I back-tracked his bloodlines and registered him in the Appaloosa Horse Club. They gave him the name "Thunder Cloud High," as close as they could come to his sire's name, "High Thunder," and to the immortal chieftan of the Nez Perce, Chief Joseph, "Thunder Rolling in the Mountains."

After this strenuous contest of wills in the darkness, never again would Chief intimidate me. It was the turning point in our relationship. I had learned if you could control Chief on the ground, you could control almost any horse.

These were my disconnected thoughts and memories as Justin Pike and I bounced on the hard seat of the pickup truck over country roads to the Horse Hospital sixty miles to the southwest.

I stood on one side of the examining room with its pale blue cement block walls and high ceilings, surrounded by sophisticated equipment for which the clinic was famous. Three equine specialists went over Chief in great detail. To my surprise, the horse endured the examination stoically. He did not seem to have the energy to resist the doctors prodding and poking.

Finally, Dr. Wade turned to me and said, "I'd like to keep him here a few days. There's more blood chemistry to be done. We'd like to keep an eye on him. I believe all signs point to a liver disorder."

The hospital stalls were all spacious, light and airy. The care Chief would receive couldn't be duplicated, but I felt heavyhearted leaving him. I patted his neck and pushed a stray lock of his sparce Appaloosa mane to one side. Chief rubbed his jaw against my shoulder. "I'll be back old fellow," I told him, swallowing the lump in my throat, trying not to appear emotional in front of the professionals.

Was it possible, I speculated, after all the years and episodes, that this scamp of a horse was a favorite? It was something I had never suspected.

Chapter 59

A Fifty/Fifty Chance

Perspiring and frustrated, I was trying to reassemble the tractor fittings before gasoline leaked onto the gravel. Standing next to little Alice, draining particles of rust and other debris from her sediment bowl, I looked up and saw an attractive young woman approaching me. She was tall, slender, impeccably dressed in a designer suit, her hair coiffed in a French twist, and with a young boy in hand. She had parked a steel grey Mercedes near the barn. Compared to my visitor, I looked very grimy and disheveled, my hands and jeans reeking of gasoline.

She began to speak in a modulated, aristocratic English accent. She was looking for a boarding facility for her twelve-year-old son's horse. She told me the horse was stabled forty miles from their home. The boy seldom saw the animal because of the distance. The board rate was high and she had learned that the twelve thousand dollars they had paid for the horse was twice his value as a jumper.

The frail youngster was silent as his mother recounted the story. He looked at me and said earnestly, "Jet's a good horse, Ma'm. Very willing. I just want to ride him. It doesn't matter to me if he's a jumper or not."

His mother interrupted with, "He's a pet, that horse. A real dear. Tommy doesn't see him often enough. We paid what they asked for him."

"Don't worry about the price of the horse," I said. "Who's to say what price can be put on a steady, reliable horse? It's over and done now."

I showed them a stall in the main barn. We spoke a few minutes more and the two of them left me with assurances they would bring the horse that weekend. If they ran into any difficulty trailering him, I was to make arrangements to have the horse brought to Arcadia Farm.

Two weeks passed and one evening Mrs. Mallory called to say they were having trouble getting their horse out of the other stable. They had been presented with a bill for delinquent board and medical fees that she and her husband found excessive. The horse had been moved to another stable and would be held there until the Mallorys redeemed him by paying the trumped up charges. It didn't sound promising to me. I doubted if I would ever see the jumper.

I was too busy to think much more about the Mallorys. Three weeks had passed when Mr. Mallory, himself, called. He wanted to be sure we had a stall available. He had paid up all the liens against Jet, and the horse would be delivered to us the following day.

About ten o'clock in the morning the following Thursday, a man called to get directions to Arcadia.

Whitney was on hand to receive the horse. Looking out the kitchen window, I saw Whitney striding across the yard toward the house. He burst into the kitchen, red-faced with anger. "Can you come out to the barn right away and see Mallory's horse? I think he will have to be put down. He's dying!"

"Dying? That can't be true!" My voice rose shrill with emotion. "Where's the man who delivered him?"

"He was a terrible-looking character. He took right off after unloading the horse."

I grabbed my outside jacket and hurried across the lawn to the empty stallion barn where Whitney had put Mallory's horse in isolation.

What I saw was a pathetic, heartbreaking sight, the remnants of a once handsome horse. His emaciated, dehydrated frame was partially covered by a skimpy, soiled blanket. His eyes were swollen shut, blood trickling from them. The horse's muzzle was so enlarged and misshapen it looked like the bill of a platypus. Dark blood oozed from his nostrils. His legs, congested with fluid, were the size of an elephant's and so sore the horse kept shifting his weight from one leg to the other.

I was as shocked as Whitney. I took out my pocket knife and cut off Jet's halter, allowing him to open his mouth. Whitney offered him water, tapping on the side of the metal pail with his knuckles, attracting the blinded animal to the location of the pail. The sad creature dipped his feverish nose into the water. He could not drink, but lapped the water like a dog.

I used the barn phone to call Thad Prince and while waiting for him I went to the kitchen to heat the tea kettle. I steamed a small bran mash and carried it to the barn. Jet was painfully chewing whisps of hay, spitting most of it out in wads. I suspected he had a very sore throat.

Whitney and I decided he would take full charge of Jet, wearing protective coveralls as a means of further isolating any disease. I would run the main barn and do all I could to protect the rest of the stock from contamination.

Dr. Prince arrived within the hour. "Poor old fellow," he said. "I'll give him a fifty-fifty chance. He's got a terribly fast heart beat and congested lungs as well."

Dr. Prince however, was not one to give up easily. He started treatment right away and suggested that Jet be moved to his clinic where the horse could have nursing care around the clock, plus the services of several veterinarians.

Mrs. Mallory met Dr. Prince at Arcadia that evening. She was aghast and tearful at her horse's condition, and agreed that he be moved to the clinic.

By morning, there was a marked improvement in Jet. One eye was partially open. He nickered softly when Whitney went into his stall to hold the water pail for him. He drank several swallows and had eaten some of the bran mash. We were encouraged to see the improvement.

Later in the morning, we loaded him in the horse trailer and he made the trip without mishap. One of us called the clinic every day to keep tabs on Jet's progress.

A week went by when Dr. Prince, himself, called one morning. He sounded defeated. "I'm terribly sorry, Mrs. K. The poor fellow's heart gave out. We couldn't slow it down."

It was Easter week. On Good Friday, Mrs. Mallory and Tommy drove out to the farm. I met them at the front door. The boy carried a salmon pink geranium in full bloom. He thrust the plant toward me, keeping his eyes averted and said, "Thank you for all you did for Jet." Then he turned away so I would not see the tears welling in his eyes.

I touched his arm gently, trying to find the right words. "Don't be ashamed to show your love for Jet," I told him. He looked at me thoughtfully for a moment, then wiping his eyes with the back of his hand asked, "Did your children ever lose a horse they loved?"

"Yes, indeed," I replied, "and so have I. You're too young to face this kind of sorrow, Tommy, but it will make you a stronger, more compassionate person. Do you believe me?"

He did not answer me right away, but when he did speak it was so softly I had to bend forward to catch the words. "Do you think the men at the other stable are compassionate now, because of Jet?"

It was my turn to look away so he would not see my tears. Knowing better, I replied, "Hopefully,they are, Tommy. "Hopefully, they are!"

Chapter 60

Deck the Barns with Boughs of Holly

It was Christmas Eve, 1978. Outside the big barn, in their winter paddock, the ponies and horses waited for their night feeding. A light sugar snow covered their backs and manes. I stepped outside among them, the ponies pressed close to me like children shoving each other in line to get closer to the teacher.

I stood with my arms around the necks of Rusty and Rickey. The other four ponies leaned against my back, pressing themselves closer to me.

"How broad their backs still are, after all these years," I thought. "Rickey's, like a flat table-top." I could picture him balancing a tea cup without spilling a drop.

Impatient, jealous Rusty nipped at Blackie's tail. I hugged the lead pony, reassuring him he was special to me. Rusty, as leader, had turned the merry-go-round wheel for thousands of children without mishap. His luxurious auburn mane still hung the full length of his shoulder. Droplets of moisture beaded the long eyelashes over his once bright eyes. Now his eyes were dimmed by cataracts, visible to the naked eye. How old he looked!

Only a few of my own horses were left, Star, the Grulla mare, Medal and Big Boy. They stood together, tolerant of the attention paid the ponies. Then they moved forward a step at a time until they were standing close to me. How little it took to make them content, only the sound of their own names.

I heard a sound behind me in the doorway. It was Whitney with a wheelbarrow and three large bales of hay. "Don't they look good?" he asked. "Nice and fat. They'll winter fine. None of them want to go in the shelter. It's not cold enough. They love it outside. See how thick their coats are. Snow doesn't even penetrate." Turning to the milling ponies, he called, "Come on, kids. Soup's on." He broke the bales up in front of them.

There was a wind chill factor of seventeen degrees below zero, but the barn was tolerable from the boarding horse's body heat. A lacy fringe of ice clung to the edge of the water pail of Gail's horse, Chief. I stirred it loose with a small piece of cedar shingle, careful not to soak my sheep-lined gloves. Chief's stall was the first one on the south end of the barn. Looking up above the horse's head I saw a festoon of cobweb, quivering in a down draft of frigid air from the hayloft above. A piece of celutex board had been loosened from the scampering and wrestling of a family of raccoons making their home in the loft. In December, they were hibernating, cuddled like pups in a corner by the silo. The protruding celutex board reminded me of the mischief they had done.

I called to Whitney from the other end of the barn and suggested, "We'd better close up that hole," pointing to the opening above Chief. "The raccoons have loosened the ceiling," I said.

"They've done more than that," Whitney replied. "Three of them got into the corn, opened all the burlap bags and threw cobs all over the bin. I found an ear of corn in Chief's stall yesterday. Couldn't figure out how it got there 'til I looked up and there were the raccoons looking down at me," Whit laughed.

"I've seen them, too," I added. "Five or six of them in the oat bin, walking across the rafters. One night, last summer, I flashed my lantern up on the ridge of the barn roof. There they were, the whole family, clinging to each other, looking down at me with those black masks and beady eyes."

My right thumb ached from pressing red thumbtacks into the stall door's hard plywood. It was time, once more, to hang red or green felt stockings and Christmas trees on the doors. A cold draft from a half open barn door scattered Christmas cards I had saved to augment holiday decorations. I sorted through the old cards, trying to choose a special one for each particular horse. I discarded some stockings with moth holes in them.

Beginning with Chief, a snowman seemed right for him. I had remarked to Gail the day before that he looked like a polar bear, he was so densely coated. There was a red stocking for Katydid and across from her a green one for the hunter, Faust. It was his first Christmas at the farm. Shannon would have a Currier and Ives winter scene, and there had to be something special for Honey, her fifteenth Christmas Eve with us. I chose a red tree with tiny gold sequins.

The horses were watching me and I found myself talking, conferring with them, asking their opinions. "What about Comanche?" I laughed. "He's not a very big pony. I imagine he still believes in Santa Claus. Yes, here's the right card . . . a jolly fat Santa, reindeer and all."

The calico cat had followed me up the barn aisle. She leaped into my box of decorations and curled up for a snooze. "Sorry, old girl," I told her, lifting her out of the box. "I'm not quite through yet."

A green stocking with tiny silver bells was a good choice for Sonny. It would jingle each time the door opened. Then, on to Chase's mare, Barbie Bar, our only expectant mother. I found a watercolor of a manger scene for her. Further down the aisle, I left a candy cane for Cocoa. I pushed the last thumbtack into her door and stepped back to admire the effect.

The whole barn had a festive air that made me recall other Christmases. One year we put up a Christmas tree in the indoor arena. The boarders brought ornaments for it. We served hot cocoa and cookies.

Carrie and Holly had knitted a bright red and green scarf for Bounty. It was two yards long and they looped and criss-crossed it over Bounty's chest. There were red ribbons for her mane and tail and a box of diced carrots and apples to share with all the horses. "Merry Christmas from Bounty," Carrie said. I wondered what happened to Bounty after Carrie died at the commune.

That year Giulio had brought the children a large, beautiful gingerbread house from his brother's bakery. It was a masterpiece with transparent sugar windows, the roof covered with sparkling gum drops. It was the first gingerbread house I ever had...and the last.

That same week, on Christmas Eve, the Zwicks, Stewball's owners, met me in the barn. They insisted I sit on the water trough cover while they played their guitars and sang old, unfamiliar carols from Appalachia. They had a gift for us too. A hand-sewn. wall-hanging, a manger scene, but all the animals around the Nativity were horses. I wanted to leave the appliqued hanging in the barn through the holiday season and hung it in front of Victor's stall. The next morning, to my dismay, Victor had been able to lip and shred one end of the linen, through a narrow space between the 2x10s. I repaired it by adding a length of two inch red cotton fringe. The manger scene was never hung in the barn again.

The barn was full of so many memories. I picked up the barn cat, a great, great, great granddaughter of the intrepid Googie, and sat down on the cover of the water trough. The memories came flooding back, all conjured up by the holiday fancifulness that filled the barn.

This was to be our last Christmas at the farm. The realization cast a shadow on what usually was such a happy season. Cradling Nancy, the calico barn cat in my arms, my thoughts turned to other special Christmases, one in particular.

Chapter 61

The Horse at the Top of the Tree

The children, Josie and I, piled into the narrow boxsledge. There were six or seven inches of snow on the ground. It was December 24th.

A few days before, Josie brought an early Christmas gift, a set of old melodious sleigh bells. He and Whitney fastened them to Dolly's harness.

It was a light task for one of the stout mares to pull the sledge over the snow and return with the selected spruce tree. Flory, the other half of the team, not used to being left behind, put up a noisy vocal protest, kicking with powerful front hooves at her stall door. I sent Whitney to open her latch, though we did not hitch her up. Flory walked and trotted next to Dolly as if she, too, was in harness. The team stood quietly in snowdrifts to their bellies while Josie and Whitney sawed the evergreen trunk with a cross-cut saw.

On our way home, the winter sunset cast a blush on the frozen fields. The children sang favorite carols and Jingle Bells over and over, Dolly's sleigh bells ringing to their accompaniment.

After supper, Whitney fashioned a sturdy stand for the fragrant spruce tree. We decorated it with Italian lights, treasured ornaments, criss-crossing garlands of fresh cranberries and popcorn. We had a family tradition of placing on top of the Christmas tree, not a star or an angel, but a small white felt horse with mane and tail of black yarn, and a red saddle blanket trimmed in gold sequins.

In early November, Gail had come back from her school library charmed by a story she had read in a book of Christmas legends. She told me the Cajun exiles of Nova Scotia believed their farm animals spoke on Christmas Eve. The legend suggests that cows, horses and other animals are blessed that night, because long ago cattle's sweet breath warmed the Christ child against the late night's chill. The legend maintains that at midnight the animals kneel and turn their heads toward Bethlehem.

I promised Gail that this Christmas eve we would visit the winter paddock precisely at midnight. There was no problem getting everyone off to bed early in spite of the excitement of Christmas Eve. Gail reminded me, over and over, not to forget to wake them in plenty of time.

By ten-thirty, the house was still except for the deep breathing of the dogs, Stuart and Ashley, curled up on a rug in one corner of the kitchen. There were a few more cards to write, a present to wrap, a last check through the barns. I kept an eye on the old school clock on the kitchen wall. At eleven-thirty, I bundled myself up in a hooded storm coat, boots and mittens, then went from room to room, waking the children.

I found Whitney had slept in his clothes. The little girls were in the red flannel nightgowns that Ida Mae, Josie's wife, had made them.

"You girls have got to be very quiet," their brother admonished them. "Not a peep, especially you, Lynn, and no giggling."

"Yes, no giggling!" I echoed his directions. Dressed in warm jackets, caps and mittens, we drew on our boots at the back door, leaving the disappointed dogs behind.

Indian file, we made our way quietly across the back yard. The crusty snow crunched beneath our feet. My own heart pounded in expectation as we crept stealthily toward the winter paddock behind the loafing barn.

There was no winter moon that night, but the sky was illuminated by the brilliance of countless stars. I could see the horses' silhouettes, each one recognizable by size and conformation, standing in different groups in the paddock, all motionless.

Tillie and the miniature pony, Miss Muffet, so tiny she scarcely reached the big mare's knee, stood off to my left with Diamond, Navaho and Colonelette. In the middle of the corral, Crystal, her pure white coat glistening in the starlight was lying down, her nose almost touching the snow. Around her, with lowered heads, all in a deep sleep, stood Colonel, Sugarfoot, Mitzi and Bobby Socks. To the right, clustered the rest of the school horse band, staunch pals, the inseparables, Big Boy, Dakotah, Star and Medal, behind them the little Grulla mare.

The ponies stood with their heads toward the center of a small circle. They formed the points of a star, all five of them, Rusty, Ricky, Blackie, Sandy and Fritz.

There was very little talking on our way back to the house. The children seemed immersed in deep thought. I heard Gail whisper to Lynn, "Did you hear anything?"

"Yes, I did," her small sister replied, nodding her head.

Suddenly we gathered around Lynn. "What did you hear?" we chorused in one voice.

"What did they say?" prodded Whitney. Enjoying being the center of attention, Lynn did not answer at once, looking up at the star-studded sky. Then she spoke. "I heard, I think it was Colonel . . . "

"Yes, yes! What did he say?" We pressed her, carried away by the possibility!

Lynn paused once more. "He said . . . he said, 'What are those guys doing out here staring at us on Christmas Eve?'"

There were gales of laughter at the logic of Lynn's reply. The children pelted each other with snowballs, racing for the warmth of the old farm kitchen, leaving me behind to savor the solitude and peace of the winter's night.

Chapter 62

Shared Feelings

The average age of the school horses was ten when I bought them from the Pike brothers or Calvin Baker. Twenty years later, many of them were close to thirty. We knew each ones disabilities and infirmities, the slow heart beat of Colonel and Navaho: Diamond's lameness: the increased fluid in Sugarfoot, Bobbysocks and Dakotah's lungs. One by one, sometimes two by two, Dr. Roper or Dr. Prince had gently eased the old timers out of this life and into the next.

At the close of the long winter I looked forward to spring, the time of budding and blooming and gentle weather. To see the horses once more on the pasture, rounding out in flesh. Maybe then I could ignore their advanced age.

Big Boy had done well through the bitter winter. I had put him into a stall, twice daily, for extra grain, then turned him back outside to rejoin his retired companions, Star, Medal and the Grulla mare. He preferred to be outdoors most of the time.

The middle of February brought a delayed thaw. The earth's fragrance spoke of an early spring and we began talking or repairing fences and enclosing new pastures. One for the broodmare, Star, due to foal any day.

Suddenly, before my eyes, Big Boy's condition deteriorated. His great carcass shriveled and he looked gaunt. His steps were feeble and he seemed confused. I was afraid he would fall on me when I was leading him.

We could not wait for "one more summer", not even for one more day. I stood by the window in the family room looking down the driveway, waiting for a glimpse of Dr. Roper's van. It was drizzling. The fine mist and fog obscured the entrance to the farm. I had made up my mind I would not cry. I would not allow myself to think of the horse. No memories were going to trap me into tears over painful farewells.

I forced myself not to think of anything in particular. The trunks of huge clusters of Norway maples, blackened by rain, reminded me I must nourish the feeder roots this spring. We had lost a companion group to it the year before. I concentrated on seeing myself drive the long, tapered chemical root-feeding cylinders into the ground around its base.

High in one of the maple's top-most branches, a lone crow clung silently, from time to time shaking out his wet feathers. What a long wingspan he has, I thought.

My attention was drawn to an accumulation of soggy leaves and branches on the lawn that must be raked up; I told myself I could do that after snow drifts melted. It was good to see an end of winter snow.

My eyes searched the long driveway almost compulsively and I saw the tan and white carry-all approaching. I did not go outside. From where I stood with the rain now running in rivulets down the window pane, I saw Whitney walk across the yard. Over his arm he carried a freshly laundered, neatly folded, pale blue chenille bedspread. He would cover Big Boy with it . . . once the horse was dead.

The day before, I had put Big Boy on crossties and brushed and curried him for an hour until there was a fair luster to his mahogany brown coat. I gently brushed the arthritic joints of his knees, combed his black tail, then wiped his eyes and nostrils with a soft, terry-cloth towel. He looked clean and well-groomed. Then, I gave him a generous grain feeding and the choicest hay I could find. From my hand, I fed him a carrot and a celery heart.

But that was yesterday. Now I stared across the back yard. Dr. Roper was coming out of the indoor arena. It was over. I knew Whitney, at that moment, was covering the horse with the blue spread.

Jeff Roper pulled his van past my garage. He leaned across the seat and opened the door on the passenger side. I slid in out of the pouring rain. Neither of us spoke for a few minutes. Dr. Roper methodically packed tobacco into the bowl of his pipe. He brushed granules of tobacco briskly from his knee. The wiper blades whined and scraped against the windshield.

Finally, I broke the silence. "He was an old, old horse, you know," I stammered, my voice quavering.

"Yes, I know he was," Jeff Roper replied.

I sensed a weariness in his voice as I plunged ahead. "I hate this responsibility, over and over again. You know what I mean?"

The veterinarian puffed quietly on his pipe. "I know what you're saying. I don't like this part of the horse business either. I've got an old roping horse I cannot put down myself. Some other vet will have to do it for me. I've had the horse so long, since I was in vet school. I roped off him all over the country." Dr. Roper clenched the pipe stem in his teeth.

The need to share my feelings was overwhelming. "I feel guilty every time I ask you to put one down. As if I had no consideration for your own feelings."

The veterinarian looked straight ahead through the windshield. He did not answer me, but leaned forward and turned the knob on the dashboard, slowing the frenetic motion of the wiper blades.

I continued, "He was the last of the school horses. Maybe the best one." Unshed tears seared my throat.

"I know. He was," Dr. Roper replied, gently. "You had him a very long time."

I groped for the door handle, opened it and slipped down from the leather seat into the pouring rain. Only then could I look at Dr. Roper. The rain splashed against my face, mingling with tears I could no longer hold back.

The red brake lights of the van disappeared into the fog. The sound of gravel thrown against its fenders faded in the distance. I felt rooted to the spot, then the distinct, clear sound of a horse's whinny aroused me. I moved slowly along the familiar path toward the barn. The rain began letting up. By the time I reached the barn door it was no more than a fine drizzle. The pungent smell of dried grasses, aromatic shavings and animal bodies hung on the moist air.

It was dark in the barn. As hundreds of times before, the comforting sound of munching horses met my ears as I moved past the boarders, stall by stall. The double-width brood mare foaling stall was in the middle of the barn. I raised my hand and snapped on the night light over the expectant mother. A quick glance took in the whole scene. Star, her nearly sightless eyes turned toward me as she stood in the back of the stall. Near her feet, on a bed of straw, under the beam of light, lay a tiny chestnut foal.

My heart beat loudly with the excitement of the discovery. I opened the stall door quietly, speaking soothingly to the gentle mare. I knelt down and examined the little creature. It was a filly. She continued to sleep with the innocent, deep breathing of all newborns.

There was a sound behind me. It was Whitney. "Where did she come from?" he exclaimed, a broad grin on his face. "She wasn't here an hour ago when I fed. It is just like that old mare to put one over on us." He knelt down beside me, bending over the foal. He swabbed her navel with iodine. "Isn't she a beauty! I'd sure like to have her. Mom. I'll take her with me to Missouri. What will you name her?"

Still kneeling beside the newborn foal, I ran my hand over the short silky hairs of her titian mane. I waited a moment to answer Whitney's question. Looking down at the filly's auburn coat I recalled the image of my father's fiery steeplechaser . . . Without hesitation I replied " We'll call her Rosebud. We've never had a . . . Rosebud."

Chapter 63

Moving On

Spring came and with it the Real Estate Tax bill, a staggering ten thousand dollars. The farms around Arcadia no longer were on the tax rolls as agricultural land. Lester's property on my north border was among the first to be sold to a developer. He and his wife had moved into town, two years ago.

I, too, had decided to sell my farm. I no longer taught riding or gave pony parties or hayrides. The rodeo arena had not held a public event for three years. There were only a dozen horse boarders left, Chase Harper and Barbie and those who had been with me fifteen years or more.

In my mid-sixties, I had learned to compromise between the things I wanted to do and the things I could do. I had begun to use a cane, some of the time, for confidence. Lynn and Gail had their own households. Josie lived with a daughter in Florida.

Each passing year had brought a steady improvement in Whitney's recovery. Now it was more than time for him to get on with his own life. He had spent two weeks traveling through southern Illinois, Missouri and parts of Arkansas. He had found rural property that appealed to him in southern Missouri and began making plans to move there.

The thirty-two foot rental truck was parked inside the indoor arena out of the weather. It was loaded to capacity with lumber from the ranch barn. Whitney had dismantled the building, board by board, by himself. He had put the indoor arena to good use.

Piles of lumber, stacked neatly according to size, almost filled the one hundred and sixty foot length of the building.

In addition to the material from the Ranch barn, there were ten-square posts from the rodeo arena and miscellaneous glazed windows of assorted shapes and sizes.

Before Whitney began to take down the structure, I walked over to the west end of the property to look at the Ranch barn for the last time. There was a beautiful sunset, as there had been so many hundreds of times before, bathing the cozy small barn with its last rays.

I fastened a swinging stall door with a piece of baling twine from my pocket, conscious this was my favorite building, even when empty. In the past, its twelve stalls with divided doors enabled the horses to look out over the lower half. The horses were protected from the elements by a wide aisle and overhang. It was a cheerful sight when you saw twelve pair of mild eyes looking at you when you came to feed and water. Sometimes there were no heads looking out at all, but after calling out a horse's name, he would nicker and stick his head out. The others always followed suit.

Some winters, the only way we could get hay to these horses was by pulling hay bales on a toboggan or sled over enormous snowdrifts. The worse the weather, the greater the challenge.

I remembered one bitter cold day, when Lynn and I struggled hard to reach the barn with the toboggan. We lost our footing in the drifts. Laughing breathlessly, the harder we struggled the more we fell. We gasped from exertion, and finally, weak from laughing and pulling we reached the horses. After feeding and watering them, we closed the top doors, content knowing the horses were well cared for in spite of the obstacles.

However, if by some unusual circumstance the underground water line or frost-free silcox froze, we hauled water on the toboggan, too. There was no laughter if water pails spilled before we reached the Ranch barn. Spilled water meant instant ice, and ice was an invitation to a hard fall. Once you fell, no one would be the wiser. Few walked near the Ranch barn in winter. I often did chores alone and worried about falling behind the barns and lying undiscovered in frigid, below zero temperatures.

This happened one February evening in the grey dusk of twenty degrees below zero. I had fallen backwards on a sheet of ice, partially obscured by snow, behind one of the corn cribs. The back of my head cracked hard against the ice. Fortunately, I was wearing a Russian caracul hat with heavy fur flaps covering my ears. The padding cushioned the blow and probably saved me from a concussion. Nevertheless, I had wacked my head severely. I lay for a minute or two, contemplating the pewter sky above me. When I moved my head from side to side, it throbbed. When I tried to raise myself to a sitting position, I became dizzy.

Ashley and Stuart were with me. At first they gambled and leapt over my inert body, delighted with the accessibility of my frozen face as they licked and nuzzled my cheeks.

In desperation, I turned on my side and began to roll over and over in the direction of the barnyard. I made slow progress, but rolling made me dizzier still. I decided to give each of the dogs one of my insulated fleece- lined gloves, hoping they would tear off to the main barn and someone, recognizing my chamois gloves, would come looking for me.

Ashley and Stu had never heard of those old Rin Tin Tin or Lassie movies. They grabbed the gloves I offered in their mouths and gleefully took off in the direction of the distant, frozen waste of the rodeo arena.

I kept rolling until I was within calling distance of the north door of the big barn. I yelled as loud as I could, "Hey! Somebody help me!"

Finally, Josie heard me. Seeing me on the ground he shook his head. "Mrs. K, what in the world are you doing on the ground in this weather?" Then, seeing the dogs cavorting in the distance he added, "Hey, you dogs! What are you doing with Mrs. K's gloves?"

Josie hadn't seen the movies either!

Chapter 64

Footprints in the Snow

The first heavy snowfall of December 1977 swirled around me as I walked the long driveway to the mailbox. The six huge mustard- yellow Laternos were parked side by side like forbidding monsters.

The excavator, his back toward me, jabbed with a sharp shovel at caked ice and clay, wedged between the treads of his Caterpillar tractor. The motor was humming. He did not hear my greeting.

The snow mercifully covered the wounds in the earth made by removal of black earth, exposing clay where once lay lush fields and pastures.

There was silence all around me as I turned back up the driveway, Christmas cards and magazines tucked securely under my left arm. I drew my woolen scarf over the lower half of my face against the swirling ice crystals.

I passed the excavator once again. Finally, he saw me. His face was ruddy from the biting cold. He raised a gauntleted hand in greeting and called to me, "I'm going home. Can't do much today. Too cold!"

"That's fine with me. You do that," I answered, glad to see an end to the gouging of my pastureland.

With the construction activity behind me, I plodded along with the aid of my pronged ice cane, past the orchard, where rabbit tracks tell me hummocks and burrows are occupied, past the towering Colorado blue spruce, their branches heavy with snow.

Through my ice-tinged eyelashes I could see the familiar outline of my house and barn, their roofs covered with snow once again.

Snowbirds were feeding at the redwood station. Two cardinals flashed in and out of the dark green yews by the family room windows. A pair of cock pheasants crouched, rump to rump, against the woven stock wire of a section of pasture fencing. They had found the golden kernels of corn I threw out early this morning.

On the south side of the house I could see the tops of two headstones, granite sills left over from when the house was built. Spring would bring patches of wild violets around them, but now the stones were almost covered with snow. The lettering on the slabs was blurred, but I knew what they read. "Dear Ashley and Loyal Stuart: Mother's Dogs."

I turned around and looked back down the driveway. The snow had completely covered my footprints. "Is it possible your own lifetime disappears as quickly, without a trace?" I wondered.

Once in the familiar pine-paneled family room, I stepped out of my snowy fleece-lined boots, put my wet mittens on the mantle to dry and sank into an easy chair. The glowing logs in the fireplace still threw heat and my toes began to thaw. The mail lay unopened on my lap. I leaned my head back on the old wing chair and closed my eyes.

Seeing my footprints obliterated so quickly by the falling snow had depressed me. My eyes scanned over the accumulation of memorabilia on the walls and mantle. There were objects from every phase of my life. In some ways, I thought, this pleasant, snug room was my life.

Behind me, on the wall, hung three hand-crafted, cherrywood canoe paddles and my father's wicker fishing creel. On the mantle stood a toy sailboat Father gave me on my tenth birthday, its varnished hull gleaming in the firelight.

Facing each other on my desk, photographs of Lynn in her nurse's cap and Whitney in uniform. To my right, hanging on the wall, were parts of Gail's Indian regalia, Chief's turquoise seed-bead breast collar, his trophies and ribbons.

Near the doorway, side by side, Big Boy and Wally's bridles, Sammy's faded blue nylon halter and Stuart's dog collar, so many reminders of the past.

I felt a desperate need to recapture and hold onto these memories. In the top drawer of my antique bureau desk I remembered a large legal yellow pad. I found it, propped it up on my knee and began to write. The tablet was soon filled and many more followed.

Winter turned to spring and I found myself caught up in the remembrances of yesterday. I scarcely noticed the roar of the diesel excavating machines. I told myself it was only Josie or Whitney putting in the field crop of soy beans.

But there were harsh changes every day. After the excavators came sewer contractors, cement crews and carpenters. I accepted the finality. Life as I had known it for more than twenty years was coming to an end.

What had begun as an exercise in recall, became for me an urgency to share it with those who were part of it and with those who had never driven up the long maple-lined lane of Arcadia Farm.

AFTERWORD

In Missouri, Whitney had built Rosebud a snug, little barn using timbers from the rodeo arena. The mare, now seven, stood quietly while I brushed her auburn mane and tail.

Six-year-old Stuart, watched me. "Why are you brushing Poppa Whitney's horse?" he asked.

I laughed. "Why? Aren't I doing it right? I'm so glad you are here. I need a boy to help me," I told him. "Here, take the bucket and fill Rosebud's water pail while I add fresh bedding to her stall."

Parked under the shed overhang, the Allis Chalmers tractor, with a fresh coat of orange enamel, looked like new. With some effort, I climbed up on the tractor seat, grasped the steering wheel, leaned over and pulled the starter. Little Alice's engine coughed once and started right up. Shifting into first gear, I turned away from the shed onto the meadowland.

I steered through a stand of meadow fescue, wild grape and Canadian thistle, scaring up a covey of ruffled grouse. The big wheels laid over wild sumac bushes and dried goldenrod. Overhead, a red-shouldered hawk soared to the top of a distant pine ridge. A pair of Cardinals, the male's crimson plumage contrasting to the cedars' emerald leaves, crisscrossed in front of me.

Little Alice moved steadily over the rough terrain. Her wheels threw globs of red clay against the sleeves of my wool jacket as they had so many times before, driving over the muddy fields of Arcadia farm.

At the top of the ridge I found myself on a gravel road. Seven wild turkeys, spooked by the tractor, scurried in front of me into a ravine. Rounding a curve in the red clay road I startled a doe and her fawn feeding in the ditch.

When I reached a clearing, a high spot, I turned off the motor. The valley stretched before me to the foothills of the Ozark Mountains.

My watch told me I had been gone an hour. Reluctantly, I turned the tractor around and headed for the hollow. Back in the shed, I turned off the engine. McNair, the labrador, came bounding to meet me with Whitney and the children close behind.

"We were getting worried," Whit said. "Had a good time, did you Mom?"

Patting the tractor's radiator cap, I replied, "One of the best of many."

"We've been waiting for you to go with us to cut the Christmas tree," the six year old said, pulling my sleeve.

His younger brother Everett chimed in. "Grandmother, we're going to take your toboggan,"

Anna, the two-year-old, nodded her head. She was the shyest of the three.

"I'm ready, let's go," I said, grasping the toboggan's rope. The four of us tramped through the woods behind Whitney. McNair ran ahead, covering the ground in big leaps. He was the only one who could keep up with Whitney's long strides. Bringing up the rear skittered Nancy, her calico pelt the depth of ermine, meowing not to be left behind.

There were hundreds of pines on the ridge from which to choose the Christmas tree. When everyone was satisfied with the decision, Whitney, with four strokes of the hand axe, felled the fragrant pine. He put the tree on the toboggan and with the children pulling and their father pushing, it was an easy trip back to the hollow.

During our absence, flurries of light, sugar snow dusted the meadowland and roof of the lodge. There was a log for each one of us to bring indoors from the woodpile. Even the "shy one" had a piece of firewood to carry.

Inside the rustic lodge, kerosene lamps cast their soft glow on weathered beams from the ranch barn. On the old round oak kitchen table, a berry basket was heaped high wlth greeting cards, many with familiar script. I recognized messages from special friends, Bud, Lester, Josie and so many others. The gift card on a bushel of oranges read, "Best wishes and happy memories from Chase, Barbie Bar and Barbie's babe."

Hissing, crackling logs in the wood stove threw cozy warmth. We set about trimming the tree with strings of cranberries, popcorn, hanging pine cones and walnuts strung with red yarn. Beneath the tree, piled high, there were wonderfully mysterious, bulky packages from Lynn and Gail.

It was time to show the children the surprises I had brought from Illinois. They gathered around me expectantly. I opened the tissue paper package, and to their delight placed the little white felt horse with the black yarn tail and red sequined saddle on top of the tree. The other box we would not open until Christmas day.

The house was still except for the heavy breathing of the lab curled up near the pot belly stove. I drew the familiar warmth of a Hudson Bay blanket against my cheek and closed my eyes. Tomorrow we would open the other package, and, at the river, I would show the children how to set the rudder on my toy sailboat from Rainbow Lake.

About the Author

Blanche Kloman, struck with polio at seven, outgrew the crippling affects of the disease through tremendous efforts of nurses, family, an Adirondack guide, and herself, to which she added grit, courage and patience. Trained for the opera stage before marriage, she picked up practical business experience as a sub-contractor and a builder in Skokie, Illinois.

All these experiences gave her the backbone to, at age forty-two with no working capital, tackle the operation of a once operable dairy farm which she boldly turned into Arcadia Horse Farm, took in boarders, built new facilities, and creatively met each financial crisis head on. From stage appearances to rolling hay bales, driving a tractor and feeding and watering 80 horses may seem a contrast, but Blanche Kloman handled it all, as well as raising children and serving her community. She also found time to write!

About the Artist

Walter M. Prosksa ordinarily sketches pen and ink creations of Barrington's churches. He uses a technique called "pecking" and claims it will take a life-time to perfect his craft. He has a good start.

When he was nine years old and immigrated to Chicago from Czechoslovakia, Prosksa received a scholarship from the Art Institue of Chicago. He took art courses at Northwestern University while he was still working, and now that he has been retired for at least ten years from his wire business, Prosksa has had much more time to develop his artistic talents. He is now 65 and has exhibited his work in several galleries.

He still likes to draw churches best. His lifetime desire would be to draw all the churches in the world.